Mystery Man

COLIN BATEMAN

ISBN: 1782922482
ISBN-13: 9781782922483

For David Torrance, without whom, etc. etc.

And for Andrea and Matthew

CONTENTS

1

There aren't many private eyes in Belfast, and now, apparently, there's one fewer. I know this because his shop was right next to mine. His name was Malcolm Carlyle and he seemed a decent sort. He would call in for a chat and a browse now and again when business was slow. *His* business, that is. His business was called Private Eye, big yellow letters on a black background. Then one day he didn't open up, and I never saw him again, and that was the start of my problems because he was still listed in the Yellow Pages, but when people couldn't get a response on the phone well, they thought, he must be good, he's so busy, he's changed his number, gone ex-directory, so they'd come down to check what was happening with their cases, find the door locked, stand back and take a look at the place and see my shop next door and think there must be some kind of a connection because you don't have a shop called Private Eye and a shop called No Alibis sitting side by side for no reason at all. So they'd come in and furtively browse through the crime books, all the time eyeing me up behind the counter, trying to work out if I could possibly be connected to the private eye they were looking for and if there was a connecting door between the shops, and whether I did this bookselling thing as a kind of respectable cover for my night-time manoeuvres on the cold, dark streets of Belfast. They'd gotten it wrong of course. Bookselling is more cut-throat than you can possibly imagine.

The first fella who actually approached me was called Robert Geary; he was a civil servant in the Department of Education in Bangor, he was married, he had three children aged from nine to twelve and he supported Manchester United. We all have our crosses to bear. He told me all this while making a meal out of paying for an Agatha Christie novel, so I knew something was up. No one had bought a Christie in years.

He said, 'My wife wears leather trousers.'

I nodded. You meet all types.

'She's forty-two,' he said, and I raised a concerned eyebrow. 'I know, I keep hinting that maybe she's too old for them, but she doesn't get it. The problem is she asked me to get them cleaned at our usual place, it's the only dry-cleaner's she trusts, except I was late for work and so I took them to this other place, do you know it — it's called Pressed for Time on the Castlereagh Road? — but they lost them and they were very nice about it and paid me what they cost, except my wife threw a fit anyway and called me all the names of the day. Then a couple of weeks ago I was out shopping and I saw the exact same trousers walking down Royal Avenue, except no sooner had I seen them than I lost them in the crowds, so I went back to the dry-cleaner's and said I'd seen them walking down Royal Avenue but they said there was nothing they could do, so I didn't want to phone the police because they'd tell me to take a run and jump and so I phoned Malcolm Carlyle, Private Eye, and he said he'd see what *he* could do, but then when I didn't hear back from him and he didn't answer his phone, I thought I'd come down and see him.

Except he's not there.'

'No, he's not,' I said.

'And now I have to get them back, because as sure as hell the wife's going to be out shopping one day and she'll see them and then there'll be blood on the streets, and some of it's going to be hers, and some of it's going to be the other woman's, and some of it's going to be mine and I can do without that. I'm five years from retirement. We retire early in the Civil Service. We're going to buy a place in Cyprus.'

'Why don't you just get her some new ones?' I asked.

'Because these were a designer pair, I bought them in America, in Texas, near the Alamo, it's my favourite film, there's not another pair like them in Ireland, and possibly continental Europe.'

'I see,' I said, and charged him £4.50 for the Christie.

He left me his number in case the private eye turned up again, and I said it seemed unlikely, but he said keep it anyway, and if there's anything you can do I'd very much appreciate it, and then he hurried out because there was another customer who'd come in and now wanted serving, so I didn't get the chance to ask what he meant by *if there's anything you can do*. The next customer was just looking for directions. He wanted to know where Queen's University was. I said I wasn't sure and sold him a street map. It was only around the corner, but the profit was the difference between burger and steak.

Over the next couple of days I was up to my neck in stock-taking and didn't give the leather trousers another thought, but then I finally got back behind the till and found the note I'd made of his number and seeing as how I'd an average of forty-three minutes to kill between customers I started thinking about the possibilities, and that's how I came to phone Pressed for Time to enquire about the mysterious disappearance and even more mysterious reappearance of Mrs Geary's leather trousers.

'And you are, who?' the man at the other end said with enough suspicion for me to say the first name that came to mind, other than my own, for I had a business and its reputation to protect: 'Lawrence Block.'

'Like the crime writer,' said the man unexpectedly.

'Like the crime writer,' I said. 'Except I'm definitely not in the book business.'

'What business would you be in then?' he asked chirpily. 'You know, I can't go giving out confidential information to just anyone who phones up asking.'

I said, 'I'm representing Mr Geary and Mrs Geary in the matter of their leather trousers, and by the by, what kind of confidential information would a dry-cleaner's have to be worried about giving out anyway?'

'Oh, you'd be surprised,' he said. 'We do police uniforms and prison officers' uniforms and . . .' And then he caught himself on and said, 'But that's confidential. I'll, ah, get the manager.'

After a bit, the manager came on and said gruffly, 'I've had it up to my back teeth with these leather trousers. Even though we don't accept responsibility for lost or damaged items we paid for them. I don't see what his problem is.'

'Well, they had sentimental value,' I said.

'Sentimental leather trousers?' he barked. But then he sighed and his tone lightened a little and he said, 'It takes all sorts. Mr Block, is it?'

'Call me Larry.'

'What are you, a solicitor?'

I cleared my throat in a positive manner and said, 'If you don't accept any responsibility for lost or damaged items, why did you pay Mr Geary for the missing trousers?'

'Well, the fact of the matter is we *didn't* pay Mr Geary, at least not directly. We send our leather items out for specialist cleaning. *They* said they were damaged in the cleaning process, and *they* instructed us to pay Mr Geary and promised to reimburse us. Although I'm still waiting.'

'Well, if they said they were damaged, how come those very same leather trousers were last seen hurrying down Royal Avenue at a great rate of knots?'

'Well, I don't know. You'd have to take it up with them.'

So he gave me their number and said they were on the Newtownards Road and I thanked him for his time and still suitably enthused, or bored, I was about to phone them when the shop door opened and a man came in and asked if I could recommend the new John Grisham and I said, yes, if you're a moron.

2

Well, it turns out John Grisham was on a signing tour of the UK, and not wanting to cause pandemonium wherever he went he was just calling at bookshops unannounced, which struck me as an inefficient way to do things, but each unto their own. His face is right there on the back of his books, so I get to look at him at least six times a day, and of course I recognised you straight off, I said, although in truth, shorn of good lighting and make-up, he looked a lot heavier and his hair was longer and unkempt and his skin was blotchy and he seemed to have some kind of a rash on his neck. It's lucky that I myself was born with an honest kind of a face, as he seemed to accept that my off-the-cuff remark was a typical example of our much-heralded Troubles humour, etc., etc.

I made him a cup of coffee while he signed copies of his books, and seeing as how he was an American and not wishing to seem overawed by his wealth and celebrity, I related to him the story of Mrs Geary's leather trousers, putting extra emphasis on the fact that they'd originated in Texas, which is somewhere in the general region of where I believe he hails from originally, but he didn't seem very interested and kept trying to steer the conversation back to exactly how many copies of his next novel I planned to order, which wasn't a subject I was keen to explore because people can snap them up for half-price in the supermarkets so there's no point in me bringing in more than a few token copies. When he finished signing his books, he moved on to signing copies of books by other authors, which I thought was a little strange, but there didn't seem any harm in it. In fact, it was quite novel and I thought it might help me to move a lot of dead stock. There probably wouldn't be a huge profit in it, but it could mean the difference between eight slices of cooked ham in a resealable packet and a fresh gammon steak. But after he had gone and I was beginning to put the signed books out on display I realised that he had signed most of his books 'Johnny Grisham' and some of them 'David Grisham' and several 'The Lord God of All Hosts' and one 'How much does your piano weigh?', and I began to reflect on the capacity of the Irish to fall for anyone with an American accent, be they pauper, paranoid or president, and whatever gibberish they might care to spout.

I was not, therefore, in the best of moods when I finally came to phone Stick to Me, the leather goods cleaners, shortly before closing time. I made a point of not identifying myself this time, saying merely that I was phoning on behalf of a client, a Mr Geary, but before I could get on to the substance of my complaint the man at the other end said, 'Is that Mr Block?'

I cleared my throat in a positive manner and demanded to know what had happened to the leather trousers.

'They got torn up by the machinery. They were damaged beyond repair.'

'And yet they were spotted galloping down Royal

Avenue.'

'We heard that. We can only presume that somebody rescued them from the skip behind our shop and stitched them back together.'

I immediately pounced on that. 'I thought they were damaged *beyond* repair?'

'Beyond the standard of repair we pride ourselves on. How close was your witness to them? They probably looked like a dog's dinner. Mr Block, Larry, the trousers are gone, we paid up, we paid up above and beyond, I think you should drop this — while you still can.'

It sat in the air for several long moments.

Then I cut the line. I put the receiver down and stood there, quite shocked by this unexpected turn of events. *While you still can.* I was being warned off. Threatened. It wasn't even a veiled threat. It was explicit, if understated, like a killer in mittens.

The phone rang and I thanked God for the distraction. I said, 'Hello, No Alibis.'

And the same voice said, 'Is that Larry?'

My own voice rose a couple of octaves as I gave him an innocent, 'Larry?'

And he said, 'Larry Block. I was speaking to him a minute ago and I got cut off and I hit caller ID and then I called the number and you answered the phone.'

'Well, I'm sorry, there's no Larry here.'

'What's the name of that place again?'

'What place?'

'You answered the phone and said hello no something.'

'Ah. No. You misheard. I said hello, Noah. Noah Alibees. That's my name. It's French Canadian originally. I design hats. Are you calling about a hat?'

It seemed to do the trick. He quickly apologised and rang off. When I put the phone down I found that my hands were damp, my shirt was sticking to my skin and my heart was beating nineteen to the dozen.

Two days a week I employ a student called Jeff to mind the shop while I sit in the back office trying to make my books balance. He's keen and writes poetry and belongs to Amnesty International, but he'll grow out of all of these things. My office is close enough to the till so that I can hear what's going on in the store, in particular if Jeff is misusing the phone to call either his girlfriend or some government agency to demand that a political prisoner not be repatriated to Sierra Leone. In light of the previous day's threat I had considered not allowing Jeff to answer the phone at all, but a cursory examination of the books told me I wasn't in any position to turn away potential business, so by way of compromise I instructed him to answer any incoming calls with a French accent, which he managed passably well, and to be as vague as possible until he was able to ascertain the nature of the enquiry. Vagueness for Jeff, truth be told, wasn't going to be a huge stretch. I made him repeat *Noah Alibees* over and over until he got it just right. Then I said that if anyone called and asked for Larry he was to reply, 'There is no Larry here, would you like to buy a hat?'

Towards noon I was just beginning to think that I might have gotten hold of the wrong end of the stick. There had been four phone calls, all of them from either customers or publishers' reps. But then the fifth call came in and my carefully constructed cover story quickly began to unravel. I heard Jeff say, 'Noah Alibees, would you like to buy a hat?' and then, 'Yes, hats, all different types.' And then, 'No there's nobody called Larry Block here.' I moved from my desk in the back to the body of the shop. 'Nope, no Lawrence Block either.' Then with a piece of inspired improvisation Jeff added, 'You'd have to go to a mystery bookshop to find Lawrence Block.' Jeff saw me; he smiled and gave me the thumbs-up. Then he said, 'No trouble at all,' and hung up. When I approached the till he said, 'You look a little pale, what's the matter?'

I put my hands on the counter to steady myself, took a

deep breath and said, 'I'm being intimidated by the owner of a shop that specialises in the cleaning and repair of leather goods.'

Jeff gave this due consideration. Then he said, 'Somebody's scrawled all over the John Grisham books.'

3

By the next day, and still being alive, and the shop not having been burned to the ground, I decided that I'd misinterpreted what the leather-care man had to say, that his threat had been more about consulting his lawyers than tanning my hide. However, I didn't wish to push my luck by calling him again to confirm this or to ask further questions about Mrs Geary's trousers, so instead I turned to the internet. I keep a database of loyal customers and send them an e-newsletter once a month. It's all about building a relationship. I try to sell them the latest releases and they burden me with their personal problems. It's tiresome but necessary. On this occasion, however, I wasn't selling anything, I merely asked those of my lovely customers living in the greater Belfast area to keep an eye out for a pair of leather trousers, and described their design in considerable detail. I included the words 'substantial reward' without specifying that it was a £10 book token plus a signed copy of *Harry Potter and the Prisoner of Azkaban,* albeit signed by Jehovah's Vengeance Grisham.

I didn't hear anything for another three days, but then, slowly, reports began to come in, and then what had been a trickle became a fast-flowing stream. The trousers were spotted again in Royal Avenue, at a cinema on the Belfast Road, at a concert in the Waterfront Hall, and twice again in Royal Avenue. It seemed like Royal Avenue was the place to be. Each of my informants who saw her there had observed the trousers between 12.30 and 1.30 p.m., and reported their occupant as, and I quote, 'a big girl' wearing too much make-up and a short white beautician's smock over the trousers. Putting two and two together, I decided to visit that purveyor of perfume and paracetamol, Boots. As it happened, I had a prescription that needed filling, so I was able to kill two birds with one stone. While standing in the pharmacy queue I kept a close eye on the make-up counters, and before very long I was rewarded with my first sight of Mrs Geary's leather trousers, which sent a shiver of anticipation, if not excitement, down my spine. I watched them for several minutes, moving up and down on the customer side of the counter as the large woman who inhabited them applied make-up to a pale woman in a pink woollen trouser suit; she was saying, 'Oh yes, that shade really suits you, and I'd tell you if it made you look like an old slut.'

The pharmacist then asked if I'd taken this particular type of antidepressant before, and I said yes, twice daily for the past fifteen years. He asked if it worked for me and I said it was early days yet. I paid for the prescription, and it now being 12.30 I was pleased to see the woman in Mrs Geary's leather trousers finish with her client and hand over her cash-desk key to a colleague. She then pulled on a short coat over her beautician's jacket and left the shop.

I hurried up to the beauty counter and said, 'Damn, I missed her . . .' The girl behind the counter looked unconcerned, but asked if she could help. 'Your colleague — in the leather trousers — she was checking out the availability of a certain perfume for me . . . but now I've missed her.'

'She'll be back at two.'

'Damn, I have to get back to work — but I could

phone to see how she got on. Who should I ask for?'

'Ask for Natasha.'

'Natasha . . . ?'

'Yes, Natasha.'

'Her surname . . . ?'

'Just ask for Natasha. Natasha on the make-up counter.'

'But in case there's any confusion, her full name is . . . ?'

'There's nobody else called Natasha.'

Mrs Geary's leather trousers were coming back at two, so there was no immediate panic.

'To tell you the truth,' I said to Laura, which was what it said on Laura's badge, 'she's not really helping me at all. I've been in three times and she keeps fobbing me off with excuses. So I'm really here to make a complaint. Can I speak to your supervisor?'

Laura looked surprised, but she nodded and went to the phone. A couple of minutes later a woman in a smart business suit approached me and said, 'I understand you wish to complain about Miss Irvine?'

Natasha Irvine returned from lunch forty minutes later. I was in position just to the left of the Boots front doors. She was a moon-faced girl with big eyes. There were flakes of sausage-roll pastry in the corners of her mouth and she gave a little jump when I said, 'Hello, Natasha.'

She stopped and began to smile but then she realised she didn't know me, and she might have blushed, but it was difficult to tell with all the make-up, which looked like the Max Factor equivalent of stone cladding.

'It is Natasha Irvine, isn't it?' Her mouth dropped open a little. 'I wanted to talk to you about your leather trousers.'

I gave her my hard look, which is like my normal look, but harder. At this point, if she'd had any sense, she should have asked for ID, and I could have shown her my

Xtravision card and my kidney donor card and then rattled my prescription at her and dribbled off into the distance ranting about this or that, but as it happened my hard look proved more than adequate.

'Oh Christ,' she said, 'they're stolen, aren't they?'

I raised an eyebrow.

'Jesus wept,' she said. 'I took one look at them and I knew he couldn't afford them. My family owns this leather repair place on the Newtownards Road, so I know what costs what. But he swore to God he saved up. Christ.' She blew some air out of her cheeks and said, 'To tell you the God's honest truth, I don't even like them, I've piled the beef on since I had the twins, and they're cuttin' the hole off me. I only wear them to keep him happy. What am I going to do now?'

I gave her another long look. A thick sweat had broken out on her brow, and I decided to move quickly in case it set off an avalanche of make-up. 'Here's what we're going to do,' I said, and this time I did take out my wallet. 'I can't be bothered with pursuing this to court, the paperwork's a bloody nightmare. As it happens, the owner's offered a reward. You tell your man they got stolen from your locker at work, he buys you another present, plus you're two hundred pounds better off.' I took out the money and held it out to her. 'Owner gets the trousers back, I don't have to do any pen-pushing, you're in the money. How does that sound?'

'Too good to be true,' she said.

'It's a once-in-a-lifetime offer,' I said.

She thought about that for just a few moments, then nodded quickly. 'But could you make it two-fifty?' she asked.

I shook my head. 'It's not your call, darlin',' I said, then held firm at two hundred and forty-five.

4

When I got back to the shop I told Jeff to take the hats out of the window, then gave him the rest of the day off. I also gave him a nice bonus. 'What's this for?' he asked.

'Danger money,' I replied. I was feeling generous.

When he'd left I sat by the till, rested my feet on the counter and unwrapped a celebratory Twix. Between the destruction of one stick and the devouring of the second I called Mr Geary.

'Guess who?' I sang.

He made five unsuccessful guesses, so I told him, and he still seemed a little confused, so I reminded him, and then he said, 'Ah, right.' I didn't plunge straight in with the good news, I wanted him to know how much work I'd put in. So I described how I'd established the crime line from the moment he'd left his wife's leather trousers in Pressed for Time: how they'd subcontracted them to the shop on the Newtownards Road, how the owner must have commented on their unique qualities to Miss Irvine's boyfriend, who'd decided that they'd make a perfect gift. He'd then persuaded the owner to fabricate the story about them being damaged and then the owner had panicked when I'd applied just the right amount of pressure. Despite being in mortal fear for my life, I'd nevertheless managed to track down the trousers and make them secure.

'I have them back, Mr Geary,' I said, raising and admiring the chocolate-covered biscuit. 'I have your wife's leather trousers.'

He seemed rather underwhelmed. 'Oh — well, that's . . . ah, that's nice.'

'It cost me five hundred pounds, but I suppose it's still a pretty cheap way to save a marriage.' He cleared his throat. I said, 'So do you want to come and pick them up?'

'Well, no,' he said.

'No?'

'Well, the fact is, it turns out she never liked the trousers in the first place.'

'But . . .'

'She threw a wobbler over my stupidity for losing them, not because of the trousers. I misunderstood.'

'But . . . they're beautiful trousers . . .'

'I know that, but apparently they cut the hole off her.'

'But I've spent—'

'Well, that's your problem, I'm afraid.'

'But . . . but what am I supposed to do with . . .'

'Perhaps you could give them to your own wife.'

The Twix was now melting in my hand.

'Yeah, I wish,' I sighed.

So I was two hundred and forty-five pounds out of pocket on the trousers, not to mention the sleepless night, the rocketing of my blood pressure and the sixty-five quid I'd spent on cheap hats from Dunnes. One day I'd meet the man who'd come up with the phrase, *if you want to get ahead, get a hat*, and I'd have a strong word or two. But in the meantime I'd a business to run. Besides, I have found that when all else fails, you can always fall back on fine writing to see you through a dark patch. The very next day an aspiring book-collector came in enquiring about signed first editions, and I showed him one of the Grishams. He turned it over in his hand as though he knew what he was doing and said, 'How much?'

'If you have to ask . . .' I said with as much disinterest as I could muster.

'No, really,' he said.

I made a quick calculation. Two forty-five, plus sixty-five for the hats, two hundred for my time and another fifty for being an unscrupulous cad. Five hundred and sixty, I said, and I could tell by the way he blanched that it was way more than what he had in mind. But I have learned over all my years in business that if you price something high enough, some sucker will eventually come along and fall for it. And so he pulled out his credit card and bought the Grisham and I was finally back in profit and also, I suppose, a wiser, more cautious man to boot.

I put the book in a nice bag for him and said if he was interested I could maybe lay my hands on another one or two. He smiled nervously and quickly changed the subject.

'I really like your trousers,' he said.

I glanced lovingly down at them and nodded. 'Thanks,' I said, 'they are nice, but they're cutting the hole off me.'

5

It was Serial Killer Week in No Alibis, and thus far the Chianti was proving way more popular than the fava beans.

I pride myself on providing a welcoming atmosphere here in the store. We have a settee and coffee and there's even a toilet if you're caught short. But this is all provided on the strict understanding that you *will buy something*. I'm not a frickin' charity. It may be something off the 'buy one, get one at slightly less than the cover price' table, or I can order some difficult-to-find item off the internet, something you'd be well capable of doing by yourself at home if you weren't such a mental invalid, or, even better, you might allow me to choose a book of distinction for you, drawing on my twenty years' experience in the crime fiction business. Life is too short to spend an hour and a half on a mystery that will ultimately be solved by a cat.

Serial Killer Week got off to an inauspicious start when the opening wine and bean evening was invaded by a former prisoner who misinterpreted the poster, but he was at least able to give us the professional's view of the genre, although in my opinion he was not up to speed on the recent rapid advances in forensic science. However, he made notes. One of my regular customers took quite a shine to him, and they left early together, amid much jolly quipping. I believe in both redemption and the power of love, but I also understand that recidivism in killers is close to 76 per cent; I suspect that we will shortly be reading either about their wedding or her disappearance.

Otherwise we have had several writers visit to give readings or lectures, with varying degrees of success. The Holy Grail, of course, was Thomas Harris, the author of *The Silence of the Lambs* and any number of preposterous prequels and sequels. I only say preposterous because my polite e-mail invitation for him to be our guest of honour was returned as spam and subsequent attempts to contact him were not successful. His loss. I'm sure he would have found my customers, a heady mix of silent-but-deadly farters, shoplifters, alcoholics and students, endlessly fascinating. Not only would the addition of his scrawl to the slowly yellowing pyramid of my unsold stock of his interminable novels have helped to finally shift them, but he might also have been able to apply his incisive knowledge of the workings of the criminal's sociopathic mind to my most perplexing case so far, *The Case of the Fruit on the Flyover.*

It started, as these things usually do, with a customer hesitantly approaching the cash desk and proffering a book for purchase. Books are precious things, and cannot be selected like tinned peas in Tesco. I had watched him pick it from the shelf without even bothering to read either the sales pitch on the back, which I happened to know gave nine-tenths of the plot away, or the review below, from the *Toronto Star,* which unmasked the killer. He then set it face down on the counter, as if embarrassed to be seen with it. In fact, it was high-end stuff, a Robert B. Parker, and it was within my rights and power and inclination to withdraw it from sale through lack of respect, but then I saw his face, which looked sad, and his eyes, which appeared hollow, so I let him have it, as Spenser is always a good remedy for melancholy, and prepared to listen to his woes.

His name was Albert McIntosh, and as soon as he said it I gave him a second look, because there was something familiar about it. He gave me the usual heartbreaking saga about being let down by the long-closed detective agency next door and that he'd heard (erroneously, I might add — I'm very picky) that I was dealing with their considerable backlog of cases.

He said he was the managing director of a small advertising agency in the centre of town. He employed fifteen people and enjoyed a reasonable turnover and a good reputation. He said, 'We're not exactly cutting edge, more middle of the road. Solid. Dependable. We've had the account for Denny's Pork Sausages for twenty-three years. The problem is, about six weeks ago I was driving to work, same route I've taken all my working life, and I have to pass under the flyover just before you go on to the West Link, and I noticed that somebody had spray-painted . . . well, had spray-painted *Albert McIntosh is a fruit* in very large letters in red paint. This was obviously most upsetting to me. Twenty thousand cars pass under the flyover every morning during the rush hour. Many of them have passengers. Then there's the buses, and God knows if you stretch your neck from the train you can probably see it too.'

He did look truly distraught. I myself pass under this flyover, and it was for exactly this reason that I thought I recognised his name. There were of course facts to be established before I could even contemplate getting involved.

'And is it the use of your name or the accuracy of the statement that most vexes you?' I asked.

'Both! How would you like it if someone did it to you? If something isn't done about it soon, Albert McIntosh will become some kind of grotesque slang for people of that, er, persuasion.'

'Do you have anything against people of that, ahm, persuasion?'

'No! That isn't the point!'

I nodded thoughtfully. 'Have you taken any action, thus far?' I asked.

'Yes,' he replied, rather testily. 'I went to the DoE and the council and between them they sent out some clod to paint over it.'

'And . . . ?'

'And, when I drove to work next day it was back. Except now it said, *Albert McIntosh is still a fruit.* I complained again, but they said it could be as much as three months before they get back to it. I can't wait that long, I'll be a laughing stock. That's why I went to see your pal next door.'

The detective next door had never been my pal, and I wasn't much taken with Mr Albert McIntosh's general demeanour, but the fact that the author of these alleged slanders had struck twice piqued my interest, because this determination seemed to me to elevate the crime into a different league — rather than a one-off act of petty vandalism or vindictiveness, this was clearly someone with a grudge, a serial painter leaving his blood-red mark as a challenge to whoever dared take him on, plus he'd done it with a certain amount of panache. I sensed that he would make for a very worthy foe indeed. He would be *my* Hannibal Lecter, my Moriarty, my minority in the woodpile.

Albert McIntosh wanted the graffiti permanently removed and the perp identified. I wanted a small extension to the back of the store. Truth and justice would meet somewhere in the middle.

6

Although as far as Albert McIntosh was concerned time was of the essence, I have learned not to rush in where angels fear to tread. A possible first step was to arrange for the removal of the offending graffiti and to then stake out the flyover and catch the phantom artist literally red handed if he or she dared to strike again, presumably in the middle of the night like all ne'er-do-wells, villains and uhm, charlatans. However, it is not a particularly salubrious part of town, and the heating in the No Alibis van has been on the blink for some time, also my night vision is not great and my antidepressants dictate that I get to bed early and at least attempt to catch up on my sleep. Besides, I was not seeking a physical confrontation with my nemesis, more a psychological contest. My weapon was deduction, his a hairy brush, and what I couldn't deduce myself — well, it was another opportunity to employ my valued and varied clientèle as my eyes and ears around the city, some modicum of payback for all the countless man hours I've wasted on them.

This is all still quite new to me, so I am not above

seeking wiser counsel. When that isn't available I occasionally consult my assistant Jeff. I would say that he works for me Tuesdays and Thursdays, but it would be more accurate to state that he appears in the store twice a week and manages to spend most of that time on the phone calling disinterested parties on behalf of the local chapter of Amnesty International. Jeff has been rather subdued since the death of General Pinochet. Human rights violations under his regime had been Jeff's area of expertise, but now that the General was gone, the spotlight had shifted on to more recent abuses in the Middle East, leaving him marginalised. He had committed the cardinal sin of failing to move with the bleeding-heart-liberal times, he was yesterday's man clinging to the vain hope that someone even more despotic would come to power in Santiago and rescue him from his do-gooding isolation. I thought drawing him into helping me with the case might rescue him from his doldrums in a way that my humming of 'Don't Cry for Me, Chile' every time I passed him hadn't.

So I outlined the facts of the case to Jeff. He then asked a series of pertinent questions. He wanted to know the exact location of the flyover, and if there was any other graffiti on it (none); he asked about Albert McIntosh's personal life (married, three children), his social life (golf club, rugby club), the state of his business (profitable) and his religious beliefs (always relevant in this city, Protestant atheist). He wanted to know about disgruntled employees (not aware of any), unsatisfied clients (difficult to be sure) and if Mr McIntosh was prepared to admit to harbouring any skeletons in the closet (literally the closet) — but no, to all intents and purposes Albert McIntosh was a model citizen and nobody had a bad word to say about him, apart, obviously, from the phantom graffiti artist.

I asked Jeff in the light of all of this information what our next move might be, while also reminding him to bear in mind that I occasionally suffer from stress-induced bouts of agoraphobia.

Jeff nodded for several long moments before giving me the benefit of his wisdom.

'It's a big flyover,' he said, 'so I would go up there in the dead of night, and right beside what he's written, I would spray in even bigger letters — *Whoever wrote this is a cunt.*'

I thought about this for a while before responding. 'Jeff, if you wrote *whoever wrote this*, you'd be calling yourself . . . that.'

'Ah . . . *right.* Then I'd write — *Whoever wrote that is a cunt,* and have a little arrow pointing at *Albert McIntosh is still a fruit.*'

It seemed to me that he was merely matching one derogatory statement with another and that might only antagonise our target.

'Exactly,' Jeff replied, 'it might flush him out into the open. And it may not even be a man. It might be a woman. In which case she might not only be one but also has—'

'Yes — okay, Jeff, I think I get your point.' I had to cut him off because that rare breed of human being known as a customer had entered the store.

Jeff, however, was not easily deterred. 'She may not only be a metaphorical . . .'

'No "c" words,' I said, indicating the new arrival . . . but also literally. And now that I think about it, maybe even figuratively as well. So actually, what I'd have to spray next to *Albert McIntosh is still a fruit* is *Whoever wrote that is a cunt, literally, metaphorically and figuratively.* And I suppose I'd also have to spray, *By the way, no he isn't.*'

We were going to need a bigger flyover.

Having wasted half of my life discussing the affair with Jeff, it was time to get down to business. With Jeff's cavalier approach to using my phone, and his lackadaisical approach to apprehending shoplifters, and his habit of giving his friends free books, and selling his own secret supplies of ethical coffee to the customers and pocketing the proceeds — thus making it unethical, I suppose — closing the shop over lunchtime and bringing him with me actually saved me money. Besides, he works out once a month, which is once more than I do, and when he's thinking about something intensely his brow furrows up and his eyes cross slightly, which makes him look quite threatening, so it was good to have him along to offer me at least some semblance of protection as I crossed from the oasis of south Belfast into the Wild West.

We drove directly to the flyover and found a parking spot just a few yards short of it. The No Alibis van is a black Volkswagen with the chalk outline of a corpse on both sides and the words *Murder Is Our Business* below. Given our location, I was rather worried about a rush of volunteers. However, much to my relief, we were left alone, possibly because of Jeff's furrowed brow and crossed eyes, which perhaps allowed him to be mistaken for a local. I jest, of course, because since they came to power their brows have been smooth as silk and their eyes straight and triumphant.

Albert McIntosh is still a fruit was written in red paint, at least a metre high, right across the flyover. The letters were well formed, which suggested that they hadn't been sprayed or painted in a rush, which surely would have been the case if it had been done from below, as the height of the flyover would have certainly required an extended ladder to be placed on the road, and then moved from left to right across it. Even late at night there would be too much traffic to make this practical. Also, the 'r' in Albert was reversed — an imperfection that didn't so much suggest dyslexia as the probability that the painting had been done from above, with the artist hanging over the edge of the flyover and, in effect, painting upside down.

We repaired to the top of the flyover and in studying the footpath there were rewarded with a trail of red paint drops leading away across the bridge and stopping abruptly just short of a small triangle of fenced-off waste ground. By pressing our faces against the wire we could clearly see, nestling amongst torn bin liners, a red-splashed pot of discarded paint. I immediately directed Jeff to climb the fence to retrieve it. I would have done it myself, but my back had not been good for several days, mostly through shifting unsold copies of *Hannibal Rising* from the front of the shop to the rear. Also, I have a morbid fear of rats, and mice, and nettles and wasps and jagged cans and rotting food and damp newspapers and the unemployed.

Obviously our budget does not stretch to fingerprints or DNA testing, so if we were to track down the culprit our clues would have to come from the information on the pot itself. Fortunately for us the man — or woman — we were seeking, perhaps never dreaming that one day he or she would have one and a half of the finest detectives in the city on his or her trail, had neglected to remove the price sticker from the pot of Dulux Red Devil Matt Finish, which not only revealed that it had been purchased from a wholesale paint supply company called, with typical Northern Irish resistance to excessive verbiage, The Wholesale Paint Supply Company, but at a brushstroke reduced our field of suspects from the entire population of the city down to just its many thousands of painters and decorators. And working on the premise that women give the orders and men do the painting, it was also hugely likely that we were looking for a man rather than a woman. We were barely twenty minutes into the case and we were already closing in for the kill. However, we were unable to immediately pursue our evidence further due to our pressing need to get back to the shop and open up after lunch. It was, in effect, a commercial break.

7

Or would have been, if there had been any customers waiting on our return. However, one must be open to the *possibility* of customers, so I flipped the *Closed* sign, paid Jeff for his assistance and sent him on his way back to college.

I took my place behind the counter and stared for a while at the empty paint pot on it. The question was, had he bought it as part of a job lot for a client or this single pot purely for use as a phantom graffiti artist? If it was the latter, then the fact that the pot was empty suggested that it may have been used elsewhere for possibly similar nefarious purposes. I don't have that many customers, but the ones I do have, that is, the ones who actually buy books as opposed to those who merely browse for three minutes so that they won't feel guilty about asking to use my toilet, represent such a broad cross-section of our society, ranging across all class, political, religious and intellectual boundaries, that I was confident that they could help me establish if the serial painter had struck previously or indeed since. The simplest and most direct route was via the No Alibis internet newsletter, through which I more usually bombard them with once-in-a-lifetime offers for books they could easily purchase on Amazon for much less money and actually receive through the post the very next day, as opposed to my own more idiosyncratic service, which might take several weeks, or months, or, in one case, a year and a half. But I think they appreciate the human touch; instead of receiving some corrugated, machine-stamped package plucked from a mile-high shelf by a bibliographic robot, they receive a crumpled, torn and reused envelope personally licked closed by a fading member of Amnesty International. So it was that I sent out an appeal to my customers asking that they keep an eye out for other possible instances of name-and-shame graffiti painted in Dulux Red Devil Matt Finish.

Meanwhile, I refocused on the paint pot and decided to call The Wholesale Paint Supply Company. I asked to speak to the manager and was immediately put through to a man called Taylor. As I like to keep a little separation between my detective work and my bookselling activities, I told him that my name was Walter Mosley and that I was an interior designer. I explained that I'd come across this simply divine shade of red paint, the Dulux Red Devil Matt Finish. It was glorious and warm and yet curiously violent, and it reminded me of my mother and the feast of the Passover and that warning they painted on doors about first-born sons or overdue rent. Perhaps, in retrospect, I sounded a little intense, but I believe that if you create a character you have to inhabit it and sell it, and I certainly did that. He responded with, 'It's only a friggin' tinna paint, mate.' I laughed heartily and told him I was interested in purchasing the DRDM Finish in bulk, but before I did I needed to know if it really was as vibrant as it looked in the pot and as mesmerising as it appeared on the colour charts; I wanted to see it in situ. To that end I asked him for the names of customers who had recently purchased it. He was a bit reluctant at first, but once I mentioned that I had the contract for the interior design of the new *Titanic* they were building next year and would be looking for a dependable supplier he changed his tune and quickly furnished me with the information I required. I jotted down the names of four decorating firms who had purchased the DRDM Finish in the past six months. Of these, only one had bought just a single pot. Dessie Martin and Son, with an address on the Ormeau Road. I asked if by any chance he kept a record of the serial numbers of the pots they sold. He said they did. I asked him to read out the serial number of the pot sold to Dessie Martin and Son. Before he did, he asked me why I wanted it. I told him I collected serial numbers of paint pots. It was the first thing that came to mind. He gave me a rather long 'Okaaaaaay,' and, perhaps with one eye on the *Titanic* contract, proceeded to read out the number. I had turned my pot over by this point, and repeated each number as I matched it to my own.

'Bingo,' I said just as he finished.

'Excuse me?'

'Nothing — I ah, I think I'll call this Dessie Martin and see just how wonderful the finish is before submitting my order. Thank you very much for your—'

But before I could finish, he cut in with, 'Dessie Martin is dead.'

That really threw me.

'Nice bloke,' he said kindly, 'asbestosis, just a few weeks back. Occupational hazard, I'm afraid.'

The trail had gone from red hot to stone-cold dead in an instant. Still, at least I would be able to tell Albert McIntosh that his troubles were over. I thanked Taylor again and was about to put the phone down when he said, 'Listen, mate, is that true enough about the *Titanic*, are they really building another one?'

'Don't be such a moron,' I said and cut the line.

The phone rang a couple of minutes later and I said, 'Good afternoon, No Alibis, Murder Is Our Business,' and a familiar voice said: 'Is that Walter Mosley?'

'No,' I replied automatically.

'I just hit 1471 and this number came up. Is this not his

phone?'

'Ah — yes,' I said. 'But he's gone. Just this moment.'

'When will he be back?'

'He won't. He's gone for good. He's accepted a job in Jerusalem.'

'So who the hell are you?'

'We share a house. But he's moved out. Just right now. He won't be back. He called me an idiot.'

'He called me a moron,' said Taylor.

'He's a bad egg.'

'If I ever see him,' said Taylor, 'I'm going to beat the head off him.'

'He'll deserve it,' I said. 'I heard every word.'

'What's that place called again?'

'What place?'

'You said hello, Noahbylies or something? And you definitely said *murder is our business.*'

I cleared my throat. 'Noahbylies — yes, indeed. It's an . . . Elvish word. Elvish for bookshop. We specialise in science fiction and fantasy novels. You know, *Lord of the Rings*. Mordor is our business.'

There was a long pause, during which my heart beat perhaps as hard as it ever has, harder even than the day I first set eyes on the girl in the jewellery shop across the road, the girl I hadn't yet had the courage to approach but with whom I was deeply in love.

'Right. Okay, mate. If you see him again, tell him he's a cheeky bugger.' He put the phone down and so did I. I immediately clapped my hands together. Once again I had outsmarted an enemy by deftly switching character and twisting circumstance to my advantage. However, to be absolutely certain I called BT and requested a change of telephone number. It would cost me several hundreds of pounds and countless man hours to change all of my stationery and inform my customers and suppliers, but it was better to be safe than sorry. I was already dealing with one insane tradesman, I didn't need another one on my tail.

That evening's event in Serial Killer Week was a competition for the most fiendish idea for a serial killer novel. Although one might think that all possible themes have already been exploited, I believe it bears comparison to the composition of love songs — every time you think the subject is exhausted, something fresh and original from Chris de Burgh comes along. However, it soon became clear that the majority of those in the audience were not treating the subject with the seriousness it deserved. I had spent a lot of time and effort organising the event, I didn't need idiots suggesting that the next big serial killer twist might be to have a character who doesn't actually kill his victims, but just gives them dead legs. Or that a great name for a serial killer might be the Coco Pop Kid. So I put the cork back in the bottle and brought the proceedings to an early conclusion. I kept smiling throughout, as one must, but inside I was seething.

Later, with the shop empty and the shutters down, I sat drinking flat Coke and slowly began to mellow out. I decided to check my e-mail and was gratified to find that my proper customers, those who weren't just interested in playing the big man or making fun of a legitimate and relevant branch of literature, had responded in considerable numbers to my request for information. There were more than a dozen examples of what was surely the phantom graffiti artist's handiwork from all different parts of the city. A foot-path on the Malone Road bore the legend *Alan McEvoy beats dogs*; a gable wall on the Andersonstown Road had *Seamus O'Hare plays away from home*; on Palestine Street the front door of a student flat had been daubed with the words *Coke dealers live here* and a parish house in Sydenham was decorated with *Rev. Derek Coates does not believe in transubstantiation*. They continued in this vein. Whether they were lies, slurs, slanders or half-truths was not my business; the only evidence I was interested in was that of their very existence, and it just galled me that their sheer volume was now of no relevance at all. Dessie Martin was dead. In fact, the effort of it all had probably advanced his demise, weakened as he was by asbestosis. But then, when I checked the very last e-mail, from a fan of Lord Peter Wimsey in the north of the city, I was suddenly brought up short — the words *Michael Lyons wears a dress* had appeared on a wall, the night *after* my request for information. For several moments I was stunned by this, but then it came to me and I cursed myself for being so retarded. The evidence had been there all along — Taylor had said it was Dessie Martin and *Son*. It wasn't the sins of the father, it was the misdemeanours of the son.

8

I rapidly checked the Yellow Pages and found the phone number for Dessie Martin and Son. Although it was well after business hours it was probably a small enough concern to have been administered from home. My call went straight through to an answering machine and, somewhat poignantly, I thought, an elderly voice, rasped out through laboured breaths, said that they were closed for the evening, but in an emergency could be contacted on the following mobile number. I wasn't quite sure what kind of an emergency a painter and decorator could expect to have, apart from dripping and peeling, but nevertheless, suffused with adrenaline at the prospect of confronting my nemesis, I called the mobile number.

He answered on the third ring. 'Jimmy.'

'Jimmy Martin?'

'Aye.'

'Your dad was Dessie Martin?'

'Aye — who's this?'

'I am your nemesis.'

'What's that, Polish or Romanian? I'm not takin''

anyone on at the moment . . .'

'No, you misunderstand. I represent a number of people you may be familiar with. Alan McEvoy, Seamus O'Hare . . .'

'Oh shite!'

'The Rev. Derek Coates . . . Albert McIntosh . . . need I go on?'

'Listen, mate, I—'

'You have slandered these men, you have sullied their reputations, they're going to sue you for millions, do you hear me?'

He was panicked and frightened, and it felt good.

'Please — you have to understand it wasn't me, it was my da.'

'Not last night it wasn't!'

'Shite!'

'We know everything, Jimmy Martin, everything.'

'Oh God . . . look, I'm sorry . . . it was my da . . . he made me promise I would finish his work, it was only the one, I swear to Christ.'

'You better tell me all about it, son,' I said with calm but threatening authority, a tone I had perfected over twenty years dealing with publishers' reps. 'How did all this start?'

There was a moment's hesitation; then, when he spoke, his voice was softer, and cracked several times with emotion. 'Look . . .' he said, 'I'm really sorry . . . My da wasn't well for a long time. He had as—'

'Asbestosis,' I cut in.

'Christ. Okay — he was sick, but he continued working right up to the end, but as time wore on it began to really get to him that the people he was working for were such hypocrites. All smiling and nice to your face, but behind closed doors, they had all these secrets. You see, Mr . . . ?'

'Mosley. Walter Mosley.'

'Like yon detective fella?'

I cleared my throat. 'Just stick to the story, son.'

'Sorry, of course — Mr Mosley, you have to

understand, we're painters and decorators. We get left alone in people's houses or offices all the time. Whenever you're gone, we go for a hoke. We all do it. Painters, cleaners, plumbers . . . We look in drawers, we open cupboards, we go into your bedroom, we switch on your computer, we check out your hidden DVDs. We don't generally steal stuff, and what we learn we keep to ourselves. It's like an unwritten rule. Tradesman's honour, we call it. We're just curious, there's no real harm in it. But my dad was dying, and he couldn't stand that his life was ebbing away while all of these people were prospering despite their sordid little secrets. So he wanted to expose them, and I knew he was doing it and I don't know if the satisfaction of it kept him going, but he certainly stayed on his feet much longer than the doctors told us he would, but as he was getting to the end he just couldn't do it any more, so he made me promise to finish his work. It's done now, Mr Mosley, there will be no more graffiti.'

It was a sad tale, and it had the ring of truth to it, but a crime is a crime, is a crime. It wasn't an accident, it wasn't a one-off act of vandalism committed in a moment of madness; these acts were premeditated, they had sullied the reputations of hard-working individuals across the city. The fact that Dessie Martin was dead was unfortunate, as was the misguided decision by his son to carry on his campaign of hate. But justice must be served.

'Jimmy,' I said, 'there are some very angry people out there.'

'I understand that.'

'And they want something done about this.'

'I know . . . but if they sue . . . if they go to the cops . . . I've a young family, I . . .'

'Would you be willing to undertake some form of community service?'

'Yes — anything.'

'Well. I will put that to them. Stay by your phone.'

I cut the line. I drank another Coke. I ate a Twix. Then

I called him back. He answered on the first ring.

'Jimmy,' I said, 'you're a very lucky man. I have spoken to the Committee . . .' I paused there for a moment, and I could almost feel him quake at the mention of this nonexistent organisation, 'and they are willing to give you a chance. We have considered several possibilities for your community service — obviously employing your professional talents — amongst them repainting the headquarters of the Samaritans or a church hall in Finaghy, but ultimately they have decided that you must first whitewash over all the offending graffiti and then you must decorate, completely free of charge and without complaint and to the highest standard, a bookshop in Botanic Avenue that plays a vital role in educating the local community. Only on completion of this will we, they, consider halting the legal process that we, they, have recently set in motion. Are you prepared to do this?'

'Yes . . . yes, of course,' he replied quickly, 'and thank you so much for giving me this last chance.'

'The pleasure's all mine,' I responded.

9

With Serial Killer Week over for another year, and the university closed for the summer, my usual trickle of customers had slowed to a turgid drip, leaving me more than enough time to contemplate both my navel and the unabashed beauty working in the jewellery shop across the road. I guessed that she wasn't the owner of the business, as she never seemed to be the last to leave or to lock the premises after her. Of course she might just have been rather accomplished at delegating responsibility, a path I had once ventured down with my trusty assistant Jeff, only to be mightily disappointed. I need not go into details here, other than to say it involved Dixieland jazz. She was petite, and when leaving never appeared to wear jewellery — at least as far as my binoculars could detect — which I thought said a lot about her. She usually walked at a steady clip, always clutching a paperback book in her hand, yet in passing No Alibis never once thought to stop in or to glance through the open door or to admire the life-size painting of Columbo that dominates the wall behind me. I had once gone a bit mad and given her a little wave as she passed, but she either didn't see it or deliberately ignored me. A shuffling drunk did notice, however, and misinterpreted my friendly gesture as an indication that I wished him to continue on his merry way. He therefore immediately and perhaps understandably entered my shop and spat on a table of books and called me the kind of names that do not feature in the average episode of *Murder, She Wrote*.

However, on this occasion I had been studying her shop window for forty-seven minutes, without detecting any signs of movement, and was wondering if after eight months of steady surveillance it was time for me to take the initiative by introducing myself to her under the guise of buying a watch or a bangle for my mother, when the door opened and my next case walked in. I reluctantly turned from my vigil and found myself nodding at a distinguished-looking middle-aged gentleman in a grey pinstripe suit and lavender tie. Without bothering to glance at the shelves of new releases, or the table devoted to titles recommended by the staff — me, in fact, because Jeff's taste is in his bottom — he immediately approached the counter and placed two hands on it as if to steady himself, before asking in a deep yet querulous voice if the new James Patterson was in yet.

'Sir,' I replied with suitable haughtiness, because I know my onions, 'the *old* James Patterson isn't in. This is a James Patterson-free zone. Once we begin stocking Pattersons we'll have no room for anything else. We may as well change the name of the shop to Patterson Books.'

I felt confident in being so flippant because I knew straight away that this man was no more interested in James Patterson than he was in the man in the moon. It was his voice: choked with emotion. And nobody has ever gotten emotional over a James Patterson novel. If I had known then that this man's visit would lead me to become embroiled in my most fiendishly difficult and certainly most dangerous investigation, *The Case of the Dancing Jews*, then I would have excused myself for several moments, darted out the back way, charged down the alley, raced across the road to the Eason's book store and bought that month's James Patterson, sped back across the road and up the alley, all the while ruthlessly peeling off their 25% off sticker, in at the rear entrance, through the kitchen, into the body of the shop and then sold it to him for full whack, all in order to avoid further involvement in the sordid events I am about to recount.

However, too late, he started to talk, and before very long he had reeled me in to a mystery that began, as with all of the others, with his employing the services of the private eye next door.

'Truth be told,' he began, 'I'm not really after a Patterson. But I understand he's very . . . *popular.* It was just an ice-breaker. You see, I'm a publisher myself.' He nodded at me, clearly under the mistaken impression that this meant that there was already some kind of a bond between us. He nodded at my Ikea shelves. 'Of course not your type of material. Local books. History. Photography. Memoirs. Some literature, a little poetry. We do a very nice calendar of Strangford Lough. We're called Beale Feirste Books.'

'Yes Belfast Books,' I said.

'No — a lot of people make that mistake. It's actually Beale Feirste Books.'

'But it's the same thing.'

He looked at me. 'No it's not.'

I knew all about Belfast Books. It was the kind of publishing I detested. It survived on Arts Council grants and donations from charitable foundations. It was a producer of decaffeinated coffee table books masquerading as a beleaguered champion of culture. Under normal circumstances he wouldn't have given me the skin off his custard, but he was clearly after something. He didn't say it, but what he meant by 'some literature, a little poetry' was that nothing I sold in No Alibis would, in his mind, qualify as literature. That I was little more than a pimp for pulp fiction. That my life's work amounted to a wasted life. That I might as well never have existed.

I hate judgemental people.

I could have told him that we publish our own calendar every year. That it has twelve months and everything. That if he cared to flip back its pages he would become the beneficiary of a spiral-bound history of crime fiction in handy captions and meticulously reproduced classic covers: from arguably the very first *roman policier* (Emile Gaboriau's *Le Crime d'Orcival*) through the Yellow Back crime fighters (like Mary Paschal in *Experiences of a Lady Detective* in 1861). He would learn about twenty-year-old schoolteacher Edward Ellis who in the same decade sold 600,000 copies of *Seth Jones*, one of the first dime novels. He would become aware of the many rivals of Sherlock Holmes — Sexton Blake, Craig Kennedy, Martin Hewitt and Baroness Orczy's *Skin O' My Tooth*. He might learn the truth about Dashiell Hammett's *Continental Op* and his newspaper cartoon strip, 'Secret Agent X-9', or about Raymond Chandler calling Mickey Spillane's I, *The Jury* pulp writing at its worst even as it sold its four millionth copy; of James M. Cain's *The Postman Always Rings Twice* being seized by the Boston police for obscenity, of fantastic evocative noir titles like *Lady — Here's Your Wreath, Kiss My Fist, Road Floozie, Night and the City, Now Try the Morgue, Murder Thy Neighbour* . . . oh, I could have opened up a whole new world to him, but there was no point, his blinkers were firmly in place.

'Okay,' I said, 'you're a publisher. We don't sell your type of books.'

'It's not about the books,' he said, 'it's about your friend next door.'

Ah.

He wasn't the first to make this assumption, and he wouldn't be the last. But at that point he wasn't worthy of an explanation.

'What about him?' I asked.

'I paid, in advance, and now he's flown the coop. You have to tell me where he is.'

'I have no idea where he is. And one should never pay for *services* in advance.'

He fixed me with a look that was somewhere between anger and despair. 'I had to,' he finally admitted. 'I had to pay for his flight. I should have known then something was up. What sort of a state does a business have to be in that its owner can't afford a ticket to Frankfurt?'

'Frankfurt?'

I think it was at this exact point that I got sucked in. It was a classic honey trap. He hadn't even explained the case yet, but already the air was rich with intrigue and the possibility of international travel. He shook his head and sighed. I could see now that his face was deathly pale and the pulse on the side of his head was standing out like a varicose vein. He was obviously in turmoil. As it happened, at that very moment Jeff appeared through the door for his lunchtime shift — although I am constantly surprised to see him. I was frankly astonished that he accepted my argument that because I only get half as many customers in the summer months he should only receive fifty per cent of his normal pay. Still, it's a hundred per cent more than he gets working for that shower of whingers at Amnesty International, and at least with me he doesn't have to hold a placard or pretend that he understands Spanish. So I quickly instructed him to take over the desk, and to keep an eagle eye on the jewellery shop across the road, before escorting the Belfast Books publisher to the rear of the store, an open-plan area where I have provided a sofa and two armchairs — rescued from premature incineration on an Eleventh Night bonfire, thankfully the smell of petrol is now fading — for my customers to sit and browse through the books at their leisure, provided they can concentrate while I give them the Death Stare from the cash desk. One must make some sort of an effort in these days when customer care is so important, but there is a fine balance — I'm not a frickin' library. I like to think the atmosphere in the store is finally balanced between the pull-up-a-chair-and-peruse-our-books-for-nothing of Borders and the reading room at Guantanamo Bay. However, the area was currently unoccupied, so I sat him down, made him coffee and on my return encouraged him to tell all.

His name was Daniel Trevor and he had set up Beale Feirste Books with his wife Rosemary fifteen years previously. They had two children, who missed their mother dreadfully. Beale Feirste Books was, he said, a reasonably profitable business, but that wasn't really its *raison d'être*; they just loved books, and the arts, and artists. Beale Feirste Books operated out of a large house in the County Down countryside that doubled as an artists' retreat, where for days or weeks or months at a time writers, painters or sculptors, composers, dramatists or poets could come to a remote outpost to work free from distraction. 'It is absolutely idyllic,' said Daniel. 'However, now the idyll has been spoiled for ever. My darling wife Rosemary has disappeared, and I don't know where to turn.'

As he said this, his bottom lip quivered. I had never spoken to the girl in the jewellery shop, but I knew I would be similarly distraught if she ever disappeared from my life.

'When was this?' I asked.

He shook his head ruefully. 'It's been nine months now.'

If his face hadn't been so terribly sad I would probably have jumped in with 'Jesus, you took your time!' Instead I gave him a sympathetic 'And no word?'

'No, nothing, no calls, no e-mails, her credit card hasn't been . . .' He took a deep breath. 'I just don't know where to turn. The police, Interpol . . . no use whatsoever. They even dug up my—'

'Patio,' I said reflexively.

He nodded. 'But I swear to God I didn't . . . I wouldn't . . . I love her more than anything.'

He settled himself for a moment, before explaining that every autumn he and his wife travelled to Germany to attend the Frankfurt Book Fair. 'It's a huge old thing . . . almost every publisher in the world, big or small, attends . . . we negotiate international publishing rights and licensing fees . . . there's something like seven thousand exhibitors from . . . oh, about a hundred countries, over a quarter of a million people visit . . . and yet . . . there are so many familiar faces, it's almost like a family gathering.'

I nodded in recognition. I had once hosted a mystery convention over one miserable weekend here in the store, which, due to a combination of bad weather, alternative sporting attraction and a lack of advertising, was, also, literally, something of a family gathering.

'Unfortunately this year, because we had an unexpected influx of poets at our retreat, and they couldn't be left on their own — honestly, they would have been hanging from the rafters — I simply couldn't go. Rosemary — reluctantly I might add, because she hates leaving the kids — had to go to Frankfurt by herself. She was selling the rights to four of our forthcoming titles, she had appointments all day, every day, but she phoned religiously at seven every night. Even though she knew lots of people there she wasn't socialising at all, went to bed early to be sure to be bright for another day's work. The last night I spoke to her, the fourth night of the convention, she was tired but happy, business was going well. I . . . and I hate myself for this now . . . I was quite ratty with her because it had been a rather fractious day at the retreat, and then when I didn't hear from her the next night I thought she was just huffing with me. Then she was due back the following day, but there was no sign of her. Well, I didn't worry, at first, you know what Ryanair is like, they say they fly to Frankfurt but really they take you to Switzerland then put you on a bus for eighteen hours . . . but when she still hadn't arrived by the next morning, well then I really did start to get worried. I contacted the airline, but they said she hadn't turned up for her flight. I called the hotel but they said she'd checked out. I was obviously very unsettled by this stage. I spoke to Frankfurt police, but with the language thing, I wasn't convinced that they understood or fully appreciated my concerns, because she's not the sort who would just go off somewhere on a whim, so I talked to the local CID here and they followed up on my behalf. I have no reason to believe that the police either here or there didn't investigate thoroughly, but the fact is, they haven't found her.'

'So then you turned to Malcolm Carlyle, Private Eye.'

'Yes, exactly, that was three months ago. He talked a good talk. I had to pay for him to go to Frankfurt, and not with Ryanair, and put him up in the same hotel as Rosemary, and that wasn't cheap. He was there for a week, even though everyone to do with the convention was long gone. He told me he was on to something. He kept asking for more money. Now he's disappeared. I am employing a missing person to look for a missing person. I feel like I've been the most dreadful fool.'

It was the first time I'd heard any indication of impropriety regarding my former neighbour. Small businesses go bust all the time, and God knows I've walked that knife edge for long enough, but thankfully those who milk their customers dry in the full knowledge that they're about to go belly up are few and far between.

Daniel Trevor was staring into his coffee. I stared into mine. Jeff stared across the road. Daniel stared some more. I stared some more. Jeff watched the jewellery store.

Eventually Daniel Trevor said: 'I need your help.'

I relaxed then. You see, I never volunteer my services. I must always be asked. It sets the dynamic for a relationship.

'I believe you . . . investigate . . .'

'Daniel, I'm a busy man,' I said, despite all evidence to

the contrary.

'I understand that.'

'But I am intrigued. People do not just disappear. Neither here nor in Germany.'

From the counter, Jeff cleared his throat. 'Six million—' he began, but then quit when I directed the Death Stare at him.

Since my own detective work had begun I had not yet failed to solve a case and my confidence had grown accordingly. So I was not bashful at all about stating: 'Daniel — I will find her. But I must warn you before I start — if you ask a question, you must be prepared for the answer.'

His brow furrowed. 'I'm not quite sure what you mean.'

'I mean, if you ask a question, the answer might not be what you want it to be.'

'I'm still not sure what you're getting at. If I ask a question, it isn't a matter of the answer being what I want it to be. The answer is just the answer.'

'Well, you're being quite literal. I mean if you ask a question, it might have variable answers. You might think that two and two makes four. But it doesn't always.'

'I . . . I believe it does.'

'Okay, bad example. I mean, if you ask what the capital of Australia is, I might immediately say Canberra, but between you asking the question and me actually going to find out the answer, it might easily have shifted to Sydney. Or Perth. Quite often the truth is based on shifting, whispering sands.'

He looked truly perplexed. The standard of my clientèle does not often match the standard of the investigation.

To further clarify I said: 'Look, if you're a lawyer, and you're in court, one thing you always have to remember is this — never ask a question unless you already know the answer.'

'What?'

'That way you'll never be surprised or look foolish.'

'But I don't know the answer. That's why I'm asking you.'

'Indeed,' I said.

In truth my head was feeling a little bit fuzzy. I realised I was past medication time. They're not that strong, but if I miss one it does cloud things.

'Look,' he said, 'my wife has gone. I love her. I need you to find her. If it takes a blank cheque, I'll give you a blank cheque.'

I took that on board.

There were obviously a lot of questions that needed to be asked, but the interview had eaten into my lunchtime, and beyond the medication my stomach was rumbling. I asked him to call back later in the afternoon — 'It'll be quieter,' I told him. *(Hah!)* He suggested instead that I might care to visit him at the Beale Feirste artists' retreat outside Dundrum. I politely declined. It was out in the country. I don't like the smell of cows, or pigs, or goats, or sheep, or chickens, or grass, or wind. Most of my cases are routinely resolved on the phone, or over the internet, or very occasionally by leaving the shop, and then almost always within walking distance, or by a short drive on roads where a 30 m.p.h. speed limit is in place.

Despite my initial excitement about the possibility of international travel, I was already experiencing a rapidly expanding sinking feeling. Deep down I knew that if Mrs Trevor was still in Frankfurt, she would most probably remain there undiscovered, at least by me, because although I like the *idea* of travelling abroad, the reality is somewhat different. I don't like planes. Or ferries. Or trains. Or buses. I'm not comfortable talking to foreigners, even if their English is passable, or even people from the countryside. I don't like strangers or, often, relatives. However, it was all immaterial. I was completely convinced that if I was to find the lady in question, it would not be via the autobahns of Germany, but by speed-bumped minor roads much closer to home. There were children involved, and my intuition and experience told me that if she was still alive, wherever she was, she wouldn't be far from them.

Just as he was leaving, I asked Daniel if he had a recent photograph of his wife. He slipped one out of his pocket. He studied it for a moment before handing it over. As I stood examining it after he left, Jeff peered over my shoulder.

'Cor,' he said, 'she's a bit of a ride. What makes you think she's in Australia?'

It turned into a long, tedious afternoon, and by the end of it I decided I didn't much care whether Mrs Trevor was ever found, blank cheque or not. All the talk of international travel, and police, and Interpol — well, it was outside of my comfort zone. I thought Daniel Trevor's money might be better spent printing posters or splashing her face over a milk carton. Every time the shop door opened and a customer came in, he tutted, and that put me on edge. He was telling me about the books she had been selling in Frankfurt, and the artists she got on best with at the retreat, but I was drifting. I was thinking about the tube of fluorescent light on the ceiling above me, and how insects ever got inside it, and why, and if they realised what they'd done or even thought much about anything at all. I had new stock to check and old stock to shift. I wanted to ask how good his printer was because I'd been thinking about publishing a limited edition by a long-neglected local writer, but I didn't get the chance because he was wittering away about his poor motherless kids. The more I heard, the more I was convinced that Frankfurt had nothing to do with it, that his wife had made her position clear, that she had run off with a poet, she wasn't coming home and she didn't much like her kids, who sounded like whiny brats.

When I walked him to the door I assured him that I would get straight on to the case, but instead I opened a Twix and thought some more about interior lighting.

10

Mystery writers toil away in an ill-rewarded and critically ignored genre that only very rarely throws up someone worthy of the bestseller list or literary acclaim, and even more infrequently, both. Ian 'Rebus' Rankin famously wrote a dozen novels before becoming an overnight sensation. So, given that they often have to scrape by on a pittance, it is particularly galling to them when someone like Brendan Coyle comes along and chalks up the kind of sales they would kill for. And yet might. Galling because Brendan was already a much-garlanded author of literary fiction when he decided to write crime under a pseudonym before being 'accidentally' unmasked. He gives the impression that it is just something he dashes off while waiting for divine inspiration to strike his real work. In reality he contributes nothing new to the genre and instead merely rehashes some of its worst clichés. Yet he sells and sells and the critics adore him. He is a vain, boorish snob, and sometimes I wonder why I ever bothered inviting him to teach a monthly creative writing class in No Alibis.

Then I remember that it's because he does it for

nothing and that I also sell a lot of books off the back of his visits. The only reason he does it for free is that I convinced him that he should be giving something back to 'his' people, and he was sucker enough to fall for it. I like to think that every minute he spends talking twaddle in No Alibis is one minute fewer spent trying to write crime, which is a blessing for us all.

His creative writing classes are artfully constructed exercises in the massaging of his own ego. When he chooses examples of fine writing with which to illustrate his thoughts, he chooses his own. When his students . hesitantly read from their work, he yawns and fidgets. When he does deign to offer advice, it is usually either irrelevant or impenetrable, or both. It is therefore rather surprising to observe how much his students love him, and staggering to have to admit that his class is oversubscribed. One day I will certainly stab him with a letter-opener. But in the meantime I must acknowledge a debt of gratitude — his name was enough to finally entice my jewellery girl into the store.

It happened on the Saturday morning after the lunchtime when I agreed to take on what would become known as *The Case of the Dancing Jews* and the interminable afternoon when I decided that what would become known as *The Case of the Dancing Jews* would actually be too much trouble. Of course I would give it a few weeks before I let him know. I might even cash a very small blank cheque to cover the stress of deciding not to investigate what would become known as *The Case of the Dancing Jews*; one must put one's mental health first. Leather trousers and graffiti, yes. Damaged pottery and wayward dogs, yes. Missing persons and Interpol, no.

During Brendan Coyle's creative writing class I sit on a stool behind the cash desk. When he mentions a book, I pick it up and show it around to try to encourage a sale. I feel a little like a game-show hostess. I was doing this before some fifteen eager students when the door opened and an elfin figure entered. I did not recognise her at first because she was wearing the woollen equivalent of a leather flying cap, pulled down low on her brow and with the equivalent of its leather side straps shadowing most of her face. But then when she pulled it off, and smiled apologetically at Brendan, I realised with a sudden flush to my cheeks, and chest, and arms, and feet, that it was her, my love from the jewellery store.

'Sorry I'm late,' she said. 'Watch stopped.'

Not an awfully good advertisement for the jewellery store, but a splendid opportunity for me, because Brendan shook his head and told her he was sorry too, because the class was already full and perhaps she could put her name down on the waiting list; even before the disappointment could register on her face I was able to saddle up and ride over the brow of the hill.

'No, no, no, not at all,' I said. 'As it happens, we have one place left.'

'No we don't,' said Brendan.

'Yes we do,' I said.

'You told me we were oversubscribed,' said Brendan.

'I lied.'

He gave me a quizzical look. 'Well, that's refreshing honesty.' I looked at the girl. She smiled at me. Brendan looked at me, smiling at the girl, smiling back at me. I looked at him. He nodded. The quizzical look changed to one of understanding. Without knowing any of the background — the countless hours spent watching the jewellery store for some sign of her, following her — Brendan *knew*. And in that moment I also knew that he would do his utmost to ruin my chances with her. He would seek to charm her himself. And if he could not have her, then he would destroy her. That was the way of him.

He immediately ordered her to the Writer's Stool.

I was helpless to intervene.

Brendan teaches that while not everyone can become a

great writer, you can train yourself to *think* like one. Or more importantly, *he* can teach you. To this end he encourages his students to take turns sitting in 'the Writer's Stool' — a bar stool in any other world — which he sets in the window of the shop. He then briefly interviews its occupant, usually seeking to embarrass him or her in some way, before turning the stool to face the street outside for what he likes to call 'the Writer's Challenge'. I have allowed him to get away with this in the past because neither the class nor his students mean anything to me, they are but a means to a paperback sale. But this was different. I was in love. *He* was approaching this new challenge with relish, swaggering with the guile of a bestselling author; she was an innocent aspirant, caught in the tractor beam of his celebrity. But what if she fell for his charm and intelligence and he swept her away from me? Or worse, what if he used her, abused her, then dashed her on the rocks of his rampant ego, hooking her like a fish and then throwing her back, still a fish, but a fish with a big hook through her cheek?

It started innocuously enough.
'Name?'
'Alison,' she said.
'Tell us a little about yourself, Alison.'
'I work in the jewellery shop across the road.'
'And how tedious is that?'
'Not at all, I love it.'
'And yet you seek fulfilment here.'
'No, just looking for some writing tips.'
'Tips?'
Brendan raised his eyebrows. The rest of the class grinned like idiots. None of them would become writers. Some of them were barely readers.

'So what do you like to write, Alison? I believe that fledgling writers should write about what they know. Do you write about jewellery, Alison? Perhaps, given our surroundings, the *theft* of jewellery, or the *jealousy* it so often inspires, or perhaps the *turmoil* of the master jeweller losing his sight? Note the keywords.'

There were nods from the class. Those were definite story possibilities.

'No,' said Alison. 'I don't even like writing that much.'

This drew *ooohs* and *aaahs*. Brendan adopted a look of fake bewilderment. He was enjoying this.

'You *don't even*

'I draw comics. The drawing isn't a problem, but my scripts are no great shakes, that's why I'm looking for—'

'*Comics?*' Brendan nodded to himself, as if giving her predicament due consideration, but when he looked at the other students I could see that his mouth was ever so slightly curled up into a sly smirk, and they returned it to him in spades. They worshipped him. I was in her corner, of course. I understood exactly where she was coming from. Comics, along with mystery fiction, exist in a literary ghetto, and in a much worse part of it at that. Unheralded. Unrewarded. But the great thing is, most of their creators don't care. Still, I felt for her. Brendan and his acolytes were awash with condescension, yet they were sitting in *my* mystery store, taking advantage of *my* largesse, belittling *my* invited guest and future bride. I *seethed.* I would have intervened, I would have led him from the shop by his ear and hurled him on to the pavement outside and turfed his gang of no-hopers out after him, but that would have affected sales, and you can't afford to be overly sensitive in this business. Besides, as it turned out, Alison was well capable of taking care of herself.

Brendan returned his attention to the pretty girl on the bar stool. He gave an overdramatic sigh. 'I suppose we must change with the times, and there is certainly a growing critical acceptance of the graphic novel as a legitimate—'

'Comics,' said Alison.

'Excuse me?'

'Not graphic novels. Comics. I draw comics. And write

them. Badly.'

'Well, *comics,* then. And you write them *badly.* So let's see if we can fix you.' He abruptly clapped his hands together. 'Turn the Writer's Stool to face the street,' he instructed. 'This is an exercise I put all of my students through; some pass with flying colours, some fail miserably.' He surveyed his class. Several heads were bowed in shame. 'Alison,' he continued, 'you, we, have something in our heads called a writer's muscle, and if you don't use it, it gets loose and flabby. This exercise is designed to pump it back up into shape. Are you with me? Are you ready to pump your writer's muscle?'

Alison nodded warily, and then turned her chair to face a Botanic Avenue busy with Saturday morning shoppers.

'Okay — these are the rules. As soon as I say go, you must describe every man, woman, child or dog who passes this window. You must tell me what they look like, where they might be going, what they might be thinking. The key to this is speed, you cannot miss anyone out. They might come one at a time, they might come in groups. You must not even think about what you're saying, you let the muscle do the work. Do you understand?'

'Yes, of course.'

'Okay, then . . . go!' He clapped his hands again. I leaned forward. Everyone leaned forward.

Alison opened her mouth.

'Faster!' Brendan cried.

'I see . . .'

'Faster!' Brendan cried again.

'Man in the leather jacket . . . there's tattoos under there . . . he's going to his mum's . . . woman with the tartan trolley, it's full of cat food . . . skinhead kid off shoplifting

'Clichés! Flex the muscle!'

'Teenager in love for the first time, he's gay . . . man with a cap, you never see caps these days, he yearns for times gone . . .'

'Yearn! Good word!

'. . . man with a briefcase, what's he doing with it on a Saturday? He's told his wife he has to work but he's having an affair, he's going to meet her in the . . . boy on a bicycle, but he's forgotten his lock, trying to decide whether it's safe to . . . masked gunmen going into my jewellery shop . . '

Everyone's head jerked to the right of the window.

'Gotcha!' said Alison.

Nobody dared smile.

'This isn't a game!' Brendan thundered.

'I thought it *was* a—'

'Three strikes and you're out, go again!'

It was getting busier outside.

'Man . . . woman . . . knew each other as kids but he's lost his hair and she can't help looking at it . . . cool dude, male model material, knows it . . . get out of my way, get out of my way, I'm king of the sidewalk

'American slang, twice, lazy, second strike!'

'Lottery ticket, but hole in trousers, this is his last chance, he'll commit suicide if he doesn't . . . old friends meet, she's afraid to ask if she's pregnant in case she's just fat . . . that's a poor excuse for a dog . . . don't see many black faces in Belfast . . . don't drop litter, you wouldn't do it at home . . . yes he would . . . sunglasses, cloudy day, she has a migraine but has to deliver . . . hat box, daughter getting married . . . cripple trying to cross the . . .'

'Three strikes and you're out!' Brendan turned from her and addressed the rest of the class. 'As we have learned in previous weeks, the secret is not allowing yourself to—'

'Excuse me?' It was Alison cutting in, her body still facing the window but turning her head back. 'Why am I out?'

Brendan smiled indulgently. 'Where do you want me to start? Undisciplined language, alliteration, propagation of social stereotypes . . .'

'Stereo what?'

'Cripple. You can't call someone a cripple.'

'Why not?'

'It is politically incorrect and it's socially unacceptable.'

'To call someone a crip?'

'*Yes.* And *that's* even worse. Please vacate the Writer's Stool. Perhaps someone else would care to . . . ?'

Every single hand shot up. I had watched them all at it in the preceding weeks, and none of them were in Alison's league. At least she'd made a stab at humour. And now she wasn't moving. She sat where she was, staring out of the window.

'Alison. Vacate the stool.'

She shook her head. 'That's not fair. You asked me to describe what I saw. I saw a cripple. I *am* demonstrating a rich use of language.'

Brendan raised an eyebrow. 'What would you know about . . . a mere comic . . .' He stopped himself. 'You've had your turn, now vacate the stool. Perhaps after class we can grab a coffee and I can explain to you the rights and wrongs of calling someone a—'

'Cripple,' Alison snapped. 'He's in a wheelchair. He *can't walk.*' She manoeuvred the bar stool round until she was facing Brendan and the rest of the class. 'He is *crippled* by injury. He worked in the Harland and Wolff shipyard for thirty-five years, labouring in the shadow of the mighty twin cranes of Samson and Goliath. On the very day the shipyard closed for good, leaving behind only inherited memories of the *Titanic,* they were shifting abandoned girders and one fell on him, fracturing his spine. He spent eight months in hospital, determined to walk again, but ultimately could not. He has *battled* to reconcile himself to his fate. He never refers to himself as disabled, or wheelchair-bound; he calls himself a cripple because it is a crippling injury, not only to his body, but to his mind. His brain is *crippled* by the realisation that he will not ever walk again, his emotions are *crippled* because he cannot adequately explain how he feels to his wife, because he does not have the vocabulary for it, and she does not have the patience to allow him to develop it. She has worked hard all of her life, always with the prospect of one day being able to retire and enjoy her few remaining years with her husband, but now he is exactly what she says he is, to herself, to her friends when she's been drinking, he's a *fucking cripple* and he can't get it up any more and she'll be damned if she's going to settle for that, she'll—'

'Enough.'

Alison stopped. Brendan stood before her. The class sat, mesmerised. I leant on the counter, in awe.

'You cannot say *cripple*. Now for the last time, get off the stool.'

Their eyes locked.

I had sweat on my brow.

'Cripple,' said Alison. 'Cripple, cripple, cripple.'

'That's it,' Brendan hissed and pointed to the door. 'Get out of my class!' he bellowed. 'I give my *time* for *nothing*, you know! I *give back*. I share and pass on my *knowledge*. All I ask in return is that I'm treated with some *modicum of respect*.'

Alison lifted her woollen flying cap from her lap and pulled it firmly down over her ears before slipping off the stool. She crossed to the door and opened it. She hesitated, looked across at me for too brief a moment, then fixed her attention on Brendan.

'If you ask me,' she said, raising her right hand, 'it's not the fucking writing muscle you need to be concentrating on.'

And then she made the universal sign for wanking, before smiling pleasantly and exiting, leaving No Alibis a wiser, richer place than before.

11

Brendan Coyle wasn't used to anything less than complete deference. He got over the initial shock of Alison's performance and miming exit, but he remained agitated for the rest of the class, and afterwards he was still something of a sweating, palpitating wreck, at least until I caved in and subdued him with a cheap bottle of white I'd been presented with as a thank-you gift from one of my cases, but which I hadn't yet dared open. Anything with the word *Tesco* and/or *WeightWatchers* on the label should be viewed with some suspicion. Wishing to steer the conversation away from Alison — I was still in a bit of a state myself, because I had at last met her, and spoken to her, and done her a favour, and she'd given me a look of gratitude, and the last thing she'd done before giving Brendan the internationally accepted hand signal for wanking was to match eyes with me and I knew that meant *something* and I wasn't about to stand there in my own shop and listen to the woman I loved being repeatedly denigrated by a man who knew nothing about crime fiction yet was still acclaimed as a master of it — I instead turned to the only thing we had in common, which was books, but even that was a dead end of disparate interests until I happened to mention that I'd had the owner of Belfast Books in the shop recently, pleading for help to find his missing wife.

'You mean Beale Feirste Books?' I nodded lethargically. 'As it happens,' he continued, 'I know Daniel quite well. They do an admirable job, encouraging *local* talent.' The emphasis on the local was very deliberate. It was Brendan saying that *he* wasn't local. He was *international*. 'Terrible shame about Rosemary. Fine looking woman.'

'So what's the gossip about what happened?' I asked. 'Did he do her in with a shovel?'

He gave me a look heavy with disdain and pity, as if he expected nothing less from a man who specialised in what I specialise in. 'I should think not. They were deeply in love, you could tell that just by looking at them.'

'A crime of passion, perhaps.'

'Absolutely not. Not Daniel.'

'Everyone can be pushed to it. Perhaps she was having an affair with one of the poets at their little retreat; they're supposed to be a randy bunch, aren't they? And they've so much time on their hands. Poems, I mean, you can knock them out in an hour.'

Brendan shook his head. 'Poetry . . .' And then he thought better of it. He took another sip of his wine, savoured it — although given its origin, God knows what he was savouring — and seemed to get a faraway look in his eyes. 'You know,' he said after a minute of embarrassed silence, 'she wasn't like that at all. She was beautiful, friendly, even flirtatious. There was a spark about her. She was funny, and intelligent, and caring. Took a notion of her myself once. A lot of red wine involved, and I fooled myself into thinking she was interested, but she soon put me straight. I really was smitten. I even told Daniel how I felt. And he absolutely understood. He said, Brendan, don't you know, *everyone* loves Rosemary. She's just fantastic. He obviously had or has something very special with her, something where he doesn't have to be jealous, where he doesn't have to worry about her being tempted by any of their visiting artists, no matter how internationally renowned they may be.'

'Perhaps he has a tremendously large cock,' I said.

I actually shocked myself. Certainly Brendan looked stunned. On reflection, all I can say is that it may have been something of a defence mechanism. Here was a man I hardly knew talking about his personal relations and feelings, and I was mortified. I mean, I only asked if he thought Daniel had murdered his wife, I didn't need to know about his own pathetic attempts at seduction. There's a time and a place for such revelations. Like your death bed. Not in No Alibis on a Saturday morning with two genuine customers and a shoplifter listening in.

Still, I have to admit, it was serving to reignite my interest in the case. Daniel had been rather modest about describing the obvious attractions of his wife. She was clearly, as Jeff had indelicately put it, and as evidenced by her photograph, something of 'a ride', and according to what Brendan had now told me, she also had men falling left, right and centre for her. Two words immediately sprang to mind: femme fatale, and they immediately opened up an entire vista of possibilities. Despite both Brendan and Daniel's assertion that she was incorruptible, I naturally suspected otherwise. She had rejected Brendan because he was a dick, and was betraying Daniel because he was too naive to believe that she would. That's how they operate. Femmes fatales find marriage to be confining, loveless and sexless, they use their cunning and sexuality to gain their independence. Flickering black-and-white images crowded through my mind. Phyllis Dietrichson like a caged animal in *Double Indemnity*, Rip Murdoch wishing aloud in *Dead Reckoning* that women could be reduced to pocket size, to be put away when not desired and returned to normal size when needed. I saw Rita Hayworth pouring it on in *Gilda* and *The Lady from*

Shanghai; the cut of her clothes, her words, her actions, her ability to hold the camera; Velma's legs in *Murder, My Sweet,* Cora's in *The Postman Always Rings Twice.* Rosemary was erotic, she was alluring, she was trouble. She was bigger than Banbridge, bigger than Belfast, she did not do *local,* she was international. If it turned out that she was sharing a caravan in Ballycastle with a drunken poet, my clinical depression would undoubtedly deepen.

By the time I shook myself back to the present, Brendan was helping himself to what remained of the bottle without so much as offering a share. Still, it was no bad thing — mixing alcohol with medication is not recommended and if not checked can lead to embarrassing situations.

I deal in consequences.

'So what do you think has happened?' I asked. 'She's run off with someone in Germany?'

He looked thoughtful for a moment, his body swaying ever so slightly. 'Mmmmm,' he said, 'Germany. Always puzzled me, that. You're aware of what they publish?' Only what Daniel had told me, but I nodded anyway. 'Beats me why they would need to go to Frankfurt. With my own books you can understand — I'm translated into thirty-two languages. But is there really much of a demand in Spain for a book about the geology of the Sperrin Mountains? Or in Brazil for a treatise on the Lambeg drum? I would expect that the market abroad for short fiction set in Newtownards is rather similar to the clamour there is here for sonnets composed by Peruvian shepherds. What exactly was she hoping to achieve out there?'

'Well, I got the impression it was something of a busman's holiday type thing. He said it was like seeing family.'

'Well, maybe there's your answer,' said Brendan, raising an eyebrow. 'All families squabble.'

12

Custom was slow even for a Saturday afternoon. If I'd closed up shop in order to drive down to speak to Daniel Trevor face to face, I'm not sure that more than half a dozen people would have noticed, and three of them only because they wanted to use the toilet. But driving was, of course, out of the question; I wasn't even sure if the dirt tracks that exist outside of Belfast would be wide enough to accommodate the No Alibis van. The alternative was to phone him for the information I was after — but he was the type to endlessly yitter around a point, and frankly I couldn't be bothered with that. So I e-mailed.

It was clearly important to Rosemary Trevor, an acknowledged (if only by me) femme fatale, that she still went to Frankfurt even though her husband wasn't going. But was it for business or pleasure? According to Daniel, she hadn't been socialising in Frankfurt at all, but taking early nights. Well, possibly. She might easily have made her reassuring calls home, and then immediately gone out partying. She might have had a string of lovers. I was quite sure there were several thousand men there who could easily have fallen for her. But giving her the benefit of the doubt, what about the books she was trying to sell? Brendan, being as self-centred as he was, couldn't imagine that a publisher from another country might be interested in anything produced in Northern Ireland, but that would surely depend very much on exactly what she had on offer. It could be a variation of the provincial journalist's eternal search for a local angle to an international story: an international angle to a local story. Perhaps she had something that originated here but *also* appealed to a global market. But even if she had, what bearing could it possibly have on her ultimate disappearance?

As I waited for a response to my enquiries, I armed myself with a Crunchie and my binoculars and settled down for a relaxing afternoon watching both the jewellery store and life in general out on Botanic Avenue. I had my notebook open beside me to jot down the licence plates of the cars parked immediately outside the shop, and for a hundred yards on either side. I have always done this. Not always, but since I was twelve and had measles and there were no books in the house because my father was a Free Presbyterian and objected to the rude words and verbs, and I had to find something to do with my time. I compiled many volumes full of car registrations, and spent hours looking for patterns in them. I still do it. I have not yet discovered any patterns, but I believe that my chances of ever finding them have been corrupted by personalised number plates, for which I have developed a pathological hatred. I routinely scratch the paintwork of cars that have personalised number plates using a nail I purchased specifically for this purpose. It is difficult to purchase just one nail, and the man in the hardware store took an age and a half to come up with a price for it; he kept trying to give me more nails for the same amount of money, but I wouldn't have them. They're dangerous. If the police were to take possession of my car-scratching nail and analyse it they would find microscopic shavings of the paint of a thousand cars, and arrest me and put me in prison. This is one reason I don't like dealing with the police, in case they discover my nail. I keep it hidden in the fridge in the small kitchen at the back of the store. When I go out shopping I take the nail from the fridge in case I find any personalised number plates. I still routinely memorise ordinary number plates and then write them down when I get back to work. However, on this occasion, I rather hurried getting the numbers down, as I had spotted that Alison was just returning to work. They say that beauty is in the eye of the beholder, but I think that that is only true in certain cases. I would defy anyone to look at the photograph of Rosemary Trevor and say that she wasn't beautiful. But out of any dozen men surveyed, perhaps only two or three would say that Alison fell into the same category. That was good for me, because I don't do well in a competitive market. I cannot imagine anyone being my sun and stars, my earth and moon, if there's even a vague possibility that someone else is going to come along and steal her away. I thanked God that she had immediately seen through Brendan's floppy hair and surgically enhanced smile. I could only keep my fingers crossed that there was nobody else in her life. I fervently hoped that her domestic arrangements were as sad as my own, that she had only known disappointment and rejection in her relationships; that she had been through her period of only liking attractive men, that she had relaxed her standards sufficiently to consider borderline personality disorders and romantic attachments that were just a few degrees south of stalking.

I am quite self-aware.

There is no sugar on my almonds.

Alison did not once glance across the road towards me. I didn't consider that to be indicative of anything. Yes, she had stormed out of my store, but it had not been my fault. And comparing what I knew about her at the start of the day — little to nothing — with what I now knew, I could not help but consider my current position to be beyond my wildest possible dreams. I had admired her from afar for such a long time. (Well, not always *afar*, as on several occasions I had actually gotten quite close to her while I followed her shopping.) But now I not only knew her Christian name — Alison, meaning 'little Alice', with Alice meaning 'of a noble kin'; a princess, undoubtedly — but also that her first love wasn't the jewellery store. She was an artist who struggled with writing. I had grown up on comics, and although I didn't stock them in the store, I had maintained a passing interest, which I was now more than prepared to fan back into life if it meant us having something in common. I Googled *Alison* and *comics* in the hope that I might suddenly be inundated with thousands of leads to further information about her, but all I got in return was a moment of stark terror — the only working comic-book artist with that first name was a lesbian called Alison Bechdel who was famous (in certain circles) for a strip called 'Dykes to Watch Out For'. However, further investigation showed that she'd been drawing 'Dykes' since 1983, which surely ruled my Alison out on age grounds, and that she was in fact American. Of course it didn't mean that my Alison *wasn't* a lesbian. There was always that possibility. I had never seen a boyfriend hanging around the shop to meet her at lunchtime or after work, and when I'd sat behind her at the movies she had been by herself. *(Hellboy* — I should have picked up on the comics connection.) But I had seen no direct indication of Sapphic tendencies, and anyway, the whole phenomenon hadn't quite caught on in Belfast the way it had elsewhere. No, *my* Alison was an artist, but perhaps her comics hadn't yet been published, or she drew them purely for her own entertainment, or she worked under a pseudonym, or perhaps . . .

At that point my e-mail pinged and it was Daniel Trevor, and an attachment detailing Rosemary's appointments in Frankfurt, together with the titles and a brief description of the books she was selling there. Obviously I ignored this until after Alison left the jeweller's at five thirty. I took the precaution of lowering the binoculars as she bade farewell to her colleagues. I was not surprised when she failed to glance towards No Alibis. If she had, she would have found me studying the PC, not the slightest bit interested in her comings and goings, whereas in fact I had my webcam pointed across the road and was watching her every move on the screen before me.

After she had gone, and I had locked up the premises, I sat in the semi-darkness before my computer and finally opened Daniel's attachment. My field of expertise is books, not people — definitely not people — so the first list I studied was of the books and their brief synopses, to see if it would lead me anywhere. Everything I really needed to know was already in the titles. These were:

The Siege of Derry — by Dr David Wilson

It Was Fine When It Left Us: the Building of the Titanic – by Michael Mercer

I Came to Dance — the Autobiography of Anne Smith

Talks about Talks: the Northern Ireland Peace Process – by Andrew Capper

It was immediately clear to me that Brendan's declaration that there would be no interest abroad in local subjects was indeed blinkered. All four titles might have put *me* to sleep — but there could certainly be *some* foreign interest in them. The *Titanic* — went without saying. The siege — history and warfare, absolutely. A successful peace process, the envy of the world, a lesson in how to do it for other conflicts? Definitely. The only one I wasn't sure about was I *Came to Dance* — and that only because my knowledge of dance was so poor that I couldn't be sure that Northern Ireland had contributed anything at all to the bigger picture. But it might have.

I next turned to Rosemary's schedule, which was indeed packed. As I perused it, it quickly became clear that there was one publishing company, Bockenheimer, that had met with her every day. She had allowed exactly thirty minutes for each of her appointments, from 8.30 a.m. to 8 p.m. — except for the last two days, where it appeared that Bockenheimer had been levered in between other meetings at quite a late stage.

I glanced at my watch. It now being 7.30 p.m., and having not so much a window as an entire glasshouse in my social diary, I decided that there was nothing else for it but to phone Daniel Trevor. A gruff, somewhat slurred voice answered and promised to get him. I hung up after five minutes and rang back and this time Daniel himself answered. 'Saturday nights,' he wearily confessed, 'and the poets are on the loose.' He excused himself for a moment as he relocated to a quieter part of the house, then picked up the receiver again. 'It's a madhouse,' he said. 'Now what can I do for you?'

I plunged straight in without any niceties. Don't believe in them. 'Bockenheimer . . . four meetings in four days seems a bit excessive.'

'Manfredd!' Daniel laughed. 'Yes of course, dear Manfredd. Manfredd Freetz. He's an old friend, and one of our regular partners, we've done quite a few books with him over the years. Usually we conduct our meetings with him over a very liquid lunch, sometimes we can barely remember what we've agreed with him. Lovely man. Enjoys his beer.'

'Does four meetings not still seem a lot?'

'Oh, I don't know. She did say something about him. I think he was undecided about one of the titles — that can happen if it isn't written yet.'

'How do you mean, isn't written?'

'Well, we might be selling an outline, perhaps a couple of sample chapters — we're really selling the idea. Perhaps it will be an expensive book to print so we have to recruit some foreign publishers to help cover the costs. A co-production.'

'Which title was it?'

'Ahm — well, actually Rosemary had high hopes of selling him the *Titanic* book, and in fact he did take that, quite a healthy price too, but then he came back and expressed an interest in the dance book as well. Anne Smith's memoir. Yes, I remember now because we joked about it. Rosemary was deliberately quite vague with him about it. She gave him the outline and one of the chapters — about the later years of her career in Belfast - but she really couldn't give him anything else because the truth is the author has been quite seriously ill and hasn't been able to deliver. I think Manfredd believed Rosemary was being coy to try and ratchet up the price.'

'But coy about what? Is anyone that interested in Northern Irish dance? Even in Northern Ireland?'

'Ah — right. I see where you're at. I may have misled you a little myself by calling it "the dance book". That's what we contracted for originally. Anne Smith is the doyenne of dance in Northern Ireland, the founder of our largest — and to tell you the truth, our only — school of modern dance. For thirty years she was our principal choreographer, she produced shows, she nurtured talent, she promoted her charges to companies all over the world. Really, I can't emphasise how important she has been to dance in Northern Ireland.'

He hesitated then.

'And . . . ?'

'Well, it seems that in her youth she was also principal dancer at the Birkenau labour camp. That's Auschwitz.'

'Fuck *off,*' I responded.

13

Monday morning, not long after opening, waiting for Jeff to come in so that I could work some more on the now reopened and intriguing *Case of the Dancing Jews,* I was idly observing the jewellery shop when I was stunned to see Alison waving at me from behind her counter. Panicked, I immediately dropped the binoculars and followed them under the counter. When I re-emerged three minutes later, and surreptitiously glanced across, she waved again. Then she stepped outside the shop and repeated the gesture. I therefore exited my own shop, taking just a moment to run a hand through my hair, and stood on the kerb opposite her.

'Hello!' I shouted across. Traffic was heavy, and loud. I held up the binoculars. 'Just got a new pair — trying them out!'

At exactly the same time she cupped a hand to her mouth and shouted: 'I wanted to apologise about Saturday. I shouldn't have . . .'

And she made the universal sign for wanking.

'No problem!' I also made the universal sign for

wanking. 'It was quite funny!'

She returned the sign again. 'I don't think yer man thought it was funny!'

'Well, he is a bit of a . . .' And I repeated the hand movement.

If a third person had been watching us from a vantage point equidistant between the two of us, and happened to be deaf, and was translating for a fourth party, he would have said that the conversation went like this:

'Wanker!'

'Wanker!'

'Wanker!'

'Wanker!'

And thought we were demented.

'Can I buy you a coffee?' Alison asked.

Result!

'Yes, please!'

She pointed along the street. There was a Starbucks about a hundred yards up. She nodded behind her, then gave me a different hand signal. *Five minutes.* She returned to her jewellery store, and I returned to my bookshop, where all the books are chosen by me and not by a committee of accountants. Jeff arrived as I was brushing my teeth.

'Look after things, I've been invited out for coffee.'

'Really? Who by?'

'Alison.'

'Alison? Who's Alison?'

'From the jewellery shop,' I beamed.

'My God, how did you manage that?'

I shrugged.

'Is she your *girlfriend?*'

'I'm just going for coffee.'

'With your *girlfriend.*'

I looked at him. 'While I'm gone, make yourself useful. I want you to Google *ballet* and *Auschwitz* together, see what you get.'

I would have done it myself the day before, but I don't work on Sundays. I promised my father. He's in heaven now, but watching.

'*Ballet* and . . . why?' Jeff asked.

'Because,' I said.

Jeff would have had a coronary if he'd known we were in Starbucks. He has marched against globalisation. I'm all for it. I'm all for uniformity of choice and familiarity. If I had my way there would be a No Alibis on every corner. I like the Starbucks menu. I start at the top and work my way through to the end. I *never* jump around. It takes me three weeks. Then I start over again. When they occasionally change their menu, it really fucks me up. Coffee is coffee to me, I don't mind what country it comes from, who picks it or under what conditions, and I really don't give a damn who serves it or what they're paid as long as they get it right. With Alison I'd gotten as far that month as a caramel frappuccino, served in a tall glass with a pink striped straw. She had a black coffee.

'I used to collect comics,' I said, 'but my dad didn't approve, so I had to keep them hidden and only read them with a torch under the bedclothes. I suppose it made it quite exciting. I had a complete run of *Sub-Mariner,* a complete *Avengers* — though only the British weekly version. My two favourite comics of all time are *Amazing Adventures 18* featuring "War of the Worlds" — you know, with Killraven, Gerry Conway wrote it, Neal Adams and Howard Chaykin drew it — and *Astonishing Tales 25* featuring the origin of "Deathlok the Demolisher". Doug Moench wrote it, Rich Buckler drew it. And anything by Jim Starlin, he's a god.'

'Jeez,' said Alison, 'you're a bit of a geek-boy, aren't you? I'm not really into superheroes.'

'Oh,' I said.

I stirred my coffee. I'd been working on my opening pitch during those eternal five minutes and was now uncertain how to continue.

Alison stirred her coffee. 'The binoculars,' she said. 'Is that to do with your investigating? I was told that's what you do in your spare time.'

'Yes, they are.'

'You're a crime-fighter.'

'Yes, I am.'

'And is that idiot boy who works in your shop . . . ?'

'Jeff? How do you know he's an idiot?'

'Because every time I pop in he tries to persuade me to go to an Amnesty International meeting with him. He should take no for an answer and concentrate on selling books.'

'I didn't realise you'd ever been in the shop.'

'Oh yeah, stacks a times. You're never there. Lunchtimes is the only chance I get.'

'Jeff never said.'

'Why would he?'

'Why would he indeed.'

'Anyway, is he your crime-fighting sidekick?'

'Well, I'm more like a PI, and PIs don't really have sidekicks. We walk these dark streets alone.'

'Do you do a lot of that? Walking dark streets?'

'Not really. I use the internet a lot.'

'So no sidekick. That's a shame. I'd love to be a sidekick.'

'It's not an absolute rule. In fact . . .'

'Holmes and Watson. The most famous of them all.'

'Famous isn't always good,' I said.

'You don't like Holmes and Watson?'

'Innovative, yes, inspirational, yes, their role in popularising detective fiction, of course. It's the, uhm, gay undercurrent.'

'In Sherlock Holmes? How'd you work that one out?'

'It was elementary.'

She snorted.

'You set me up for that,' she said.

'Not at all, I really believe the books are rendered largely unreadable by . . .' And then I hesitated. 'You're not offended?'

'By what?'

'In case you're . . . you know.'

'Would it make a difference?'

'To what?'

'To me becoming your sidekick.'

'No. Not at all. So are you?'

'Why do you ask?'

'No reason.' I'm always aware when colour creeps up my face, and I'm certain that other people are too. It's like a petrol gauge. Starts around the neck and works its way up to my ears, then across my cheeks and up to my forehead. I changed the subject. 'Do you not like frappuccino?'

'Never tried it. I just like . . . coffee.'

'It's great, really' I moved my glass forward and angled the straw towards her. 'Go on. Have a suck.'

'No. No, thanks.'

'You do know how to suck, don't you?'

'Yes, of course.'

'You just put your lips around the tip, and do what comes naturally.'

She held my gaze for fully five seconds before suddenly tearing the straw out of the glass.

'This,' she spat, 'would be a very skinny cock.'

She stood, threw the straw at me, and stormed out of Starbucks.

I sat for a while. I studied the menu board. Tomorrow I would have a cinnamon dolce frappuccino.

14

Whenever personal things get me down, I find great comfort in my work, either the continuing survival of No Alibis or my part-time investigations into cases of mystery and intrigue. For every misjudged disaster like Starbucks, there is the comforting knowledge that at the very moment where my life seems bleakest, there is someone somewhere clapping their hands together and thanking the Lord for my intervention. My purpose is not to waste time on short-term, no-return personal relationships, but to return light to shadowed lives. Sometimes there is some crossover, when I am forced to apply my Sherlockian skills to my own problems. For example, it was but a few weeks since I had investigated the cause of a quite distressing burning sensation in my armpit area. At first I was convinced that one of my nemeses was attempting to poison me. Any other crime-fighter thus suffering would surely have alerted National Security and insisted on a radiation sweep, or at the very least rushed to the casualty department of their local hospital. But with the battery dead in the No Alibis van and my GP having explained to me on several occasions just how packed his appointment book was, I decided instead on a calm and rational analysis of the facts. I examined the situation, the circumstances and the timing, and after due rumination these led me to deduce that by not immediately donning my glasses when emerging from my shower each morning, I had not in fact been spraying deodorant on to my steaming body as I had thought, but Windolene.

It is the little triumphs like this that get me through the difficult times.

On this occasion, however, it was much more difficult. With my dreams of love, marriage, or even a girlfriend completely in tatters, the shop suddenly seemed particularly drab and unexciting. Jeff, never a comfort, was uncharacteristically smiley when he saw my downbeat look, and I knew why. I obviously did not tell him any of the details of my coffee with Alison. He didn't ask. He *knew* it had been a catastrophe. I was on the verge of sacking him for wilful deviousness. But then I remembered that old Maxim Jakubowski: *keep your friends close, but your enemies closer.* I would keep the evidence of his attempted betrayal for another time, when it might have more value as a bargaining tool. Besides, he was cheap, and he could lift boxes of books where I couldn't, with my back. Sometimes you must make these dark moments work for you: *The Case of the Dancing Jews* was a sombre business, and I now had the perfect mood for it; and Jeff, being well used to wallowing in persecution at Amnesty International, was at least a sympathetic sounding board. He was the human equivalent of a squash-court wall; blank, but occasionally capable of throwing the ball back at interesting tangents.

Jeff had Googled as instructed while I had been out making a fool of myself, but the results were rather meagre. The only dance-related reference was to a French-Jewish choreographer, René Blum, who had died at Auschwitz in 1942. There were no references to any dancers who had actually *performed* in the camp. So, for the meantime, all we had to go on was Daniel Trevor's rather vague account of how his wife came to uncover the fact that Anne Smith had been the principal dancer in a performance of the sentimental comic ballet *Coppelia* in the most notorious death camp in history.

Daniel had explained that Rosemary made several visits to Anne Smith's home in Hillsborough to encourage her to complete her work on her autobiography. Anne was in her late eighties, not very well, and though Rosemary thought the manuscript was in reasonably good shape, the author had proved reluctant to part with it. Although described as an autobiography, it was just as much an official history of dance in Northern Ireland that then segued into Anne's own life story. She was a teacher at a Belfast secondary school when her choreography for a sixth-form show received such a good reaction that she was encouraged to nurture her ideas through her own dance classes, which gradually grew in scope and ambition to the point where she won Arts Council backing to establish a school for ballet and dance. It became a national institution. Daniel had read most of the manuscript himself and described it as 'not terribly interesting and not particularly well written'. However, on one of Rosemary's visits Anne was carrying in a tray of coffee when she stumbled and everything went flying. Anne reacted by swearing in fluent German. When Rosemary asked her where she'd perfected her accent, Anne surprised her by telling her that it was perfect because it was her native tongue, that she had grown up as a Jew in a German community in the Democratic Republic of Czechoslovakia. Her real name wasn't Anne Smith but Anne Mayerova. As a teenager she had trained to become a professional dancer and enjoyed a meteoric rise and critical acclaim. Her last performance had been in Molière's *Le Malade Imaginaire* in 1939 at the National Theatre of Prague — and then she corrected herself . . . no, it wasn't quite her last performance . . . and became quite emotional.

'When Rosemary asked what she meant,' I told Jeff, 'Anne responded by rolling up her sleeve and showing the number tattooed on her arm.'

Rosemary was understandably shocked by this revelation — and also quite incredulous that Anne hadn't thought to chronicle it in her memoir. Anne was reluctant at first to talk about what had happened, but pretty soon it all started to come out. It was, Daniel reported, a tale of incredible courage and survival — and also one that was quite surreal, culminating as it did with her choreographing, rehearsing and dancing in a Christmas show in Auschwitz attended by both the prisoners and their SS guards.

'Bloody hell,' said Jeff, 'Ticketmaster could have made a fortune out of that one. And she really hadn't mentioned any of this in her autobiography?'

'She genuinely didn't seem to think that anyone would be interested.'

'Meanwhile there were probably dollar signs flashing in Rosemary's eyes.'

'Well, you can understand. And it does open some interesting lines of enquiry.'

'How do you mean?' And then the penny dropped. 'You think it might have something to do with Rosemary's disappearance?'

'Well, think about it. She goes to Frankfurt, she tells this *German* publisher that she has a book about a dancer with an interesting past, but she can't reveal too many details because she doesn't know them yet. She tells him what she can — perhaps Anne's real name and how she danced for the SS in Auschwitz — and somehow this means something to the publisher, and maybe he becomes determined to find out more. You know, like in *The Odessa File* — the journalist investigating the Holocaust turns out to be the son of the only good Nazi in history? Well, maybe there's some sort of personal connection here as well — but when Rosemary won't reveal what she really doesn't yet know in any detail, the publisher reacts angrily and *murders* her. Or he reports what she has discovered to the Odessa and *they* have her killed.'

Jeff shook his head. 'You're the one always complaining about me having loony conspiracy theories. Have you heard yourself?'

Perhaps he had a point. Nazi conspiracies had been briefly popular in the early seventies when many of them were still on the run. Now, although some octogenarian Nazis were undoubtedly still being hunted, it seemed unlikely that the Odessa still existed, or if it did, that it could be much of a threat to anyone. But it didn't mean that the publisher *wasn't* somehow involved with her murder, I just had no realistic possibility of proving it. And, of course, there was no body yet. Rosemary Trevor could still be living it up in that caravan in Bally castle.

Intrigued as I was, as much of a crusader for justice and champion of the unjustly maligned as I was, I still had my business to consider. I was a bookseller, first and foremost, with a duty to promote and sell mystery fiction in a difficult market. I could not go running off to Germany to look for a missing woman, no matter how alluring she was. Nor could I close No Alibis temporarily — what were the good people of Belfast going to do for advice about what to read? It was okay to slip out for five minutes here and there to solve some of my other cases, but this was different. I certainly wasn't going to leave my pride and joy in the charge of a two-faced idiot like Jeff for days on end. It might have been different if there had been a personal angle to the case, but there simply wasn't. I wasn't Jon Voight investigating what had happened to his father. I wasn't missing a wife or a mother or even a distant cousin. What I did in my spare time was a *hobby*. I was free to adopt or reject cases as I chose. I owed Daniel Trevor *nothing*. There were new books to be ordered and a sales strategy that might entice more customers into the store to be determined. And Christ knows, if there really were Nazis conspiring out there, even if they got about on Zimmer frames, what would worrying about them do to my precarious health? I'd had ulcers over *The Case of Mrs Geary's Leather Trousers* and a bad asthma attack from paint inhalation during *The Case of the Fruit on the Flyover*. The Third Reich would probably finish me off.

I thought about it some more after Jeff left and decided the best course of action would be to quietly withdraw from the case. I would cite ill health. I was going to phone Daniel Trevor to tell him personally, but then I thought better of it because a sound argument or contrary opinion can easily win me round. So I sent him an e-mail instead. I also decided not to answer the phone for the rest of the afternoon in case he decided to call me about it.

My e-mail was simple and succinct. I told him I had reviewed the evidence he had provided for me, and though it was far from certain that something dreadful had happened to Rosemary, in my opinion the police should be talking to Manfredd Freetz of the Bockenheimer publishing company about his pressing interest in *I Came to Dance*. I wished him all the best and assured him that I'd torn up his blank cheques and that I wouldn't be charging anything more than the going rate for my time.

I'd only been open for ten minutes the next morning when I saw Daniel Trevor on the other side of the road, waiting for a gap in the traffic. There wasn't even time to lock the front door, let alone pull down the shutters and hide under the counter. In just a few moments he was across and entering the shop.

Immediately I said: 'Daniel, how are you? I was thinking about my bill, and it's really quite ridiculous under such sad circumstances to charge you for my time, so let's just forget about it and in addition I'll make a donation to the charity of your choice.'

I don't think he even heard me. He was visibly upset and breathing hard. He dabbed at his sweaty brow with a tissue.

'I tried to call you!' he cried.

'Yes, there seems to be a fault on the—'

'Manfredd Freetz is dead! *Murdered!*'

15

Everything came tumbling out of him in an excited, terrified jumble, but all I could think about was that it had nothing to do with me any more, and please get out of my store. I stopped him mid-flow.

'Daniel! Calm . . . calm down . . . it's truly awful . . . but let's just slow down for a moment. Daniel — listen to me. Do you still have the business card I gave you?'

He looked momentarily confounded. Then he patted his pockets. My business card has my shop and home and mobile phone numbers on it. And my website address and e-mail. And the chalk outline of the body and the No Alibis logo and the *Murder Is Our Business* tag line.

'Why . . . yes, of course . . . but I don't under—'

He fished the card out of his wallet. I immediately ripped it from his damp, shaking hand and tore it in half. And then into quarters and threw them behind me, like salt. I quickly explained that I was having my numbers changed and if he kept it, it would only lead to confusion.

'Never mind that! What are we going to do about Manfredd?'

'We?'

He did look very frightened, and I felt sorry for his predicament, but *Murder Is Our Business* was never supposed to be taken literally. I reiterated to him that the fragile state of my health simply did not allow for my continued involvement. I was unwell. I couldn't travel. I didn't speak German. He would have to take it up with the police. I was finished with the case.

'You *can't be!*' he cried. 'Not *now!*'

'I'm afraid I've decided, and I never change my mind.'

'But I told Manfredd only last night that you were—'

'You told *who what?*'

'Manfredd! After I got your e-mail last night I called him immediately and confronted him with your suspicions

'Jesus Christ!'

'And now he's dead! Pushed in front of a train!'

Fucking dominoes!

If Manfredd Freetz had been murdered, then Rosemary Trevor probably had been as well, both of them to protect someone or something. And Daniel Trevor had implicated me! The selfish *bastard!* He had brought murder into *my* store, threatening me, my customers, my livelihood and my future. I was swamped by a sudden return of the black dread. All my old feelings of paranoia and xenophobia and claustrophobia came crowding back. The world closed in and then expanded and contracted. I wasn't born for excitement or thrills. My pacemaker could cope, but my brain couldn't. My legs were like jelly. I gripped the counter for support.

'What *exactly* did you tell him?'

'I told him about your theory that Anne's book might somehow reveal—'

'About *me*, not the fucking book!'

'I . . .'

'Did you mention my name or where I worked?'

He looked confused. 'I'm sorry, I don't see the relevance of—'

'The *fucking relevance* is what if he told his killer who—'

At this point the shop door opened suddenly and I immediately took a step back. A useless move if it was a hired killer, but instinctive.

But it wasn't. It was Alison. Beautiful lovely Alison.

Immediately I said: 'Perhaps we should just try and stay calm, Mr Trevor, then we can examine the facts again.'

Daniel said, *'What?'*

Alison said: 'Sorry — don't mean to disturb. Wanted to apologise. Our misunderstanding.'

'I'll just be a minute,' I said.

I settled Daniel Trevor on the couch at the rear of the store then returned to Alison. I folded my arms and gave her a look, although not before sticking my head out of the door and checking both ways for vehicles with European registrations and Aryan-looking men with bulges in their jackets.

'Well?' I asked.

She was wearing a white shirt with a name tag and a black pencil skirt. 'You look so angry,' she said. 'Perhaps another time?'

'No. I'm fine.'

She sucked on her lower lip. 'The misunderstanding. With the frappuccino?'

'The frappuccino?'

'Please. I'm trying to apologise. Y'see, I thought you were just being pervy. I hardly know you, and you start talking about . . . that . . . and I thought . . . you read about people . . . and I just thought you were trying . . . I just thought it was a bit creepy.'

'Is that your apology? Because it's really shite.'

I wanted to yell. Not at her, particularly, but someone. *Anyone.* I wanted to shout and rave about how stupid people were.

But then she gave me a nervous smile, and that broke me.

I smiled back. I had to, because I was in *love* with her.

My feelings of dread and terror and paranoia were already evaporating. Seeing her there in front of me was like the sun coming out. It made me realise how ridiculous I was being. Manfredd hadn't been *murdered.* He hadn't been stabbed or shot or garrotted, he'd been run over by a train. Daniel had already described him as a drunk, he'd probably just stumbled and fallen. It was an *accident.* It was only its timing that made it look suspicious. And as for Nazi conspiracies? I'd already concluded that if the Odessa still existed, it was comprised of old men with dodgy hips and cataracts and there was no real reason to change my mind. If it really had dispatched an assassin from Frankfurt after killing Manfredd, he was probably still on the bus to Switzerland to get his Ryanair flight. If he ever made it as far as Belfast, his hands would be so shaky and arthritic he wouldn't be able to hit a barn door with a bazooka. I had *nothing* to worry about. I had to remain grounded in reality. My psychiatrist has told me repeatedly that it's important not to drift. Rosemary was still just a bored wife on the run, Manfredd a coincidental traffic accident. Daniel was a stressed, cuckolded publisher trying to raise a young family by himself. I was just an armchair detective who happened to have a good-looking girl beaming up at him.

'I really am really, really sorry,' she said. 'When I went back to work yesterday I was upset and my boss wanted to know what was wrong. She was a bit wary of me meeting you anyway because she'd heard . . . it doesn't matter what she heard, she just advised me not to go, but if someone says that I'll invariably go the other way . . . so I met you, and you said what you said and I went back all in tears and I eventually told her what you'd said and she just burst out laughing and said haven't you ever seen Bogie and Bacall and I didn't know what she was talking about and she said that you were just quoting lines from a movie everyone in the world seems to know about but me. That you were only joking and didn't you work in a mystery bookshop and all that kind of smart dialogue and double talk is exactly the kind of thing you'd know all about. And I thought you were like deranged or something. So now I know you're not, I was wondering if by way of apology we could go back to Starbucks and I'll buy you whatever you want and even if it's one of those exotic ones I'll have one of them myself. And we'll both put our lips together and suck them out of straws and have a good laugh about how we got started. What do you say?'

I glanced back at Daniel Trevor, sitting on the sofa, staring into the void.

'Wait till I get rid of this clown,' I said.

16

'Are you sure it's okay to leave him? He looked quite upset.'

'He'll be fine. Honestly.' I'd done my best to usher him out of the shop, but he wasn't going anywhere. He was petrified. 'How's your cinnamon dolce frappuccino?'

'Cinnamon-*ey*. What was his problem? Is it a case you're working on? I was thinking if anyone ever comes to you with a case about stolen jewellery, you'd need to consult an expert.' She pointed at herself. 'I charge by the hour.'

'It's not about the money,' I said.

'Oh right. So you're like a public service?' I nodded. 'In my experience, most public services are crap. Are you crap?'

'Generally. Yes.'

Tell me about him.'

'He's just a nut.'

'A nut you've locked in your shop, with the shutters down.'

'We're just closed for lunch.'

'You don't normally'

'I was meeting you, I've no cover today, I felt sorry for him.'

'Please tell me. I'm interested.'

'His wife did a runner and he wants me to find her.'

'And can you?'

'Can. Won't.'

'Why not?'

'It's complicated.'

'How complicated?' I looked at her. 'You want me to mind my own business?'

Well, I was in two minds. Now that I seemed to be back on good terms with her, and she had made it abundantly clear that she wanted to be my sidekick, I was wondering what harm there might be in allowing her to indulge her little fantasy. If I wrapped the case up as quickly and efficiently as I normally did then she was bound to be impressed, and that might even lead to kissing. On the other hand, I hadn't liked Daniel Trevor from the start, he was clearly unbalanced, and it seemed like he was becoming something of a sticking plaster precisely when I wanted as much free time as possible to spend with Alison.

'Complicated because he's a bit paranoid. He thinks Nazis killed his wife, and that they might be after him now, and, by association, me as well.'

Nazis? German Nazis?

'The best kind, yes.'

'But why does he think . . . ?'

'Because he's delusional. I think he's traumatised by the fact that his wife ran off on him and he's been left to look after the kids. Although, now that I think about it, I've seen no evidence that he actually has children.'

It wasn't exactly how it was, but I was in a difficult position. It was important that she didn't know what I was like. As I said, I'm quite self-aware. No sugar on my almonds. But there are times when one has to sprinkle a little.

'Oh, you have to tell me more!'

So I told her all about what I was already thinking of as *The Case of the Dancing Jews*.

When I was done she said, 'Oh, you've the patience of a saint! I would have thrown him out ages ago! If he loved her at all he would go off to Germany himself and look for her. He doesn't like leaving Northern Ireland? He doesn't like talking to foreigners? He doesn't like wide-open spaces? He has a bad back? Oh, he's such a pathetic little wimp.'

I shrugged helplessly.

'Although,' she added after another suck of her cinnamon dolce frappuccino, 'the German publisher guy . . .'

'Manfredd . . . yeah, it is a bit of a coincidence.'

'And the story about Anna . . . what's her name?'

'Anne Mayerova

'May-er-ova . . . it is remarkable.'

'Yes it is. If it's true. He could be raving.'

'Well, I suppose you could always find out? She's still around, isn't she?'

'I believe she's been unwell, but yes.'

'Well perhaps you could solve *The Case of the Dancing Jews* by actually talking to the Dancing Jew herself. At least you could decide if it has any relevance at all.'

'I'm not sure if that would be appropriate.'

'Why not?'

I had absolutely no idea. Apart from the fact that I don't particularly like talking to strangers. And I especially don't like talking to old people. I don't like having to shout to be heard. I don't like their turned milk and soft biscuits. I don't like their fishy cats and Youth Dew perfume that smells of mothballs. I don't like that they groan every time they sit down or stand up, or how loud they have the television and how much they complain about what's on the television or how they boast about having their own teeth or why I should be interested in the fact that they can still spell when they're eighty-nine years old. I'm with the Eskimos putting their useless grandparents on ice floes and waving goodbye. This may be a monstrous slander on Eskimos. It could just as easily be some other tribe with access to large bodies of ice, or just plain water, with crocodiles.

But I couldn't tell Alison any of this, obviously.

'It might be a mistake to indulge his fantasies.'

'But what if they're not? I mean, even paranoids have enemies.'

A fair point. I had *hundreds* of them.

'Besides, I'd like to meet her.'

'Why?'

'Because she sounds inspirational. And maybe I could write a graphic novel about her life.'

'I thought you didn't call them graphic—'

'Oh, I was only winding that wanker up. Did you ever read *Maus?*'

'Mouse! Is it like a murder mystery? That's my field of expertise . . .'

'Six million murders, no mystery. *Maus,* it's a graphic novel by Art Spiegelman. It's incredible. It's all about Auschwitz. Except instead of human beings he draws the Jews as mice and the Nazis as cats.'

'Really? Are there any dancing mice?'

She smiled. 'It's better than it sounds. Really moving. I'll lend it to you.'

I liked the sound of that.

I liked the thought of *us.*

It was like sewing one piece of material to another. They're quite separate, but gradually you build the connection until eventually they're inseparable.

Of course it was by no means a foregone conclusion that we *would* end up together. I would have to tread a careful path through the realities of my life; as long as I kept Alison on that path she wouldn't need to know about the perilous swamps that lay on either side of it.

I paid for the coffee. She looked impressed, although slightly less so when I insisted on waiting eight minutes while they worked out how to fit a new roll of receipts to the till.

17

On the walk back down towards No Alibis Alison said: 'What if, while we were sucking cinnamon dolce frappuccinos, a Nazi hit man broke into the shop and assassinated Daniel Trevor? What if his brains are sprayed all over your painting of Columbo?'

I smiled indulgently. I was just pleased she'd noticed the painting of Columbo. It really hadn't been there for that long. The artist is quite well known and it would have cost me in the region of £4,000 if I'd actually been foolish enough to commission it, but he'd done it for free (albeit after some serious hinting) in gratitude for me solving *The Case of the Vanishing Easel.*

We were almost at the shop door when Alison stopped and looked thoughtfully at the former premises of Malcolm Carlyle, Private Eye. The big yellow letters were smattered with grime; the pull-down metal shutters were plastered with fly posters. There is nothing as sad as an abandoned business. If you write a poem and it doesn't work, nobody knows. If you design a hat and it doesn't fit, nobody cares. If you open a business and it fails, it just sits there shouting, *I'm no good, I'm useless, I hadn't a clue,* sometimes for months and years. It's part of the reason I keep battling away with No Alibis. I refuse to fail.

'Do you think you've been ignoring the bigger picture?' Alison asked suddenly.

'How do you mean?'

'All these little bitty cases you've been solving . . . ?'

'They aren't bitty to me . . .'

'Don't get defensive. I just mean they're not earth-shatteringly important, are they? They're about trousers, and vandalism, and missing plants and that one about the rat . . .'

'I said cat.'

'You know what I mean. Haven't you asked yourself what these little cases have in common?'

I looked at her. 'No.'

'They're all connected to this guy Malcolm Carlyle, Private Eye.'

'Well I know *that.*'

'But is *he* not the real mystery here?'

'*No.* He went bust and then got offside so he wouldn't have to deal with the fallout. That's not a mystery, it's normal business practice.'

'That's what you *think* happened. Tell me this, how many of his customers have you had in asking about him?'

'Dozens by now.'

'Does that sound like a business in trouble?'

'Well, no. But what does it matter *why* he closed? Maybe he was fed up with *itty-bitty* crimes.'

'Because it was so sudden. *Overnight.* We arrived for work one day, and he didn't. His shutters never went up. I saw it, you saw it. He was in our shop the day before, just chatting, but not a peep out of him about closing down.'

'Maybe he didn't want to say *my business is a flop and I'm going to leave all my customers in the lurch.*'

'But nobody ever came and cleared it out, I never saw the furniture go or filing cabinets, and to this day there's been nobody looking round it wanting to open a different business, there's been no for-sale sign. And this is prime retail. Don't you think that's strange?'

I stared at her. Who did she think she was? She sold *bangles,* and by all accounts — Jeff's, in fact, although he may have had a chip on his shoulder — not very good ones.

But there was no stopping her.

'Maybe the big mystery, the mystery you were born to solve, is right next door to you. What really happened to Malcolm Carlyle? Why did he close so suddenly? Where did he go?'

'Yes,' I said, 'it's certainly a big mystery.'

I admired her passion, but passion can be misplaced. Maybe she was deciding that as well. I studied the footpath and its patterns. I liked her immensely but I *would not* be railroaded into something that wasn't *me.*

'To tell you the truth,' I said, 'I kind of prefer the itty-bitty crimes. They're like little animated crossword puzzles. They take a couple of hours, they focus the mind, they make the day go a little quicker and there's like this nice feeling of satisfaction when you solve them. Then they're out of your mind and you look forward to the next one. Nobody gets hurt, what's right and what's wrong is pretty clear. These crimes are at my *level.* I don't like *bigger pictures.* I'm not interested in panoramas, I'm fascinated by small portraits. That's why I'm not interested in what Daniel Trevor thinks is happening in Germany, and why I can't get excited about what may or may not have caused Malcolm Carlyle to close up shop and disappear.'

'*God,*' Alison said, 'where did all that come from?'

I shrugged.

'Did anyone ever tell you you were very intense?'

'Yes. Sorry.'

'Don't apologise. I like a man who knows what he wants. Even if he's wrong.'

'What do you mean, *even if he's wrong?*'

'Stalin was wrong, but he was absolutely convinced he

was right.'

'*What?* Are you comparing me to *Stalin?*'

'Absolutely not. He led hundreds of millions of people. You lead an idiot boy. He looked at the bigger picture and reshaped the world. You like small portraits and, well . . . You have nothing but the courage of your convictions in common.'

I studied her. 'Are you serious?'

She studied me.

Then she burst out laughing. '*No!*' She gave me a friendly but nevertheless painful dig in the arm. 'I think the problem is that you're *dying* to take on a major case, but now that you've met me you just don't want to expose me to danger. And *that* is sweet. But I'm much tougher than I look. You have to be if you work in a women-only jeweller's, because there's hardly a month goes past without some pissed-up Spiderman staggering in and trying to grab a tray of earrings.' She held up her elfin hands. 'I could kill you with one blow.'

I took a step back and she laughed. She couldn't have known that I have brittle bones.

She turned to study Malcolm Carlyle's premises again. 'Do you know what we really need to do?'

'No.'

'We need to get inside.'

'*Inside . . . ?*'

'Don't you see? It closed down overnight. So if nothing came out, then all his old files are still sitting there. And if you get hold of those, you might be able to answer whatever questions come walking through your door right away.'

'But that would be like someone telling me the answers to the crossword. The fun is—'

'Oh *shush*, it'll give you time to tackle bigger fish. Didn't you say Malcolm Carlyle flew off to Frankfurt and claimed to have found something out? Maybe it's *in the files.*'

'What're you suggesting? We *break in?*'

94

'Maybe we don't have to *break* anything. Maybe if we thought we heard intruders and in the spirit of public service we went to investigate

'No, Alison. Absolutely not. No *way.*'

She smiled again. It was lovely and warm. But misleading. I knew now that she was capable of extreme violence. She had hands of death. I'd spent the last few days looking for a femme fatale, while all the time there was one right under my nose.

'Oh, look at your face.' She reached up and touched it. Her hand was soft. 'I'm only teasing you. Shouldn't you be opening up? Are you not worried about Looney Tunes messing up your precious books?'

She had a point. It was well past lunchtime now. Any other business along this street might have had a queue of impatient customers waiting to enter.

I had none.

As I pushed the shutters up Alison said, 'I should be getting back myself, but I have to see if he's been murdered.'

'He hasn't been murdered,' I said.

As I punched the combination, then undid the bolts, then turned the five keys in a particular sequence, she said, 'In those sick books you sell, the murder victim is quite often displayed in some gruesome fashion, you know like he's been crucified or his organs are laid out in alphabetical order.'

'Don't be ridiculous,' I said.

I opened the door.

I stepped back and allowed Alison to enter first.

I am a gentleman. And she is a self-confessed trained killer.

It was gloomy inside. And quiet.

Nothing moved.

The clock ticked on the wall above Columbo.

Tick.

Tick.

Tick.

We stood side by side.

We said nothing for six more ticks.

There was no blood.

No smell of cordite.

No stench of death.

'Do you think . . .' Alison whispered, but before she could finish, a noise came from the small kitchen at the back of the store. There was a shadow of movement across the gap at the bottom of the door, which slowly began to open.

Alison's hand found mine.

Daniel Trevor appeared. 'I hope you don't mind,' he said, 'but I made myself a cup of tea.'

18

It was the first bodily contact I'd had with a woman since 2002, and that was my mother slapping me in the chops for failing to send her a Valentine's card. My hand-holding with Alison lasted for about eight seconds before she let go. I was *elated*. For Alison I think it wasn't anything remarkable. I was learning that she was quite tactile. To be able to touch someone like that without even considering the likelihood of them being a carrier of bubonic plague, well, I could only perspire to that.

Daniel volunteered to make us both a cup of tea. When he returned to the kitchen I said, 'See, alive and kicking.'

'And not obviously deranged,' said Alison. 'Although in the sort of books you sell, they're all sweet one minute, then they plunge a knitting needle through your eyeball the next.'

'You have a very poor opinion of the books I sell.'

'You forget I come in here at lunchtimes.'

'Yes, but with idiot boy as your guide. I could show you fantastic things.'

'I know. But what about the books?'

Reader, I blushed.

Alison had to go back to work, but asked if she could return later. Instinctively I replied, 'Why?'

She gave me a funny look and said, 'If it's not *convenient*...'

I talked my way out of it. Of *course* I wanted her to come back. I was just a little bit wary of being alone with her. Starbucks was different. There were other people there. Distractions. Even being in my own shop with her was different in daylight, with Daniel there and the remote possibility of customers. But alone, after closing time, with the shutters at least half down? What would I say? There was *The Case of the Dancing Jews* of course, but it couldn't all be about that. There would have to be chit-chat. I've never done chit-chat. That or I could ask her to stand with me and look for patterns in the spines of the books, and I don't mean alphabetically. But it was probably a bit early in the relationship for that.

Relationship. I liked the sound of that. It was so *alien*.

When she'd gone I spent another twenty minutes talking to Daniel. He had calmed down considerably, and after we'd looked up a German newspaper on the internet — like Rosemary, he was quite fluent — and read an account of the death of one of the country's best-known publishers, he was quite relieved to learn that the police were not treating Manfredd's death as suspicious, but, as I'd kind of known all along, an unfortunate accident.

'I've been so foolish,' he lamented. 'But you have to understand . . .'

'I do understand. It's a very difficult time.'

'But at the end of it, we're no nearer finding her, are we?'

'I wouldn't say that. I think the dancing Jew is an interesting lead.'

'The what? Oh — Anne. Yes. Possibly. Does that mean you're not giving up the case, that you're going to keep looking for her?'

He seemed impossibly sad. It was like looking in a mirror.

'Of course I'll keep looking for her,' I said. And then

added, 'As long as you keep signing the blank cheques.'

He smiled gratefully. Sometimes when things seem impossibly bleak, when you think they can't get any worse, the tiniest little light, nothing more than a candle flickering in a strong breeze at the far end of a lengthy tunnel, can mean so much. Daniel Trevor had *me*.

I had Alison.

And *lithium*.

He was going to return to his country retreat. He was going to tell the poets to *shut up* and go for a lie-down. He was exhausted by nine months of worry and despair.

He should inhabit my shoes.

I kept a surreptitious eye on the jeweller's via the webcam, and worried some more about what to say or do. But she didn't look over, not once. She was a cool one indeed. When there was a lull in business — *hah!* — I popped out and bought dips. When Alison arrived, she had changed out of her uniform and had that ridiculous woollen flying cap on her head.

She said, 'Wow, are you having a party?'

I had been unable to decide about which dips, so had bought every variety. They were laid out on a trestle table, which was covered in a disposable cloth. There were paper plates and plastic cups and four bottles of wine.

'Book launch,' I said, 'but they cancelled at the last moment. Have a Quaver.'

We munched.

After a while she lifted her handbag and opened it. 'We should probably get started,' she said, removing a flashlight from within.

'Started what?'

She raised a speculative eyebrow before indicating for me to follow her across the store. We entered the kitchen. 'If this place is anything like our place . . . and they look identical . . . then . . .' At the end of the kitchen there are stairs leading up to three rooms on the first floor. 'Yip, here we go.' She started up. I followed. Each of the rooms was stuffed full of unsold stock. She stopped in the hall and looked up at a panel in the ceiling. 'Drop-down steps?' I nodded. There was a stick with a hook on the end of it resting against the wall. She lifted this and prised open the panel before carefully lowering the steps. 'Light up there?' I nodded. 'Floored?' I nodded. 'Hot water tank by the dividing wall?' I nodded.

'Excuse me,' I said, 'but I didn't order a plumber.'

'We have to do this,' she said.

'What?' I asked as I began to follow her up the steps. 'And why?'

She pulled herself up into the roof space and tugged on the string light. As I clambered up myself, fearing at any moment that the vertigo that had stopped me becoming a paratrooper or window-cleaner might strike, Alison shimmied her way through more boxes of books until she was standing to the right of the tank, facing the wall that separated No Alibis from the vacant detective agency next door.

'Okay,' she said, tapping the wall, 'exactly like ours. A child could get through it.'

'Excuse me?' I said, coming up beside her.

'Unfortunately we don't have a child.' She put her hands on her hips. 'Look, we owe it to ourselves to do this.'

'We owe . . . *ourselves* . . . to do *what?*'

'*This.*'

She swivelled and *kicked* the wall. I had not noticed until this point that she was wearing DM boots. A lump of plaster immediately came away.

'Please stop,' I said. 'The insurance

'Insurance, *inschmurance . . .*'

She kicked again. More plaster cracked and fell. The wall behind now had a visible crack in it.

'Alison, please. You can't just . . .'

Her third strike went through. Her boot was next door while the rest of her was still in my roof space. 'I believe I just did,' she said, and then held a hand out to me to stop herself from falling back.

I took it. 'This is *insane,*' I said.

'Well you're the expert,' she said.

There wasn't time to think about *that* then — though it had the potential to keep me awake for days — because she immediately used me as leverage to pull her boot back through before renewing her assault on the wall. She rained half a dozen further kicks against it until she'd created a hole large enough for her to squeeze through.

And me. If I chose to.

'Are you coming or not?' she asked from the other side. I could already see the beam of her flashlight criss-crossing my neighbour's roof space.

'No,' I said. 'It's illegal. It's . . . *wrong.*'

'It's an adventure.'

Please, Alison

'Oh come on . . . it's just some harmless fun . . .'

'I really don't think it's—'

'OH JESUS CHRIST!'

Her cry was sharp and piercing.

'ALISON!' I threw myself through the gap into the dark interior. No flashlight. No sound. 'ALISON!'

The torch flicked on, under her chin, illuminating her smiling face. 'I thought I saw a spider,' she said. 'Still, while you're here . . .'

She angled the beam to the floor and began to search for the ceiling panel that would allow her, *us,* access to the office below.

There is a thin line between love and hate.

Very thin.

Alison led the way down bare, creaky stairs, my heart in my mouth, dust mites conspiring to ignite my allergies. Running a bookshop I fight a constant battle to stop the place smelling musty; unsold books can do that. Even after six months, Malcolm Carlyle's offices smelled fresh. If I ever met him again I'd ask him his secret.

Before I could stop her Alison flicked on a light switch as we entered the front office. Surprisingly the power was still on. There was a desk and a switchboard, although I'd never seen a receptionist. I think it was all just for show. He was strictly a one-man operation, although if he'd asked he could have borrowed my idiot. There was a set of filing cabinets behind the desk that lay open; files spilled out of the drawers; many were scattered across the floor. As I crouched down to examine them, Alison moved across to check out the main office.

I was looking for the *Ts* — Daniel Trevor or Rosemary — but they were all jumbled up. I did find the Geary file, but I'd already solved that one. From somewhere behind, Alison again said, 'Jesus Christ.'

'I suffer from arachnophobia,' I said. 'You'll have to sort it out yourself.'

She repeated, 'Jesus Christ,' a little louder.

'Alison, I'm not falling for—'

'Jesus Christ!'

Something about it made it sound as if she wasn't swearing, but literally appealing for help and guidance. As I glanced round I saw that she had reversed out of Carlyle's office to the point where she was now steadying herself against the door jamb.

'Alison?'

She stared back into the office.

There was still a fair chance that she was attempting to stitch me up again, so I just smiled and stood and carried several of the files across to her, determined not to be sucked in, but also curious. 'If we're going to go through all of these we'd be better taking them back to my place rather than—'

Then I saw what she saw.

Malcolm Carlyle was sitting in a leather swivel chair, the flesh rotted off him, and hung with hundreds of Pine Fresh air freshener trees.

'Jesus Christ,' I had to agree.

19

No Alibis was warm and welcoming and all laid out for a party for two, but neither of us felt much like dips. We were both shaking with adrenaline and fear and disgust. Ever the trouper, Alison opened the wine.

'What the hell, what the hell,' I was saying, 'what the hell, what the hell, what the hell . . .'

'Please,' Alison pleaded, 'stop pacing, you're making me seasick.'

'Shouldn't have gone in, shouldn't have gone in, shouldn't have gone in . . .'

'Listen to me — he might just have had a heart attack after closing up for the night.'

I stopped. 'Yes, and Rosemary is off on holidays and Manfredd is careless around big speeding trains! God!' I started again. 'Shouldn't have gone in, shouldn't have gone in, shouldn't have gone in . . .'

'Look . . . look, you're right, but it's done now . . . what difference does it really make . . . we found his body, maybe we'll get a pat on the back.'

'No! They were all murdered! The only pat on the back we'll get will be with a huge fucking pickaxe! Shouldn't have gone in, shouldn't have gone in, shouldn't—'

'Please! Just settle down!'

I glared at her. It was all her fault. There was a wall between our two stores for *a reason*. It was *private* property.

She put her hands together, as if in prayer. 'Okay, he was *probably* murdered. But that was six months ago! Nobody knows we've been in there, can't we just close up the hole in the roof space and forget about it?'

'Forget about it? Don't you know *anything*?' I didn't really care that she looked hurt. She had put me in this *position*. I was implicated. I was a suspect. I was an accessory. 'I shouldn't have listened to you, I shouldn't have listened to you . . .' I stopped. I tried to control my breathing the way they'd taught me. 'We're screwed, we're really screwed . . . every way you look at it we're screwed . . .'

'I don't see how . . .'

'Then listen, you halfwit . . . ! Sorry . . . sorry . . . it's just . . . just because nobody's found the body yet, when they do, *when they do,* the police, the *police* will seal the place off and their forensic people will go in and they'll find *our* DNA, our fingerprints, *we* will be accused of killing him!'

'We could go back in and wipe it up and—'

'No, you moron, it doesn't work like that! And we may not even survive long enough for them to find the body anyway. Don't you see? Everything I thought in the first place is right! There's a murderer out there, and he's killing everyone who knows about the book, he's killed Rosemary and then Malcolm and now Manfredd and it's like he's ticking them off and it's only a matter of time before he comes looking for Daniel and me. *Me!*'

'So I'm okay?'

'No! As soon as we're arrested for next door, he'll find out about you, and he'll just add your name until there's no one left. We're all up shit creek!'

She nodded to herself. *'Or.'*

'Or?'

'Or because I've only just met you, and have nothing to do with your crime-fighting, and nobody but you knows that I even know about it, and because Malcolm Carlyle had customers in there all the time, so that's how my DNA got in there, you could just stand up like a man and take all the blame if the police come calling, that way I won't be involved in discovering the body and I won't be on the killer's hit list. What do you say?'

'Fuck off! You got me into this, it's your fault, I didn't want . . .'

But she was holding up her hands. And bloody *laughing.* 'I'm only joking.'

'This isn't a time for jokes!'

'I know . . . I know . . . but *of course* I'm in this with you. And we'll work it out. Honestly.'

'How?'

'I don't know . . . but we will. We'll solve it. We really will.'

And then she came forward and gave me a hug.

And it was quite one of the most wonderful things that has ever happened to me, so I forgot for the moment that I hated her and that I was in imminent danger of being murdered, and luxuriated in her embrace, because it couldn't last for ever, and didn't.

She let me go, shook her head and said: 'Fucking pine trees. Piece of genius or what?'

I was trying to work it out in my head, while Alison quickly got drunk.

I rarely drink. It reacts with the medication. For this, I needed to be in control of all my remaining faculties, because now I knew that at any moment of any day from here on in the killer might strike. I had no idea if the Odessa still existed — I mean, it wasn't as if it had a website — but even if it did, Malcolm Carlyle's death seemed like the work of just one man, probably a German. Rosemary was killed in Germany, so was Manfredd, and Malcolm had gone there to investigate Rosemary's disappearance. He had surely then been followed back to Belfast and killed in his own office. The fact that the killer had left the body *in situ* suggested that he wasn't confident enough to try to dispose of it in an unfamiliar city and/or that he didn't have the physical strength to lift it himself. Malcolm Carlyle wasn't a huge man, but a dead weight is, literally, a dead weight, and extremely hard work. I know this because I'd dragged my father's body from the bathroom where he collapsed and died to the bedroom where I laid him out. He had been delirious, and weak as a kitten, but it says much about the moral core of the man that he had forced himself up and into the bathroom to use the toilet so that he wouldn't soil the bed. His last words to me, as I hovered near the door, were, 'Tumbling into the darkness.' He could see death coming. My mum's last words to me were, 'Comb your hair.' She wasn't dead, we just weren't speaking. But Dad wasn't a big man either, yet so heavy in death that I staggered under the weight of him. I fell and his corpse fell on me, and I had to crawl out from beneath him and start again. Unless Malcolm Carlyle's killer was some kind of weightlifting champion, he would have struggled to dispose of the body.

Alison was pouring another glass of white. She paused when it was half full, a thought suddenly striking her. She put the bottle down and turned: 'You're wrong,' she said. 'It's not just you and Daniel and possibly me on the list — who are you forgetting?'

'Jeff?' I suggested hopefully.

'No — Anne Mayerova.'

'Bloody hell. *Of course.*' She was the source of it all. And if he got to her then he'd have the main witness to whatever it was that was annoying him. I took a deep breath. 'That's it,' I said. 'This can't go on.'

I lifted the phone and began to punch in the numbers.

There were only the three of them.

'What're you doing?' Alison demanded, crossing from the trestle table to the desk.

'What do you think? I'm calling the police.'

She reached out and cut the line. 'No.'

'What do you mean, *no?* It's my case, it's my life, it's my shop and it's my phone.'

I punched the numbers in again.

The operator said: 'Which service, please?'

Alison shook her head. I covered the mouthpiece and said: 'I *have* to. I do itty-bitty cases. There's a corpse next door and a killer on the loose. I don't deal in lead, I deal in paper.'

'We can do this.'

'We will *die.*'

'Which service, please?'

'Not *yet,'* Alison said firmly. 'It's going to be hard enough explaining about Malcolm Carlyle. If we start into the whole German, dancing Jews, Auschwitz thing they're going to think we're mental, and even if they don't they're going to take their time checking it all out, and meanwhile the killer's going to be free to find old Mrs Mayerova. We have to get to her first, we have to warn her, after that, okay, call the cops in then. But at least let's give her a chance.'

I looked at her, with her big lovely eyes, pleading, and I looked at the phone.

'Which ser—'

'Oh fucking buggery,' I said, and cut the line.

20

There was no right way to do things, of course. My gut instinct, based on my father's regular beatings, designed to instil in me the sanctity of the law and God as the ultimate arbiter of justice, was to go to the police and confess all. But our story had the whiff of fantasy about it already, and I'd read enough fiction to know for a fact that once they gained access to my medical records it would be as good as making a signed confession. Nor would it help if they searched No Alibis, as they surely would, and discovered my nail for the scratching of cars with personalised number plates. Getting rid of it wasn't an option. It was precious to me. There was also the fact that the forces of law and order had nothing to do in Belfast these days, which made it difficult for officers seeking promotion to stand out. They would be falling all over themselves to secure a conviction for *anything* and *quickly*. It wouldn't even be good cop, bad cop, it would be bad cop, bad cop, and they would twist everything we said until we somehow implicated each other.

So really we had no choice, although I did think briefly

that one possible solution would be to finger Jeff for the murder next door. I could quite easily take a book impregnated with his DNA and fingerprints and place it in the dead fingers of Malcolm Carlyle. It would be a just and fair reward for his attempts to steal my girl.

'What?' Alison asked.

'What *what?*'

'You mumbled something about *stealing my girl.*'

'No I didn't. Concentrate on the road.'

My girl, who was driving at speeds way beyond what I felt were safe. I didn't know if she normally drove this quickly, but we were certainly *moving.* I would have driven in daylight, but with my poor night vision and my nerves it simply wasn't safe for me to take control. In some situations a drunk driver is better than a hesitant one. A drunk driver focuses and concentrates to prevent him — or herself from crashing. A hesitant driver prevaricates and ends up causing crashes. A drunk driver indicates half a mile before junctions, which is a big help to those following behind. A drunk driver never goes through lights on amber. Alison was breaking all of these rules. But I did not tell her this, of course: I just threw her the keys and told her I wanted to go through the files we'd stolen from Malcolm Carlyle's office and which were now piled untidily in my lap and at my feet. We had decided that we had nothing more to lose by going back in and scooping up as many files as we could carry. I didn't look at the deceased again. There were doubtless things I might have deduced, but I didn't have the stomach for it. On our exit we stacked up boxes of books against the hole Alison had kicked in the dividing wall in a rather poor attempt to disguise our burglary.

We were on our way to visit Anne Mayerova in her new home — Purdysburn Hospital. Daniel Trevor had told us where she was, although only after he'd gotten over the heart attack he suffered when we told him that actually he *hadn't* over-reacted to the news of Manfredd's sudden death, and that we now believed there *was* a killer on our trail, and that he should take steps to ensure his own continued well-being.

He said, 'I'm surrounded by poets and there's a sculptor in the back bedroom. He wouldn't really attempt anything here, would he?'

Poets, not largely known for their fighting ability.

'I'm sure you'll be fine,' I said. 'Do you think her husband will be at the hospital?'

No, was the answer. His name was Mark Smith, but they'd been divorced for twenty-five years and had two grown-up children. She was a teacher, so she probably told people that she had *thousands* of kids, like Mr Chips. Teachers did that. It was bollocks.

As we drove, flashing through amber lights and taking off over speed bumps, with Alison passing time between them by doing a passable impression of the weaver bird, she said: 'Purdysburn, is that not where all the nut jobs go?'

'I believe it has a wide range of patients.'

'I always heard it was all the psychos. When I was growing up you were always teased about going to Purdysburn. If you did anything stupid people would say, you should be in Purdysburn. If you acted the eejit they'd say—'

'I understand it's changed.'

'Well I hope she's not barking, we need to know her secret.'

I still wasn't convinced that we actually did. There is sometimes a great comfort in ignorance. For a long time I didn't know that Canberra really was the capital of Australia, then for a long time after I did find out I worried about why it was. Anne's secret was not our business; our only duty was to warn her about the imminent possibility of her dying violently.

About a mile away from Purdysburn I came across the Rosemary Trevor file, or at least the manila folder that had once held it. It was impossible to say if it had been deliberately taken, or was lying mixed with the many hundreds of pages I'd left on the floor of Malcolm Carlyle's office. I am methodical to the point of obsession, but the circumstances of our second visit next door were hardly conducive to an organised search, what with my dust allergy and the mouldering body in the next room. Alison registered my sigh of disappointment, but did not comment.

We pulled into a hospital car park busy with people arriving for evening visiting time.

As Alison parked, and then switched off the engine and opened her door, I said: 'We should have just phoned.'

She looked at me. 'What's the point in that? We have to look in the horse's mouth and check its teeth.'

'I feel a bit carsick,' I said.

She closed the door again and sat beside me. 'It'll settle in a minute,' she said.

'If you want to go on in, I'll catch you up.'

'Me? I'm the sidekick, you're my main man.'

I *liked* that. Not *the* main man. *My* main man. It was time to step up to the plate. To release the hounds. To marshal the troops. To gird the loins. It wasn't about saving an old woman's life . . . well, yes it was . . . but it was also about impressing this young lady. About showing her what I was capable of. That I amounted to more than the sum of my parts. My only problem was that I couldn't quite get out of the van. I was torn. I often suffer this problem in car parks, particularly at night. It's the way headlamps flash across the jagged rows of licence plates causing some to *jump!* out at you. I had a notebook in the glove compartment. I didn't want to write them all down. That would be mental. I just wanted the ones that called to me. There weren't that many of them. Given the circumstances I thought I was probably better to just sit there for a while and memorise them and then jot them down later. The problem was that some of the cars were parked facing out, and some facing in, and I couldn't be sure that the magic numbers worked at both ends, and what it meant if they did, or didn't.

Alison said, 'Are you coming?'

'Yes,' I said.

'You're always thinking, aren't you?'

'Never switch off,' I agreed.

Alison went up to the reception desk and told them who we were here to visit. These days Pursdysburn was Bedlam Lite, but it didn't mean they wouldn't spring the butterfly net on you if they didn't like the cut of your jib. I hung back. She said we were cousins, that we hadn't seen Aunt Anne in a long time and felt bad about it. The receptionist said she was sure it would be okay. Then she smiled at me and asked how I was.

'Fine,' I said.

'Friendly,' said Alison as we walked to the elevator.

It was an old Victorian redbrick that seemed to resent the presence of a modern elevator. We rattled up to the third floor. I held my breath the whole way. I always do. I once nearly expired in a twenty-seven-storey office block.

On the walk along the corridor to the ward a doctor nodded at me and said, 'How're you doing?'

'Fine,' I said. To Alison I said, 'He comes into the shop.'

'Popular man,' she said.

We had to be buzzed into the ward. It was really to stop those within from getting out, but it worked both ways. This nurse looked at me oddly, as if unsure if I was coming or going. Alison asked how Aunt Anne had been and the nurse gave her the soft-shoe shuffle, the way they're supposed to.

There were eight beds in the ward. Anne Mayerova was in the last on the right, curtained off. Two of the other women had visitors; three were asleep. The light was quite low. There was no wailing television. The smell was antiseptic mixed with canteen food. The nurse pulled the curtain back slowly and said, 'Anne, dear, look, your niece and nephew are here to see you!' with exaggerated bonhomie.

Anne Mayerova sat in a chair by the side of the bed and regarded us with hooded eyes. Her liver-spotted arms, thin as sparrow legs, jutted out of a pink nightdress. There it was on her inner arm — the vague tattoo of a serial number. Her skin was pulp-magazine flaky and her white hair was long at the back and wispy on top. She looked like the old woman in *Titanic*, the one you wanted to push over the rails.

'I've never seen them before in my life,' she said.

'Of course you have!' The nurse moved around, smoothing down the bed covers, and in an only slightly lower voice said to us, 'She gets confused.'

Anne Mayerova's eyes flitted towards her. There was confusion there, but also defiance. 'I don't have any brothers or sisters.'

The nurse smiled indulgently and left us to it. Anne Mayerova looked at us suspiciously. 'Nieces and nephews,' she said, 'would have brought grapes.'

'Nieces and nephews wouldn't,' I said, 'in case you choked on them.'

I meant it to be caring and concerned, but Alison looked at me. I was nervous. My heart was palpitating way above the normal palpitations. It was hot and sticky in the ward. The fluorescent light hummed irritatingly. There were bugs stuck in there. Stuck, or plotting.

'Miss Mayerova,' Alison said, 'of course we're not your niece and nephew. We work for your publisher, we just weren't sure if they'd let us in if we weren't relatives.'

'For Rosemary?'

'Yes, Rosemary.'

'She doesn't come to see me.'

'She sent us instead.'

'Why?'

Alison glanced at me, and then thought better of it. 'Because she's unwell.'

Anne Mayerova shook her head sadly. 'I haven't done my homework.'

'Well you haven't been well either, have you?'

While Alison engaged Anne in conversation I took advantage of the distraction to examine the chart at the bottom of the bed. I flicked back to her medication list and saw that she was being treated with a heavy dose of Effexor XL, which I knew to be an anti-depressant, and Priadel, which I knew to be lithium, for bipolar disorder, and Solpadol, a codeine phosphate, for pain. In the old days they would have given her a lobotomy and left her to rot.

I've had a close shave with a lobotomy, but that's a different story.

I had a private flashback. When I reconnected, Anne was almost in tears. 'But what am I supposed to do? They don't let me write, not in here. When I was at home . . .' She stared out of a window that overlooked the floodlit fields surrounding Purdysburn. On the bright side, I supposed, at least the lights weren't ranging back and forth.

'Don't worry about it,' said Alison.

I didn't like it here; even passing through reception it had felt like someone had reached into my chest and was squeezing my heart. It was time to cut to the chase.

'We think someone may try—'

Alison immediately cut off my *to kill you* with: '. . . to help you out.' She gave me another admonishing look and knelt down beside the old woman. She softly cupped one of her spindly hands. '*Us*, in fact. We thought that if *you* told *us* what you still had to write in the book, then we could take that to Rosemary and she could decide exactly what to do.'

'But I told her already.'

'Well because she's been unwell she's forgotten a lot of

it and she'd really like you to tell us again, if you can. I know you don't like talking about it, but perhaps just this one more . . .'

'No . . . no, I *do* . . . it was my greatest performance, you see.' There was, suddenly, a light in her eyes. Alison patted her hand. 'Mark said it was magical.'

'Your husband?' Alison asked. 'He was in the camp with you?'

'Of course. We were *lovers.'* And despite her years, the smile she gave us was that of a girlie teenager. Alison grinned up at me. She indicated the edge of the bed for me to sit. I remained where I was. I was agitated. I was blinking rapidly. I wanted to say hurry up, get on with it, this isn't *Jackanory,* visiting time will soon be over and if we don't get out quick we may be overlooked and they may seal off the ward and shut the gates and turn off the lights and we might never again know freedom. In the echoing halls of night the soldier ants in leather boots would march up and down, making sure nobody ventured from their rooms, or spoke or breathed any more than they had to. I wanted to say this, couldn't. I stood there sweating and palpitating and edging towards a faint. But then Anne Mayerova did what I had least suspected she would be capable of: this confused old woman began to tell us her story, and we were mesmerised.

21

A shocked sobriety had descended on Alison. She drove more carefully than I normally did. It was nearly eleven o'clock and the roads were damp and quiet. We were the last to leave the hospital. Our attention to Anne's story had been so rapt that when she finished and closed her eyes, and the tears of joy were on her cheeks, I turned away to wipe my own eyes, and only realised then that we had an audience, that two of the ward nurses and three other patients had quietly moved up to listen.

Now, with the streetlights easing past, I glanced several times at my sidekick. I didn't like to see her so quiet. She was usually so chirpy. She was my antidote.

We turned off the Lisburn Road and pulled up in front of a three-storey house that had been converted into apartments. In the past, in all the times I had followed her, I had never quite made it all the way to her home; partially out of fear of what I might discover, or do — standing in a garden and peering through a window has gotten me into trouble before — but usually because I'd become distracted, either by licence plates or the changing sequence of traffic signals. Now as she switched off the No Alibis engine she nodded across and said, 'Mine's the bottom one. It costs me an arm and a leg.'

I nodded.

'You're thinking about them, aren't you?' she asked.

'I can't imagine you without an arm or leg.'

She tutted. 'All those poor people.'

I nodded. Actually I'd been counting the lamp-posts between Purdysburn and where we were now. I can compartmentalise. What had happened to Anne Mayerova was filed away, to be dealt with during the long hours of sleeplessness later. For now I sat waiting for Alison to get out so that I could sidle over into her place for the drive home.

She said, 'After something like that, it doesn't feel right to be alone.'

I was studying the petrol gauge. The van was precisely half empty. Although that presumed that the reading was accurate. And that I hadn't been cheated with pirated, watered-down fuel.

'Do you want to come in?'

'No.'

'Okay.'

She still didn't move.

The van was diesel, but remarkably quiet.

'Are you sure? You could meet my husband.'

My eyes flitted up.

'Only joking,' she said. And then, after another long silence, she added: 'I mean, you could meet my wife.'

After another while I said, 'Your wife?'

'No, *stoopid.*' She smiled. 'How do you like your toast?'

'Burned,' I said.

'So would you be coming in for that, or will I bring it out on a plate?'

I was wondering why, if the engine was switched off, the petrol gauge was continuing to give a half-full reading. It may have been that it was not only inaccurate, but completely malfunctioning. That as soon as I drove away, the No Alibis van would run out of fuel and I would find myself marooned in the wastelands of South Belfast.

'Tell you what,' Alison said, 'I'm going to go in now, but I'm going to leave my front door on the latch. If you decide you want some toast, you just come on in, okay?' I nodded. She leant across and kissed me on the cheek. I didn't know where to put myself. Hand-holding and a kiss on the cheek *in one day*. 'Listen,' she said, 'don't let it get to you. It was sixty, nearly seventy years ago. You can't beat yourself up about history. She's a lovely old woman with a sad and happy story. We may not know exactly what the big secret is, but at least we've tipped off the security people there to keep an eye on her. There's nothing more we can really do.'

I nodded.

'So I'm going in now. Raspberry or strawberry?'

'Raspberry,' I said.

'Butter or margarine?'

'Butter.'

'Crusts on or off?'

'On.'

'I think we're a perfect match,' she said. She smiled again. Then she slipped out of the van and hurried up to her front door.

I sat where I was for another minute. I watched the lights come on in the downstairs apartment, then in what I took to be her bedroom. I caught a glimpse of her throwing down her coat, and then moving back out of the room. She had held my hand and kissed my cheek. It was more than I had ever imagined. Father always taught me that God crushes those who dare to hope, and life had shown him to be right.

I moved into the driver's seat and started the engine.

Then I drove home.

Anne Mayerova had spoken with unexpected clarity

and so far as I could judge her recall seemed absolute. There was no vagueness, nothing half remembered. She might no longer be capable of living alone or of combing her own hair, but she was certain about the events that had defined her life.

She had arrived at the Birkenau labour camp at Auschwitz in April of 1944 with her young husband Mark. She was branded with a serial number, though she said it didn't seem particularly painful — possibly because she was already in shock. Conditions were of course appalling, although that didn't stop those who were already there taking great satisfaction in describing how awful life would be and what would happen to her. Everyone expected to die. Those who had arrived the previous September, for example, had been worked into the ground until March, and then exterminated. Six months was as long as anyone survived.

Anne was surprised to meet an old acquaintance, a man called Alfred, who was working as a kapo in the laundry. He quickly got her a job there, washing the clothes taken from the new arrivals — but as most of these were already clean and packed in suitcases it wasn't particularly hard. She readily admitted that she had grown up cosseted, and even in the camp it took a while to knock that out of her. One morning she was late for work and Alfred threw her to the ground and beat her very badly — because if she was late, then he got into trouble — although he later went down on his knees and begged her forgiveness. His own parents had only recently been sent to the gas chambers. Although she was in a women's barracks, she was still able to meet with her husband during the day — she didn't tell him about the beating and he didn't tell her about his own appalling experiences. Several times they were even able to make love.

On 6 June the Allied invasion of Europe changed things in the camp. Hitler declared that as workers were needed, no longer would *everyone* be sent to be exterminated — only the sick and the weak, the very old and the very young. But that meant *selection*. By this stage Anne had fallen seriously ill with typhoid and could barely walk. Her husband helped her to strip with the other prisoners and then join the inspection lines, dogs barking all around them, SS guards barking orders, and Dr Mengele watching everyone like a hawk. One quick glance at her emaciated, fevered frame, and Anne was selected for death. Mark could say nothing. It would mean his own death. There were two parallel lines — those who would live, and could reclaim their clothes; and those who would remain naked and be taken to the gas chambers. But the two lines were quite close together. Realising what was coming, and knowing that she had nothing left to lose, Anne just closed her eyes and stepped out of her death line into that of the living. And nobody noticed. She had a brief moment with Mark before he was marched away to the men's camp.

Anne and her fellow prisoners were also taken out of what had been a family camp into an all-women camp. Even the SS officers in charge were women — in this case the cruel and barbarous Oberaufseherin Elsa who regularly oversaw beatings and took great joy in dispatching anyone she took a dislike to directly to the gas chambers. They survived on watery soup, served in bowls without spoons so that they had to lap out of them like dogs. They were formed into small groups called kommandos and set to work carrying bricks, running with them along a path, depositing them, and then running back for more. Their hands bled and the wounds did not heal. They were given a lump of bread at night, and they were always torn whether to eat it all at once or to save some for the next day, which meant running the risk of having it stolen during the night. They were freezing and hungry and in such total despair that many of the prisoners literally gave up: they volunteered for the trucks leaving for the gas chambers.

Even in the midst of such degradation, there was still defiance. When it came time to celebrate Yom Kippur, the women prisoners decided to observe it by fasting for twenty-four hours. Their SS tormentors were furious, but the inmates stuck to their plan, even though at the end of it the guards refused to hand over their evening meal, which meant that these already starving women went without food for thirty-six hours. There were other tiny pinpricks of light in this universe of darkness. There was one SS guard known as the Mechanic who rode about the camp on a bicycle repairing broken-down vehicles and machinery. He would occasionally stop and talk to the women, and offer a kind word. It was remarkable how important even little things like this became. Anne had been suffering from dysentery and was barely able to work, but she had no choice. On one particularly bad day, the Mechanic saw her distress and actually gave her his lunch. He suggested she go to see the camp doctor, without apparently realising that once you went to see him, you didn't come back. She was so unused to the relatively rich food that she immediately threw it back up. The Mechanic knelt beside her and whispered encouragement: that he believed that life was like a great wheel, that some days you were moving up on that wheel and some days you were moving down. She was down right now, but one day she would be on the top of the wheel while he would be at the bottom. After this he took to coming every day and surreptitiously giving one of them part of his lunch.

As Christmas approached, Elsa, the Oberaufseherin, decided that a programme of entertainment should be mounted, featuring dramatic sketches, music and dancing. Auditions and rehearsals were held in the early hours of the morning. Anne was dragged there by friends, just to watch, and with no desire to take part — she was far too ill and weak — but when she saw the selected dancers perform she forgot herself and shouted that they didn't know what they were doing. She had, after all, been a professional dancer — and those on the makeshift stage reacted by telling her that if she knew so much, she should show them how to do it. Thus, barely able to walk, she made it to the stage, and as the musical accompaniment began — an accordionist — something miraculous happened. She felt power in her legs again. She felt adrenaline course through her pathetic body. She danced the *valse* from *Coppelia* in her torn and stinking pyjamas, with block clogs on her rancid feet. It must have looked bizarre indeed — but it worked. Anne was not only recruited as the lead dancer, but to choreograph the entire production.

A week before Christmas it was announced that the Ober would be attending the rehearsal to see how her great idea was progressing. She duly clapped and laughed through the entire show, until it came to Anne's turn to dance. She watched without reaction — and at the end simply got up and walked out. Anne naturally feared the worst, especially when, the next morning at roll-call, her name was called out and she had to step forward. But then it was announced that from now on she would be excused from outside work and would receive an extra portion of soup every day.

The show took place on Christmas night, and Anne remembered it better than anything else in her life. Hundreds of women prisoners crowded into the hall, dozens of SS were there as well — not to guard them, but to enjoy the show. The sketches were greeted uproariously, everyone sang along to the music, and then the climax of the show — Anne dancing *Coppelia* — and for a few minutes she and the entire audience were transported to another dimension. They gave themselves up to the grace and passion of the music and the movement; the horrors they were all living through were forgotten, and she danced as she had never danced before. The bare wooden stage was better than any stage in the world, the heavy-fingered accordion more powerful than a great orchestra;

as she danced she glimpsed snow falling through the hall windows, almost as if it was washing away everyone's sins. She felt love and hope and knew that it didn't matter if she survived, that her life's purpose had been fulfilled, that she had given hope to the poor people around her and perhaps given pause for thought to their tormentors. When she finished the audience stood as one and cheered so much that she was forced to perform an encore, this time a South American tango. It was a triumph. Afterwards the cast were treated to soup with real meat in it.

In the telling of this, Anne Mayerova had raised herself on her spindly legs and did her best to ape the movements she had performed on that Christmas night in Auschwitz; we made space for her to shuffle back and forth. She looked like a *nut*.

But she absolutely lived it again.

Alison was sobbing. It was powerful stuff. You couldn't imagine what it had been like in those camps. Although I would do my best. After Anne's recounting of what had happened at the show, a lot of the life went out of her; in her eyes the rest was an anticlimax. Her story-telling became more vague, and quite listless. She said that the 'good times' could not last, and very soon she was back with her kommando, working outdoors. The difference was that she had several weeks of comparatively healthy eating behind her, which made her better able to cope, at least for a short while, with the appalling conditions.

Within a few weeks, however, their situation changed again. The war was all but lost, and the Russians were closing in on the camp. The SS, frightened of what the enemy would do when they discovered what had been going on, forced the prisoners to go on what became a death march, walking for days at a time without food or shelter in freezing weather and without any apparent destination. If a prisoner stumbled and fell, they were shot where they lay. Anne became so ill that she began to hallucinate and soon could no longer walk. She lay down to die. But instead of her being murdered, an Allied air raid distracted her guards and in the confusion she found some last surge of strength, just enough to allow her to find a hiding place. Her fellow prisoners were marched off to their deaths, and she was taken in by a Polish farmer. She hovered between life and death for several weeks, but eventually recovered enough strength to be handed over to the by-now Russian victors; and from there she made it home to Prague, only to discover that she was the only one of her family who had survived the war. But then only two days later another miracle — her husband, her Mark, whom she had presumed dead in Auschwitz, walked through the door, like a ghost. They had both survived.

I sat at the kitchen table and worried. This was not unusual. I had a hot chocolate and a Twix. Neither was this. I worried about what Alison was thinking of me, and about whether she was thinking of me at all. After all, how important was supper with a vague acquaintance compared to the astonishing story she had just listened to? She was quite probably entirely consumed by that. It was an epic of survival that spoke volumes about the power of the human spirit. It illustrated exactly how art could raise you up out of the most dispiriting situations imaginable. No, Alison wasn't wasting any thought *at all* on this mystery-bookshop owner. She might not even have noticed my sudden departure. If she remembered tomorrow and asked what had happened I would say, *There was a family emergency, I had to get home.* And if she didn't buy that, then I would have to reconcile myself to the end of our nascent relationship. It didn't mean I wouldn't see her again. I had the webcam, and *stealth*.

Yes, I worried about Alison, but mostly I worried about moral ambiguity.

If you took the old woman's story at face value it was evocative, emotive and uplifting. It was, ultimately, a triumph of good over evil, which, rather than dwell on man's inhumanity to man, is how we like to deal with our Holocausts. I have to admit I *was* quite carried away with her story — at least until the climactic dance when she described how she'd glimpsed the snow falling outside, and that was when I realised that she was giving us a version of the events warped by both time and ego. *Of course* it wasn't snow falling picturesquely at Christmas; it was ash from the crematorium chimneys. And when I thought this I also thought of the preposterousness of their mounting a Christmas show at the behest of and for the entertainment of their SS captors, the monsters who were doing their very best to destroy the entire tribe of David. These poor cretins, who could hardly stand, whose loved ones were being exterminated even as they hoofed across the stage, somehow deluded themselves that *auditioning* for, *rehearsing* for and *performing* in comedy sketches and dances was somehow a *good thing*, to be remembered fondly. It was *The Bridge on the River Kwai* in ballet shoes, without the saving grace of 'What have I done?' at the end.

Did it make Anne Mayerova a collaborator? Probably not. Did it make her a hate figure amongst her fellow prisoners? Chosen for special treatment, excused hard labour, given extra rations? To do what — *dance? Of course* they hated her. She remembered it as her finest moment, but was it anything like that? Was there wild applause and encores?

No!

No, no, no, no, no, no, no, no, no, no, no, no!

No, no, no, no, no, no, no, no, no, no, no, no, no, no, no, no!

I sat at my table and ate my Twix and attempted to cry for the Jews of Auschwitz.

Couldn't.

Malfunctioning tear ducts.

I moaned for a bit.

After a while Mother came through. We still weren't

speaking, but she had obviously heard me from upstairs and had taken the trouble to jot down a note of support. She set it on the table before me and then went to fill the kettle.

It said:

Go to bed, you fucking loser.

22

I drove nervously to work the next morning. I always drive nervously. There are too many cars and the roads are too narrow and cyclists should be forced to use the footpaths instead of giving qualified drivers the shakes. But these were extra nerves. They were to do with the probability of seeing Alison again; they were also to do with *The Case of the Dancing Jews* and its consequences for my own health. I have a radio but will only listen to it when completely stationary, otherwise it is distracting and my speed will creep up into the thirties. If I'd had my radio on I would undoubtedly have heard the news at nine a.m. and would then have been prepared for what was coming.

As I passed under the flyover at the West Link I noted that the graffiti that was supposed to have been removed now read: *Albert McIntosh is no longer a fruit.* That was just plain wrong. It would be dealt with. But at least it was my kind of problem. My *size* of problem. Not Nazis. Not murder. Just some numbskull with a paint brush. It was a problem I could dwell on that wasn't so major that it distracted me from my driving, unlike the Alison problem, and the killer-on-the-loose problem, and the dead-body-next-door problem, which all might have contributed to vehicular negligence.

The traffic on Botanic Avenue was unusually heavy. But then, as I drew closer to the shop, I realised that it wasn't really — it was just slow because of the rubberneckers staring out of their cars at all the police activity. The offices of Malcolm Carlyle, Private Eye, had been cordoned off; there were half a dozen police cars parked up on the footpath or in *my* parking bay. There was a hearse with an undertaker leaning against it, smoking. There were forensics guys in white. There were two news crews and several photographers. There was Jeff standing in my doorway, looking nervous. Behind him, four mysterious rectangular black holes had been blasted in my pull-down shutters.

It was too much for me to compute all at once.

I kept driving.

How could I park the No Alibis van near the shop when the place was swarming with police and reporters and the van had *Murder Is Our Business* on its side? Would it not be a surefire indicator that I was involved in the murder of Malcolm Carlyle? How many milliseconds would it be before the long arm of the law grabbed me by the throat? And it wouldn't even require a long arm. A short arm. A stunted arm. A police officer suffering from growth hormone deficiency in the general arm area would throttle me the very instant he saw the No Alibis van with its *oh so witty* catch line.

I needed to think. I needed to gather information away from the glare of scrutiny and interrogation.

I hid the van in a public car park on Great Victoria Street and having failed to find a Starbucks in the immediate vicinity made do with an ordinary café. I ordered a hot chocolate and bought a Twix. Throwing caution and brain tumours to the wind, I removed my mobile phone and called Jeff.

'Jeff,' I said, 'what on earth is going on?'

'Where are you?' he barked in response. 'The police are looking for you. They've found your man next door, he's been there all along, he's been rotting away in there while we've been—'

'Why are they looking for me? Do they think I killed—'

'You? Why would they think you—'

'Jeff, what did they say?'

'They wanted to check if it was okay to use your parking space.'

'They *what?*'

'They have pretty strict guidelines about where they can park, you know, on private property and—'

'Jeff. What have they said about Malcolm Carlyle?'

'Nothing. Why would they say anything to me? Where are you anyway? Why aren't you opening up? They want into the shop.'

'*My* shop? *Why?*'

'Well I asked them if they wanted a cup of tea — they can't make it in his place because of the forensics. But that was when I thought you'd be here in a minute and now I feel stupid because I can't get in. And they also think it's pretty strange about the toast.'

'The *what?*'

'When I arrived here this morning they were looking at our shutters. Someone has stuck four pieces of burned toast to them. I mean, you could understand chips or pizza or something some drunk's going to buy on the way home, but where do you get toast from unless you go home and make it and then take it out with you? What retard is going to do that?'

'Do they think the toast is in some way connected to the murder next door?'

'Why would they think that? I think it just made them hungry. Who said it was a murder anyway?'

'Jeff . . .'

'So are you coming in this morning at all? Because if

you're not I don't want to hang around here like a suspect or something. Don't they say killers always come back to the scene of the crime? Don't they always offer to help out? Christ, I shouldn't have offered them tea, should I? What was I thinking?'

'I'll be there shortly,' I said, and hung up.

My hot chocolate arrived.

It was not up to scratch. It wasn't Starbucks. There was no finesse. It was spoon, stir, deliver.

Okay.

Settle.

The relevant point was that I had done nothing wrong, apart from a spot of burglary. I had not killed Malcolm Carlyle. The police did not think I had killed him either. They had no reason to. No reason to suspect anything.

Not yet.

But how did they know to even look for him? Why today of all days? Had somebody seen us enter Private Eye? Perhaps spotted the lights going on inside? Or, please God, no, what if Alison had tipped them off in revenge for the toast incident?

No.

No.

Absolutely not.

She was as confused and concerned as I was. She was surely at that very moment staring across the road from the jewellery store at the crime scene. She might even be wondering if the police could extract DNA from toast and then connect it to what they found inside? Was she thinking that if questioned I would choose to spread the blame and incriminate her?

For the ten millionth time I cursed myself for not following my instincts. I knew *The Case of the Dancing Jews* was out of my league almost from the very start. I should have rejected it completely and concentrated on my bookselling; but oh no, a chance to impress a pretty girl, and now I was up to my oxters in trouble. Even last night, when we'd discovered Malcolm Carlyle's body, I'd gone against my own better judgement by not following through with my 999 call. There was a world of difference between *immediately* telling the police what we'd discovered and going to them *after* they'd already located the body. It was more than suspicious. It was *damning*.

So what to do?

Buy more time.

Figure it out.

Act dumb.

Act *normal*.

How hard could that be?

23

I pushed through the crowd of gawkers. Some fellow shopkeepers tried to engage me in gossip, but I said nothing. Jeff was relieved to see me. I unlocked the shutters and pushed them up, in the process removing the toast from scrutiny. I punched in the code and released the dead bolts. We entered the shop and switched on the lights.

Thirty seconds later a man came in.

Jeff gave him the thumbs-up and said, 'I'll put the tea on.'

'Forget the tea,' said the man.

He was of medium height, in a charcoal suit, with a black moustache and grey-flecked hair. He put out his hand and said, 'Detective Inspector Robinson, CID.'

I tend not to shake hands because of the risk of plague, but on this occasion my hand was out and grasping his before I could stop it. 'How're you doing?' I enquired. 'I hear you have a stiffy.'

Shut up, shut up, shut up, shut up, shut up, shut up . . .

His brow furrowed. 'We have discovered a body next

door. We believe he may be—'

'Malcolm Carlyle,' I said. 'We were wondering where he'd gotten to. Six months he's been missing. Poor man. He was in here a few times but I didn't know him that well. I get his clients calling in from time to time looking for him. I help them out when I can. Are you sure you don't want a cup? We have coffee. There's Ribena in the fridge.'

DI Robinson nodded slowly. His eyes ranged around the interior of the shop before settling back on me. 'You would appear to specialise in murder.'

Jeff laughed.

I aped him. But louder. 'Well you know what they say, those who can, do, those who can't, teach, and those who can't teach, teach PE.' His eyes were stuck to me. 'So Jeff tells me you're concerned about my parking space. Park away. I haven't the van with me today anyway. You'll probably be here a couple of days, but that's fine. The traffic wardens can be a bit—'

'So, I understand you called the emergency services last night.'

I cleared my throat. My pacemaker *whirred.*

'No, I . . .'

'Call was logged at seven thirty p.m. from this location.'

'No, I . . .'

'Were you on these premises at seven thirty, last night?'

'No. And yes. I wasn't exactly aware of the time . . .'

'Did you phone the emergency services at seven thirty last night?'

His eyes bored into mine. I have a terrifically inbred Presbyterian tendency to deny *everything,* even in the face of perfect evidence to the contrary.

'No,' I said.

'It was me.' It was Alison, standing in the open doorway. 'I phoned.'

I pointed at her. 'Yes, it was her.'

If she was prepared to shoulder the blame, if she'd already made the decision that she was going to be the martyr, then it was my duty to do everything in my power to support that decision.

DI Robinson studied her. 'And who might you be?'

'I work in the jeweller's across the way. I was over having a drink with my boyfriend . . .' She nodded down at the trestle tables, still set up for a party, while I concentrated on trying to stop my head rolling off my shoulders. Had I heard her right? Yes — I'd heard her right. But I was careful not to get carried away with it, or to clap my hands and jump on the table and propose marriage. I knew, or suspected I knew, that she was just saying I was her boyfriend as a means of adding more weight, more credibility, more *heft,* to the pathetic explanation that was bound to follow. It meant that we were no longer blaming each other, that we were a team, partners in crime. We would go down together. Bonnie and Clyde. '. . .and I persuaded him to take a look next door — we were worried about the smell.'

'The smell?'

'Pine,' she said. 'An overwhelming smell of pine.'

DI Robinson looked from her to me. 'Pine,' I agreed.

'Why on earth would that worry you?'

'Because it was so unusual,' said Alison. 'If we'd smelled something rotting . . . we would have thought it was just the drains . . .'

'Or the bins out the back,' I said. 'They never pick them up on time . . .'

'But we're in the middle of the city,' said Alison. 'You shouldn't be smelling pine that intensely.'

'So his plan actually backfired,' I said.

The detective's head literally jerked towards me. 'Whose plan?'

'Whoever killed him and hung pine trees on his body.'

'Am I understanding you correctly?' he asked incredulously. 'You were next door? You saw it? You've actually been in there?'

I looked at Alison. She rolled her eyes. 'Yes,' she said, 'we went in. There's a hole in the roof space. We thought the place was empty, and if we could pin down the smell we'd at least know what to complain about . . .'

The DI shook his head. 'Well this is a turn-up for the books. I thought you dialled 999 and then decided not to waste police time, so you hung up. But you actually entered the building next door? Both of you? You *broke* in.'

I studied the carpet. Most shops have carpet tiles so that they can be easily replaced when dumb customers walk in shit and stuff. I had insisted on one single piece of fitted carpet in plain beige. If there had been lines or patterns or both I would never have gotten any work done.

When I chanced a look up, DI Robinson was staring at me. He raised an eyebrow.

'Yes, we were in there,' I said.

'To find the source of the pine,' said Alison.

'I want you to tell me exactly what you saw.'

'Do you want me to draw you a picture?' Alison said.

The detective's demeanour visibly darkened. 'Watch your attitude,' he snapped, waving a warning finger at her. 'A murder has been committed and—'

Alison held up her hands. 'No, I mean literally draw you one . . . I'm an artist . . . I could . . .'

She trailed off. He was shaking his head. He had heard enough. 'I'm not quite sure exactly what I'm dealing with here,' he said grimly. 'Either you two are up to your necks in this, or you're complete blithering idiots.'

The truth, of course, lay somewhere in the middle.

'We didn't expect to find a body,' Alison said weakly.

'And we didn't murder him,' I added.

24

For the moment there was nothing much DI Robinson could do beyond chastising us for breaking and entering and possibly contaminating a murder scene. He directed a more junior officer to take statements from us. He warned us he'd be back to see us once the forensics evidence was analysed. 'In the meantime,' he said, 'if I were you I wouldn't be making any plans to leave the country.'

As *if.* I hadn't been out of Belfast since 1985, and that was to Lourdes, which is no place at all for a Presbyterian; I was coachsick and seasick on the way there, and the same on the way back. If there was a miracle, I couldn't see it for all the boke.

As DI Robinson didn't yet know how the cards were going to fall, he also demanded a statement from Jeff, who acted like he was furious, but seemed to rather enjoy being slightly to the left of the centre of attention. The prospect of running a campaign to free *himself* from prison excited him in a way that merely protesting on behalf of obscure lefties a continent away hadn't for a long time. The way he slowly tramped out of the store just before lunch would make you think the ball and chain was already attached to his ankles. As he stood at the door, having collected his £12 for standing behind the counter doing *nothing* all morning, he raised a fist and punched the air defiantly. I gave him a similar salute, but utilising just two fingers.

As he left, I glanced across the road and saw Alison at her window. She pointed to her left and held up five spread fingers. I nodded. As soon as she'd given her statement she'd had to rush back to work; and as I'd still been busy giving mine we hadn't been able to speak openly either about the events of the previous evening, or the dramatic developments of the morning.

I thought we might walk up together, but by the time I pulled the shutters down, peeled off the toast and deposited it in a street bin, she'd already left the jeweller's. I just caught a glimpse of her entering Starbucks. The police remained busy next door, and the pavement outside was still cordoned off. The hearse was gone.

Starbucks was busy. Everyone was talking about the murder. I caught little fragments of it as I looked for Alison. I found her upstairs, at a window table for two; from her chair she could look back along Botanic Avenue to the shop, and the police activity. I sat with my back to it.

'I bought you a skinny cinnamon dolce latte,' she said. 'They'll bring it up in a minute. Busy.'

I smiled my thanks. It was a false smile. It was *not* the next beverage on the menu. She had skipped two. If I even touched it, it would negate three weeks' work.

'I'm sorry about the toast,' I said. 'There was a family emergency.'

'*I'm* sorry about the toast,' she responded. 'It was a childish act of revenge.'

I nodded. She nodded.

'Last night,' she said, 'what a story.'

'Six million Jews,' I said, 'what a bummer.'

'I would love to have seen her dance,' said Alison. 'It

must have been . . . *transcendent.* What kind of family emergency?'

'My mother. She takes funny turns.'

Alison smiled. 'You make her sound like a comedian. Funny turns.' I nodded. She was far from a comedian. 'Is she okay?'

'Yes. Of course. Thank you for asking. She never has a headache, it's always a stroke, do you know what I mean?'

'And the one time you do ignore it, it *will* be a stroke.' She understood. I was off the hook. The skinny cinnamon dolce lattes arrived. 'So what are we going to do?'

'About?'

She rolled her eyes. She leaned forward. 'The *case*. The *murder*. The *assassin.*'

'Not an assassin,' I corrected. 'An assassin murders important people.'

'So *what*? What are we going to do about him? Why didn't we tell the police? Am I going to spend the rest of my life looking over my shoulder? Are you going to have to keep a gun underneath your counter? What's going to happen to Daniel Trevor? Is Rosemary really dead? Who killed Manfredd? Is Anne safe in Purdysburn?'

'I'm allergic to cinnamon,' I said.

'Since when?'

'Childhood, but I have good days.'

She studied me for a long time. She shook her head, but it did not seem unduly negative. 'There's just something about you, isn't there?'

'Is there?'

'Sometimes you are absolutely manic and there's no talking to you. Now you have this kind of Zen calmness and there's still no talking to you.' I shrugged. 'It's just washing over you. It's like someone throws a stone in a pond and there are all these waves, and the people who own the toy yachts get panic-stricken, yet you know that very soon everything will settle down again. I wish I could be like that. I hardly slept last night. But seriously, what are we going to do?'

I shrugged again.

'Of course being all Zen can be really annoying when you're trying to have a serious conversation. *What are we going to do?* What do you think of that detective? Do you think we should trust him? Because we can't go on like this, can we?'

'Well,' I said, 'maybe we can. Maybe we can afford to be a little bit more relaxed. Look — now that the police have discovered Malcolm's body, well they'll be investigating a murder, won't they? If they're any good at all that will lead them to Rosemary, and that will also then become a murder inquiry. So I'm thinking that the killer must be lying low. Most probably he's back in Germany. And anyway — we were worried that we were next on his death list, but really, who's to say we're even on it? The reason he killed Rosemary was because she was planning to publish a book that might have revealed some secret about him. Perhaps for safety he killed Malcolm and Manfredd as well. But maybe that's where it ends — it's pretty clear that Anne Mayerova isn't going to ever write the rest of her book; and even if she did, Daniel has had too big a fright to even contemplate publishing it. The secret is safe, maybe he doesn't *need* to kill anyone else.'

'But what if he thinks you're still investigating . . .?'

'We don't know for sure if he's even *aware* of me. Daniel told Manfredd that I was involved, but we don't know that Manfredd told his killer, or if he did, how much. Why would he?'

'So what are you suggesting?'

That we let the police do their job. If they don't uncover the whole thing about Rosemary well, we can make an anonymous call. We keep a reasonable eye out for trouble, but I really think we should just try and forget about the whole thing. One of these days another case, a much easier one, is just going to walk into the shop, and maybe we can tackle that together. It'll be fun. What do you say?'

She thought about that. She took a sip of her latte. After a while she said, 'So you're just going to let *The Case of the Dancing Jews* remain unsolved?'

'Absolutely,' I said.

25

Over the next few days things began to return to abnormal in No Alibis. Our summer sale was not a huge success, even with the 5% off stickers I had Jeff attach to our least popular books. I wasn't particularly worried. I see the *need* to attract customers into the store, I just don't often feel the *want*. Yes, I could go crazy and push it up to 7 or 8 per cent, but what then to do with the riff-raff it was sure to attract? Those who poke their heads through the door and say, 'Oh I'm just looking for something a bit rubbish to read on the beach.' Or even worse, 'something light'.

Fuck off!

Of course, I don't turn sales away, but more than once I've slipped a Henning Mankell into their bag of books, telling them he makes the master, John D. MacDonald, 'look like a shit', in the full knowledge that it won't be disturbed until they're lying in the sand. Only then do they discover I've sold them the original Swedish version. Sometimes I just laugh and laugh.

We actually closed for the Twelfth of July holiday. *Really* closed, the first time since No Alibis opened. Usually

I would just have the shutters pulled down three-quarter-length so that the bully boys in band uniforms wouldn't accuse me of treason, but those in the know were *in the know*. You cannot just cut off an addict's supply, there must always be an outlet. So four or five times during the day a customer would saunter past the store, keeping an eagle eye out for military-looking Protestants and then when absolutely sure that the coast was clear, dip under the shutters and inside for their fix of hit lit, like dress-down Sherlocks slipping into a Parker Knoll version of an opium den.

But not this year.

This year Alison took me on a picnic.

I warned her beforehand that I didn't want to go out of Belfast, having in mind the flies and the cows, and she laughed and said, 'What're you frightened of, Dutch elm disease?' It was seventh on my list, but there was no point in mentioning it. I don't like being made fun of. That was also on the list.

As a compromise, we sat in the grounds of City Hall. She'd made sandwiches. I picked through the ones my stomach could handle while she showed me several of the comics she'd drawn. I thought they were fantastic. I am not biased. I know what I'm talking about. I asked where I could buy them and she said, don't be silly, you can *have* them. I said, no, I mean, to sell in the shop and she said she only had a few copies she ran off from her computer printer.

'And you're *giving* them to me?' She nodded and smiled. 'There is no such thing as a free picnic,' I observed.

She lay back on the blanket, shades on, enjoying the sun. 'Well,' she said, 'I may want a kiss later.'

'You'll be lucky.'

I laughed. She laughed. She laughed because she thought I was joking. I laughed because I knew I'd be home long before that, broken hearted and embarrassed and full of anger because I'd done something wrong or stupid.

But before the hour was out she rolled over beside me and screwed her face up and said, 'What's wrong with your eyes?'

'I'm myopic.'

'No, I don't mean . . .'

Then there were the cataracts and diabetes and . . .

She was leaning over me. 'No . . . I think there's . . . close them a moment.'

I closed them.

She kissed me on the lips.

Then she lay back.

It is a mark of how shocked and yet comfortable I was that I did not even think of reaching for an antiseptic wipe.

With the country virtually closed down for the next two weeks — one day of official holiday the rest to recover — DI Robinson returned from somewhere doubtless cheap and nasty sporting his Ulster tan, red faced, peeling and with his freckles standing out like liver spots, and somewhat sheepishly revealed that he no longer needed to talk to us about the murder of Malcolm Carlyle, because they were no longer certain that it was in fact a murder. The body had been so decomposed that it had been impossible to establish a cause of death, and in the absence of any evidence to the contrary — no bullets or fractures found during the autopsy and no obvious signs of a struggle (the files on the floor might easily have tipped over when he collapsed, perhaps from a heart attack) — they did not intend to pursue the matter unless new evidence emerged. I pointed out that he had been decorated with several dozen Pine Fresh trees, which wasn't something he was likely to do to himself, unless it was some new and extreme perversion that hadn't yet come to public attention, though it might well have its own premium rate website, and DI Robinson said, well, all we can guess is that it's someone's idea of a joke. Maybe kids broke in not long after he died, and decorated him for a laugh. Kids these days — they're like that. They're so inured to death that it doesn't faze them at all. Every day they're killing people.

'What's that game . . . *Grand Theft Auto*? Shooting pregnant women in drive-bys, the mind boggles. Have you played it?'

I shook my head. I don't play console games. The bright flickering lights can induce my epilepsy.

He said, 'I heard on the grapevine that you do a bit of detecting in your spare time.'

'Not really,' I said.

He nodded around my shelves. 'That's what I'd like to do, good old-fashioned detective work, without all the bloody paperwork, without the need for back-up, or forensics, or to have to prove everything in a bloody court. Just to use your brain to work it out, invite all the suspects to a meeting, and explain how you solved the case and then point out the guilty party who then conveniently takes the gentleman's way out. Isn't that how it should be?'

Every once in a while you meet an idiot who fantasises about living in an Agatha Christie world, but it's rarely an actual detective. It displayed, however, a softer side to DI Robinson, which was, I suppose, welcome. Still, I remained on my guard, aware of the dangers of entrapment — he might well have been trying to lull me into a false sense of security so that I would reveal what my involvement *really* was, or indeed he might have somehow stumbled on my secret night-time activity and been after my nail for the scratching of vehicles with personalised number plates, which was still nestling in a tub of I Can't Believe It's Not Butter in the fridge.

As it turned out, he was surprisingly knowledgeable about crime fiction and confessed to being an admirer of Georges Simenon, unusual these days, and to have once attended a performance by the musician and detective novelist Kinky Friedman. Although I'm not a great admirer of Mr Friedman, I do stock him, and thought it would be an interesting experiment to offer DI Robinson one of his books.

'As it happens,' I said, 'I have a copy of *The Love Song of J Edgar Hoover* here, signed by Kinky himself. Going for thirty quid.'

I fetched it down for him.

'Do you know,' he said, turning it over in his hands, 'I just might.'

'Tell you what,' I said, 'I'll do it for twenty-seven.'

'Deal,' he said.

He handed over the cash and I put it in the till and said, 'Would you like a receipt?'

Now if you give someone a receipt automatically, that's fair enough; but unless you think there's a chance you might want your money back or want to exchange something you would surely automatically say no, especially if it has to be written out by hand. I mean, you can understand wanting a receipt for a pair of trousers that might not fit or a shirt that your wife might not approve of, but who ever takes a *book* back to a shop, particularly a shop that has a sign taped to the wall that says *No Refunds Under ANY Circumstances*? So I thought', if he asks for a receipt, then that's a sure indication that the cash he's paid me is from police funds, that he's using it to butter me up so that I'll spill the beans about Malcolm Carlyle, but he needs a receipt to satisfy the number-crunchers at CID, to claim the money back from them. Obviously if he was going undercover doing drug deals with Belfast gangsters he wasn't going to ask for a receipt, but under *these* circumstances he probably thought it wouldn't raise the slightest whiff of suspicion.

'No thanks,' he said.

It was the classic double bluff.

I put the book in a No Alibis bag and he thanked me. He took another look around the shop. 'Nice spot,' he said. 'I'm sure I'll be back.'

I nodded. I was sure he would. And it would have been sooner rather than later if he'd known that I'd spent 90 per cent of our conversation with one hand beneath the counter, curled around the handle of a meat cleaver, because it had suddenly struck me that he might not just be an innocent book-collector or a nosy cop, he might also have been hired by the Odessa to murder me now that two weeks had passed and the heat was off *The Case of the Dancing Jews*.

The meat cleaver belonged to my father.

He wasn't a butcher.

He just had an interest in cleaving meat.

26

Leaving affairs of the heart to one side, it was around this
time that Alison showed that she was more than just a
pretty face by proving her worth as a sidekick through her
contribution to the solving of a mystery I have called *The
Case of the Missing FA Cup*. This case was not quite as
glamorous as it sounds, but it does illustrate that
sometimes the fairer sex can provide something unique: a
woman's *intuition*. You don't learn that at detective school.
Although I would undoubtedly have solved the case
entirely by myself, Alison's involvement certainly speeded
it to its conclusion.

It began, as these things do, with me buzzing another
unlikely-looking customer into No Alibis. I had taken to
keeping the door locked when I was alone in the shop; it
just allowed me a few seconds to take a good look at
whoever wanted in, in case they were of an unsavoury
type: an obvious drunk, a begging Romanian or anyone in
Nazi regalia. I am a good judge of character (perhaps that
is one reason why I despise myself) and on this occasion
the man pressing the buzzer appeared harmless enough.

He looked to be in his mid-to-late thirties, in a banker's suit and carrying a considerable amount of weight. His cheeks were flushed from walking and his black hair sat damp against his forehead. He nodded thanks when he came in and immediately began to examine the shelves opposite the counter. I knew he wasn't really interested in the books because he was looking straight ahead instead of inverting his head to one side to read the spines.

I said, 'Can I help you with anything?'

Normally I hate people who approach me in shops like this, because if I wanted help I'd bloody well ask, and because invariably those who do approach aren't really the slightest bit interested in what *you* want, but are pushing something or other that they've been instructed to push, or are on commission or know nothing about the product itself but everything about the insurance policy they insist you have to have because the item in question is bound to blow up in your face. I'm different, obviously, in that I offer what might once have been called a bibliographical bespoke service, because if you don't *know* mystery it can be a minefield. *You can't judge a book by its cover* isn't a cliché for no reason. Every book *claims* to be the greatest thing since sliced bread because no publisher is going to put 'distinctly mediocre' on the cover even if it's a fact; I have to provide some kind of quality control, because a returning customer is a happy customer, and a happy customer is a returning customer.

'Actually, it's not really a book I'm looking for.'

'Oh, okay,' I said, and then knowingly added, 'I also sell mugs with reproductions of classic Penguin covers. A tenner each, or five for the chipped ones.'

'No, I . . .'

I was only jesting, obviously. They're all chipped. Jeff dropped the whole box. Some of the chips you wouldn't notice, and others have hairline fractures you'd only notice when you got home and boiling coffee began to drip on to your bare legs.

But this man, this Garth Corrigan, was actually the first of my clients not to come to me via the dead detective next door, but had arrived at my store purely on the strength of my growing reputation as a solver of mysteries and a stopper of crimes. He was very apologetic about bothering me, and he said he understood if it was far too insignificant a case for me to take on, but he just didn't know where to turn. Even before he described it to me, I had a fairly good idea that I would agree to investigate, because my first impression was that he was an honest, unassuming type struggling to cope in difficult circumstances that did not immediately smack of danger.

I said, 'I'm sure it isn't insignificant.'

'In the grand scheme of things . . .' he said mournfully.

'In the grand scheme of things, a butterfly beats its wings in New Delhi, and in New York a building falls down.'

'I'm not sure . . .'

'If Lee Harvey Oswald had been turned down for a part-time job in the Texas Book Depository, then maybe President Kennedy would still be alive. Little things affect the bigger picture, usually you just don't know it at the time.'

'Well, anyway, I've split up with my girlfriend and she's disappeared and I need you to find her.'

The last thing I needed was another dame on the run, but I could at least do him the courtesy of hearing him out.

'Look, Mr . . .'

'Childers, Erskine Childers,' I said, assuming the identity of the author of the classic spy thriller *The Riddle of the Sands,* for I have a business and its reputation to protect.

'Mr Childers, I'm just an ordinary bloke, work in a bank, not particularly high up, not a very exciting life. Never really been in love, was married once, didn't work out. So I was single for two or three years, really not much interested in meeting anyone, not much of a social life either. Most of my friends are married, you know how it is . . .' I cleared my throat. 'Only real interest is football. I'm a big United man, live and breathe them. Anyway, once a week, a Friday, I treat myself to a Chinese meal in this restaurant not far from here, The Blue Panda, on the Ormeau Road?' I shrugged. I don't venture *that* far out of downtown. 'I go early, just after it opens, so it's pretty empty — don't like it later, sitting with all the couples or the stag nights, it looks a bit odd, right?' I nodded stiffly. He just needed to get on with it and stop enquiring about my personal life, which, incidentally, was on the up. 'So I go early, and over the weeks and months, I got kind of friendly with one of the girls working there. Just a kind word and a joke here and there. Her name is May, obviously Chinese background but born and bred in Belfast, perfect local accent, and I have to tell you, I thought she was the prettiest woman I ever saw. But I know my limitations when it comes to women, and she was way out of my league. And yet every time I went back it was always May that served me, and I kept noticing that when she brought my meal, there was always *more* on it than last time. Every week the servings just got bigger and bigger. I thought it would be impolite *not* to clear the plate, because she was obviously doing this to be kind, but at the same time if they kept growing like this I was going to suffer a coronary. Anyway, one day I just had to say something. It was kind of embarrassing, but I explained that I loved the food here, and I appreciated the lovely big portions, but I just couldn't eat that much, and I hoped she didn't take it as a mark of disrespect if I left some on the plate. Well, she was embarrassed as well, and she didn't know where to look, apart from at the floor. But then she said, very quietly, 'It's only because I like you.' And I could just have melted. This great beauty liked *me*. I couldn't believe it. Well, we got talking after that, and it turns out that she's almost as big a United fan as I am. So I tell her the pub around the corner is showing tomorrow's game if she fancies having a drink and she jumps at the chance. And more than that, she actually turns up, and more than that again, we have a fantastic time and we begin *dating*. Result! Are you with me?'

'I'm with you so far,' I said. It wasn't rocket science, but it was time-consuming. He was lucky there were no other customers queuing to be buzzed in.

'Anyway . . . oh God, this is the embarrassing bit, I've never told anyone . . .' He took a deep breath. 'Anyway, anyway, we're soon going steady . . . but I'm kind of rusty, a bit backward about coming forward on the um, er, sexual front, if you know what I mean?' I just looked at him. 'And she's kind of reticent as well because as it turns out she's not what you would call . . . experienced.' He nodded to himself then, for several moments, his eyes fixed on the counter. 'A real beauty, yes she is. A real beauty.'

He fell silent.

'But . . . ?'

'But . . .' He sighed. 'She *is* a real beauty. I wouldn't change her for the world. But . . . I don't quite know how to put this . . .'

'I'm not a police officer, Mr Corrigan, I don't judge people. Just saying it is the simplest way.'

He nodded gratefully. 'Thanks, Mr Childers. You see — she has these ears. They're — large. They're large and they bend outwards. They're large and they bend outwards from the side of her head — I mean, where else would they bend out from? But that's how they are. Not huge. But large. And obviously I noticed them. I noticed them in a good way, because they're absolutely fine. Look at me, I'm no oil painting. But she *is* an oil painting, she's beautiful, every part of her. I don't have a problem with her ears. Honestly.'

'Okay.'

'Thing is. We were getting along brilliantly, my life is suddenly superb, and we're both leading up to that moment when we . . . well, when we . . .' He cleared his

throat.'. . . *consummate* the relationship. We wanted
everything to be perfect. We're at my place. She cooks me
a lovely meal, we have a few glasses of wine, we light
candles, soft music . . . it *was* perfect . . .'

'But . . .'

'Well — *God!* — it was the best night of my life, Mr
Childers, we were making love, and I knew I was
absolutely *in* love, and that I wanted to spend the rest of
my life with her, and I believe she felt exactly the same way
. . .'

'Except . . .'

'When I was coming to the . . . coming to the moment
of climax . . . and I was on the greatest high any man can
experience . . . when I surrendered all control and gave my
very soul to her . . . at that precise moment . . . I grabbed
her by the ears and shouted, *I've won the FA Cup* . . .'

He was staring at me, bug-eyed with horror, and I was
staring right back.

'I know . . . I *know* . . . where did it even come from? I
was mortified, *she* was mortified . . . I mean, I mean . . . I
tried to argue it was a compliment, that finally making love
to her was . . . was like winning the FA Cup . . . but she
was kind of quiet, and then later we just lay there and I fell
asleep . . . and when I woke up she was gone. I tried to call
her, but there was no reply, and I went to the restaurant
and they were very frosty and told me she had gone away .
. . and I've been calling ever since and watching the place
but she really isn't there . . . and I don't know what to do.
I've been very, very stupid, and I love her, and I just want
her back . . .' There were now tears rolling down his
squirrel cheeks, and mine, although for a different reason.
'Please, Mr Childers, I have to make things right . . . you
have to help me get her back . . .'

27

Just because I have not travelled, it does not mean that I am *unworldly*. My books have educated me about this planet of ours, and fine writing has shown me places richer in colour and sound than any complicated train journey or intrepid adventure on the back of a yak could. You do not have to listen to jazz to appreciate it. I could talk for months about the mercurial talents of Dizzy Gillespie, yet I wouldn't recognise a note of his if it came at me unexpectedly in an elevator. Similarly, I have read enough about Chinese culture — *The Mystery of Dr Fu Manchu* by Sax Rohmer was the first of many novels featuring that master criminal that I devoured in my childhood — to understand that the elusive May had fled from the arms of her lover not to some mysterious retreat, but into the bosom of her people. And I don't mean China itself. That vast, overpopulated country would be as foreign to her, born and bred here in Belfast, as the freezing South Atlantic would be to a trained circus seal. While *they* were catching fish and frolicking on ice floes, she would be clapping her flippers together and balancing a beach ball on her nose. No, I was pretty sure that May was still in Belfast, being jealously guarded by our own not insignificant community of Chinamen. And as she was a waitress by trade, it seemed pretty obvious that the key to tracking her down lay in visiting as many of their eating establishments as I and my girlfriend could possibly manage.

This would be tricky enough, because my stomach reacts badly to Chinese food. And Indian food. And Italian food. I could quite happily survive on Irish stew, jelly and anything that might come in either a Cadbury's or Mars Selection Box, but I do have to sometimes take chances by ordering food in restaurants that I know will not agree with me. It is exactly the kind of sacrifice I am prepared to make to solve a case.

Garth Corrigan left me a picture of his girl. As I studied it he peered over my shoulder and said, 'Look — I should have realised how sensitive she was, her hair is covering her ears.'

'It's unfortunate,' I agreed. 'If they'd been out, it would have made her easier to recognise. Chinese people all look the same to me.'

Mr Corrigan gave me a look. 'Don't you think that's a bit . . . ?'

'No. Not at all. I believe in calling a spade a spade.'

'Don't you think *that's* a bit . . . ?'

'Mr Corrigan, when it comes to justice, I'm colour-blind.'

'Yes, of course.'

'But they do all look alike, at least until you get to know them. It's like puppies, you think they're all exactly the same, but gradually you get to tell them apart, the one with the wet nose, the one with the waggily tail . . . and I'm sure they say exactly the same about us. But by the time I'm finished with this case I'll be able to tell a Ching from a Chong at fifty paces.'

He looked at me some more.

'And incidentally,' I added, 'I *am* actually colourblind. Every time I go through traffic lights it's like playing Russian roulette.'

He wasn't sure what to make of me, but he was sure that I was his last best hope of getting his girl back. To help me I had the lovely Alison, whose first task was to pop across the road at lunchtime so that Mr Corrigan could describe to her his missing girlfriend's ears. Alison was able to draw what we know in the trade as an artist's impression of the said appendages, to approximate scale, detailing the shape and size of the lobe, the position and number of piercings and type of earrings worn, the layout of the tiny bones within the ear itself, and some indication, albeit in just two dimensions, of the ears' curvature from the skull. Some of this information was necessarily hazy. He had not made a particular study of May's ears, and in fact the inner bone structure was pure conjecture. But at least we had something to go on. We had one good clear photo of May, and two A4 sheets of white paper, each bearing a drawing of an ear. They were like mirror images of each other.

That evening we were to begin our trawl through the city's numerous Chinese restaurants. I was at home getting ready to go pick up Alison when the doorbell rang. I let it ring, because I tend not to answer doors when I can avoid it. Besides, I was halfway through shaving. Whoever was there was persistent, however. And I am obstinate, so it would have continued to be an impasse if Mother had not yelled from upstairs, 'Answer it, you little shit!' with such venom that my Mach 3 blade skidded along my top lip and caught the edge of my left nostril, opening up a slit that immediately began to bleed profusely. This was, understandably, distressing for someone suffering from haemophilia and with an exceedingly rare blood group to boot, but nevertheless I hurried as instructed to the front door, dabbing at the cut with a white towel and with red-tinged lather still caking my cheeks. When I opened it, Alison was standing there.

She smiled widely. 'Hey, Freckles, who's been slapping you around?'

'No one. What are you doing here?'

'We have a date. Or a job to do. I thought I'd pick you up. I'm hungry.'

'But . . . how did you know where I live?'

She laughed. 'Why, is it a closely guarded secret? I used my *detective skills*. Are you not going to invite me in?'

'No.' I had instinctively adopted a defensive position, both physically and mentally. 'Mother . . . she has a migraine . . . lying down . . . any noise sends her . . . you know how it is. Why don't you wait in the car and I'll be out in a minute?'

Alison raised an eyebrow. 'Are you sure you haven't some other woman in there?'

'Yes,' I said.

'Yes you have, or yes you haven't?'

I was dripping blood on to the doorstep, it was no time for word games. 'I really haven't some other woman inside. Now I'll just be a minute.'

I turned back inside and closed the door behind me. From upstairs Mother shouted, 'Who was it?'

'No one.'

'It was some little slut, wasn't it?'

'No, Mother.'

Five minutes later I joined Alison in her car. It was a Mini and it suited her. The number plate was RLC 216 L which sounded like it *could* be an ego plate, but clearly wasn't. As she started the engine she looked at me and nodded approvingly. 'I like it. But I'm not sure if it'll catch on.'

I pulled the passenger mirror down and studied my reflection. The bleeding was liable to start again with the slightest encouragement, like breathing, so I'd cut an

Elastoplast down to a narrow strip and stuck it across the slit in the edge of my left nostril to stop the flow. To keep it in place it arched over the tip of my nose and was secured on the other side.

'It looks suitably *mysterious,*' said Alison.

'It's practical,' I said. Then I showed her my wristband. 'If anything happens to me, all the relevant information is in here.'

Her brow furrowed as she glanced at the plastic band. 'Anything happens?'

'If I faint or collapse or lose too much blood, it's all in here — my blood group, the fact that I'm allergic to penicillin.'

She nodded. 'Are you expecting to collapse or lose too much blood?'

'Forewarned is forearmed,' I said.

There are one hundred and twenty-six Chinese restaurants in Belfast, three hundred and eight Chinese carryouts, and no Chinese plumbers. If you asked me, they were putting all their eggs in one basket. They may have also been running opium dens and gambling houses, but they weren't advertising. However, the sheer volume of eating establishments meant that we were on a hiding to nothing unless we were able to somehow narrow it down. This was where Jeff came in. During another relentlessly quiet afternoon I got him to phone as many restaurants in the immediate downtown area as he could pick out of the Yellow Pages, and to come up with some pretence to ask for the family name of the owners and then match it with May's own surname. I was fairly certain that if she'd transferred to another restaurant she'd have used a family connection. Jeff managed to track down eight restaurants and three carry-out establishments that carried May's name, and it was on these that we concentrated our attentions.

We ate lunch, we ate dinner, I discovered a certain

tolerance for curry, we put on weight. We studied the ears of waitresses. We got nowhere fast. But it was not a waste of time. I got to know Alison, and she did her best to prise information out of me.

'Sometimes,' she said, 'it's like getting blood from a stone.' Then she smiled and said, 'That sounds like the title of one of your books. *Blood From a Stone.*'

'By Donna Leon, actually. Just a couple of years ago.'

Alison smiled. 'Was there ever,' she asked, glancing around this latest restaurant, the Hong Kong Palace, at the bottom of Great Victoria Street, 'a Chinese detective? I remember one on TV, don't I?'

'*The Chinese Detective.* David Yip starred as Sergeant John Ho on the Beeb. It was the early eighties — you were probably about three years old.'

Alison shook her head. 'Repeats, then. But boy, you're a mine of useless information, aren't you?'

'No information is useless. It all has a purpose.'

'God, and now you sound like a Chinese cracker.'

I nodded around the restaurant myself. 'Then there was Charlie Chan.'

'Shhhh,' said Alison. 'You can't go saying Charlie Chan in a Chinese restaurant, it's offensive.'

'Why?'

'Because it is. Wasn't he just some fat white guy with his eyes taped back?'

I sighed. 'I'm not talking about the rubbish movies. I'm talking about breakthrough novels — Earl Biggers wrote them just after the First World War. He was in Honolulu and read in the local newspaper about the exploits of a detective called Chang Apana. He wrote six books about him all told; it was only when the movies got hold of Charlie Chan that . . .'

'*Shhhhh . . .*'

I don't know why she was bothering to *shhhh* me. She was the one who'd gone on at length about cripples. How was this any different?

This was the sixth out of the eight restaurants. As the waitress set down our starters, Alison studied her intently. When she'd gone I continued.

'. . . he became the clown we all remember. But the books are actually still surprisingly readable, though they're quite difficult to come by . . .'

Alison nodded, but also reached for her handbag and took out May's photo and her artist's impression of her ears.

'But of course,' I said, 'it was still a Western take on Chinese culture, and a somewhat Westernised version of that culture. If you go back far enough, it turns out that some of the first detective stories came from China. We tend to think of Poe or Wilkie Collins as the originators of the genre, but in fact there is a strand of ancient Chinese detective fiction — *Di Gong An,* if I'm not mistaken, which translates as *Celebrated Cases of Judge Dee* — that was extremely popular in the seventeenth century. Of course, as you might expect, they're very different from our detective stories — they're what is known as inverted detective stories, with the criminal and the reasons for his committing his crime introduced right at the start. There is also quite often a supernatural—'

'Would you ever *shut up*?' Alison hissed. 'I think that's *her.*'

It was good timing, actually, because I was starting to reach the bottom of my well of information on Chinese detective fiction. Instead I studied our waitress, who was just crossing to a nearby table. She lifted two plates, then turned and walked past us, face-on. She certainly looked very similar to the May in the photograph, which Alison quickly rechecked then surreptitiously showed to me. Yes, indeed — but she was wearing her shoulder-length black hair over her ears, so it was difficult to be absolutely certain.

We ate our first course, then our main course, all the time with our eyes on the waitress, waiting for a moment that we knew would come: the big reveal. She was sure at some point to sweep her hair behind her ears, or to even just reach up to fix it or scratch her head, any movement that would reveal the hidden appendages. Eventually, when we were ordering dessert, and Alison asked for something off-menu, the waitress had to think for a moment to see if it was possible, and in so doing slowly pushed her hair back behind her left ear.

We only saw it for a moment. It was larg*ish*, but flat against her skull.

It was a very disappointing ear.

We changed our minds about dessert and quickly settled up.

I drove Alison home. We sat in the No Alibis van outside her apartment. She said, 'Do you want to come in?'

I shook my head.

'I don't bite, you know.' I stared at the dash. 'Or perhaps that's what you'd like.'

I glanced at her. 'Do you have any idea how many germs there are in the human mouth? If you bite someone you might as well inject them with botu—' I cleared my throat. I smiled. 'Only teasing.'

Of course, I *was not*.

'You're playing hard to get,' said Alison. 'Usually it's the other way round.'

I shrugged.

'But I like that in a man. I like a challenge. I don't like everything on a plate right from the start. There are girls out there who'd give you a blow job on your first date as easy as a kiss on the cheek. But I say one swallow doesn't make a summer. Do you know what I mean?'

I had an idea, but was too flustered to respond coherently. I grunted.

She kissed me on the lips. Just quickly. She looked at me again and nodded. 'Yes, indeed,' she said, 'you're *definitely* a challenge.'

Then she slipped out of the van.

She phoned me at three a.m. I was still up looking for patterns, but faked a yawn for her benefit. She told me we had to go back to the Hong Kong Palace.

'Why? The food wasn't that—'

'The waitress. It's her. I'm certain.'

'But you saw her ear . . .'

'I know. But we still have to go back.'

She didn't give it a name, but it was a woman's intuition.

Naturally I mocked it, but she was convinced. And I was quite happy to go along.

She then said, 'So are you in bed now?'

'Yes.'

'What do you have on?'

'My pyjamas.'

'Do you know what I have on?'

'No.'

'The radio.'

'Why?'

'I don't really. I have no clothes on. I am naked.'

'Okay.'

There was a long pause.

Eventually I said, 'What time tomorrow?'

'Lunchtime.'

'I have to go now,' I said. 'Mother's calling.'

'I don't hear anything.'

'She may have fallen out of bed.'

'If a tree falls in the forest, and nobody hears, does it still fall?'

'What?'

'It doesn't matter. I'll see you tomorrow. Don't be going to sleep thinking about me being naked.'

'Okay'

I put the phone down. There was no doubt about it. She was as odd as begot.

The Hong Kong Palace was a good-sized restaurant; busier at lunchtimes than it was at night; upholstery like a hoor's handbag. We had to wait a goodly while for a table. When we were eventually seated, Alison said she had a plan, but refused to elaborate. Instead we talked amiably while we both kept a watchful eye on our waitress. Alison told me about the unusual customer she'd had that morning — an absolute gentleman, charming, well mannered, well dressed, actually listened to advice, handsome too.

'And what was unusual about him?'

'*All of the above,*' Alison laughed. 'It was so refreshing.'

'Did he buy anything?'

'No, no he didn't.'

'There you go.'

'But he did ask me out on a date.'

My blood froze. My throat contracted. I managed a raspy, 'Really?'

'Of course I said no, but even so, it was rather nice. Don't you think the standard of people has gone down in recent years?'

'I don't think it was ever particularly high.'

She had turned down a charming, well-mannered, well-dressed, handsome man, for me.

'They're ignorant, and smelly, and devious,' Alison said.

'They're loud, and arrogant, and opinionated.'

'They steal and swear and . . .' She turned suddenly to one side, just as our waitress passed. '*May . . .*'

The waitress's head snapped towards us.

'. . . we have a menu?'

'Yes . . . yes of course.'

She gave one to each of us. As she left, Alison grinned across the table at me. 'See?'

'Proves nothing,' I said, though in truth I was impressed.

'It's her.'

Today the waitress's hair was back in a ponytail,

allowing us to see both ears. Neither of them was sticking out. Nobody was going to mistake her for the FA Cup, or any kind of silverware with handles. Alison was watching her closely, nodding almost imperceptibly as she finally understood — something.

'The son of a bitch,' whispered Alison.

'Excuse me?'

'Don't you see? Look what he made her do.'

'You've lost me.'

'Staring right at you. Look at the way she's tossing her head from side to side. The way her hair is tied right back. She's showing off her ears. She's had them done. Pinned back. The son of a bitch hurt her so much she went out and had plastic surgery on her lugs.'

I studied the waitress as she went about her work, but really couldn't tell. 'Are you sure?'

'Certain. That's her. Yesterday she had them covered up, they were probably still sore from the op. I know girls who've had it done. It isn't pleasant.'

'God. Do they cut them off and sit on them for a while and stick them back on?'

'No. You idiot. She's had them cut and sliced and pinned back and today is the grand unveiling.'

'Well, she seems happy with them.'

'Yes, of course she is. But that isn't the point. He made her feel so bad, she thought she had to do it.'

'I'm not sure I agree. He liberated her. He gave her the confidence to go and make a change.'

'So if you didn't like my nose you'd make cracks about it until I had it straightened. Do you want to liberate me through verbal abuse?'

'I like your nose the way it is. It doesn't need straightening, much.'

Her eyes narrowed, cute, not *that* serious: 'People in glass houses . . .'

'Are you ready to order?'

May was back at our table, smiling down at us.

'Yes, we are,' said Alison.

'But first,' I said, 'can I have a word in your ear?'

Though I might occasionally play the chauvinist, I had taken on board what Alison was saying. Also, I wanted to stay in her good books. Either way, I felt obliged to tell May who we were and what we were at and to give her the choice of whether we reported back to my client that we'd found her. If she decided against it, then it was no loss to me; I could still sting him for the price of half a dozen curries.

As we spoke to her, May's hand wandered occasionally to one ear or the other; though fixed flat against the sides of her head, they were still clearly very red, and now that I was able to study them up close, somewhat swollen. She said the operation was *horrendous*. They had told her she would experience some discomfort, but it felt like her ears had been fed through a mangle. When we told her about her ex-boyfriend she was sweet but mortified. Sweet that we had taken the trouble to track her down, mortified that we knew about her ears and how the falling-out had come about.

Alison was quick to jump in with, 'I don't blame you for dumping him. He sounds like a big fat loser to me.'

May's fingers gingerly traced the outline of her left ear. 'He . . .'

'He abuses you, makes you feel like shit, he more or less forces you under the surgeon's knife, and then has the gall to hire us to find you. You should tell him to—'

'You misunderstand,' May cut in, nervously bending a menu between her hands. 'I love him very much. I have not *dumped* him. I knew he would not approve of me having the operation, because he does not wish me to suffer any pain; also I did not want him to worry about me having it; so I merely withdrew from his company until I could have it and I was sufficiently recovered to be the old me again, the me he loves. I was very ill after the operation

164

and it took me longer to recover, but I did not think he would miss me so much that he would hire private investigators to find me. But that is him all over. He is so good to me and I love him so much and I cannot wait to see him with my new ears.'

'I think that's *so* romantic,' Alison said immediately.

28

The Case of the Missing FA Cup was exactly the kind of investigation I was interested in. No particular exertion required, barely a whiff of danger, no extensive travel, very little in the way of having to talk to strangers, and a resolution based on observation and deduction. *The Case of the Dancing Jews* was its polar opposite, and, more to the point, unlike the girl with the formerly sticky-out ears, it simply would not go away.

Towards the conclusion of the former case, I was returning from a lunchtime curry with Alison to relieve Jeff when I observed to my horror that Daniel Trevor was in the store. Jeff was behind the counter, studiously ignoring him, while Daniel was pacing back and forth at the back of the shop. He was muttering, 'Yes, this will do rightly, yes it will. Absolutely.'

I was attempting to back out of the doorway when he turned suddenly and spotted me. He clapped his hands together and exclaimed: 'The very chap I'm looking for! Come on in!'

Daniel Trevor, beckoning me into *my own store*.

'Mr Trevor,' I said, 'how can I help you?'

'Very easily, my friend, very easily indeed! I want to borrow your shop!'

'Borrow?'

'Absolutely! You host book launches, don't you?'

'Very occasionally.'

'Perfect! I want to do one right here!'

'Well, I'm not sure if that's going to be poss—'

'Of course it is! You can't be booked up every night from here to eternity. Just tell me whatever night is free and book me in. This is the ideal location. The School of Dance is just a few hundred yards away, the staff and students will be able to nip in and—'

'Whoa there, Mr Trevor. You're doing the book? Anne Mayerova's . . . ?'

'*I Came to Dance.* Yes, I am. I'm making a stand. Anne Mayerova stood up to terrorism in her own way, and now I'm going to stand up to it in mine. I'm going ahead with publication.'

'But it's not finished, and you didn't like it anyway, and what if it stirs up—'

He held up a hand to stop me. 'Relax, my friend, everything is going to be just fine. I'm publishing exactly what we contracted for, Anne Smith's history of dance in Northern Ireland.'

'Not the dancing at Ausch—'

'It won't even be mentioned. I think on reflection that part of her reason for not including it in her life story is that she refuses to let her life be defined by such barbarism, she doesn't want to give them credibility, even after all these years. She's a remarkable woman to be able to put it in perspective like that, and I admire her for it. It will be a tribute night to Anne Smith, to Anne Mayerova, and also to my dear departed Rosemary. Neither of them will be able to attend the launch, but I, sir, know how to run an event and I'm quite sure that every student of dance in this mighty province of ours will be making their way to your delightful premises on whatever night you see fit to grant us, and every single one of them is going to buy one, two or three copies of *I Came to Dance*. A night of tribute, and a night of profit, sir. What do you say to that?'

'I can do any Thursday in August,' I said.

I am not purely driven by financial gain, but one must be practical. I may not always enjoy the good health I enjoy now. Books do not grow on trees, and must be purchased, and where cash is not readily available, credit must be employed; let us just say that my credit is not always good. That is the lot of the small business. I could have cut and run the way so many others have, but I have stood and faced and fought to keep No Alibis open, and it would be criminally negligent of me not to reluctantly accept a profit when it presents itself. Bookselling is like prostitution, you sell your wares, you close your eyes, and you never fall in love with the clients. You also keep your fingers crossed that they won't ask for anything perverted.

A date was agreed two weeks away. When I told Alison about it she laughed and offered to provide tray bakes 'for a price'. She told me I had no principles. She is wrong. I have lots of them. I keep them in the safe at the back of the shop and only take them out when required. She said that I seemed to have gotten over my fear of Nazis. I said they were coming to the launch until they heard about the tray bakes.

Oh we laughed. It was a golden period.

Daniel Trevor was handling the publicity and the invitations, he was providing the wine and the music. I also advertised through the website, though I doubted if any of my regulars would bother turning up for what I jokingly referred to as 'an evening of dance crap'. I had to negotiate the borrowing of two dozen chairs from a local hotel. It took me about half an hour to explain the concept of *borrowing* as opposed to *purchasing*, and I had to invoke the Blitz spirit of all small traders sticking together to finally ensure their delivery. When the blokes from the hotel arrived and stacked them in the back room, one of them took a fancy to the new Michael Connolly and asked if he could borrow it. I told him I wasn't a library. Honestly, the riff-raff I have to deal with.

Everything proceeded apace. Not only that, but there was a general upturn in business thanks to some unseasonably good weather — sunshine in summer, thank God for global warming! — and the days flew by. Alison and I continued to meet for lunch and things continued apace on that front as well. She was pleased with the display of her comics in the shop and could hardly keep up with the demand. I told her she was soon going to have to employ the services of a proper printer. When I handed over the cash from their sale — minus my commission, obviously, because I'm not a charity — she looked like I'd given her the keys to the bank. She peppered me with kisses. If I'd known she was going to do that I'd have opened the till and given her a fiver weeks ago.

But.

I should have known better.

Golden days are known as golden days because they are valuable and rare, and another way of saying they are rare is that they are few and far between, and when they do come along they are fleeting. I was happy and smiling one moment, and the next the phone rang, and I should have known better than to answer it. Almost as soon as the man at the other end of the line spoke, my Spider-sense tingled.

'Hello — is that No Alibis, yes?'

An elderly voice, but with a thick German-sounding accent. I was so thrown by it that I agreed that this was indeed No Alibis instead of instantly claiming a wrong number.

'I understand that you buy and sell rare books?'

'Yes . . . yes, we do.'

'And you have a number of these in your store?'

'Yes, of course.'

At that very moment I was alone, and I *felt it*. Even though this caller was only on the end of a telephone line, I felt physically threatened.

'I wonder if it might be possible to make an appointment to come and see you? I am a collector, and would appreciate the opportunity to peruse them in private, with your personal attention.'

'Well I don't really . . .'

'I am an old man, with the traffic, the pushing and shoving . . . really I would prefer . . . shall we say seven p.m.?'

'Well, I'm . . .'

'Very well. Seven p.m. it is.'

He cut the line. I hadn't even thought to ask his name. I was shaking and sweating. But strange as it may seem, I was also curious. Until I had started investigating these cases I had never been curious about *anything*. Now, particularly with this one, there was a need to know. He could of course just be an old duffer with a foreign accent and an interest in books. But he had made an arrangement to see *me*, in *private*, *alone*, by *myself* at a time when I had only recently been living in fear of murder by an elderly German assassin. (And I mean assassin, because like it or not, I am an important person, albeit in the shrinking world of independent bookselling.) It was surely just too much of a coincidence. He was coming for me. It was *The Night of the Jackal*. My Reichenbach Falls. My date with destiny. I would conquer fear and I would deal with it. It would be a meeting of minds. I would outwit him. I would be that bloke in that Swedish film sitting down to play chess with the Grim Reaper and confounding him with logic. And if that failed I would use the meat cleaver beneath the counter.

I would also have back-up.

I wasn't stupid. He might be old, but at point-blank range a gun doesn't care how old the trigger man is. First of all I called Jeff and explained the situation. He said that was scary and he'd love to help but he'd arranged to go swimming. I told him to rearrange or he could kiss goodbye to his job and say hello to an invoice for all the books he'd sold to his mates at less than cover price. He said he'd be there before seven. One of my favourite private detectives, Spenser, calls on a huge jive-talking black man called Hawk when he needs back-up. Hawk scares everyone and the ladies love him. Jeff, who occasionally lifts some weights, *only* scares women, and being from Amnesty International I suspected that he was less likely to tackle an assassin than mount a campaign for his release after he had killed me, although if the assassin was going to kill me, then he could just as easily kill Jeff as well. So safety in numbers was required. I called Alison and told her and she said I was mad letting him into the shop, that I should call the police, it was better to appear foolish and live than be brave and die. It was a good point. But alerting the police *in general* was only going to be time-consuming and would require frankly fantastical explanations, at the end of which I would be no nearer to solving *The Case of the Dancing Jews* but considerably closer to appearing in a local court charged with wasting police time or being sued for making false allegations about an elderly book-collector.

However, there was, I thought, a way of attracting police protection without actually tipping them off.

I phoned DI Robinson. As I had previously imagined there to be a small possibility that he was in the employ of the Odessa, I first asked him if he was busy that evening. He said, 'Apart from protecting Ulster from evil, no.' Satisfied, I explained to him that I was having a special private viewing in No Alibis for some of my favoured clients, and wondered if he would like to come. A number of very rare and immensely collectable titles would be on sale, with discounts well into the double figures (in my mind's eye that was 11 or 12 per cent). Even if he had purchased the Kinky Friedman in order to maintain his cover story, this would surely allow him to get even further into my good books, while at the same time providing me with a modicum of protection. So I wasn't particularly surprised when he thanked me, and told me I was very kind, and yes he would be very pleased to come.

Thus adequately protected in the store — I presumed that while the assassin was prepared to kill me, he would not be foolhardy enough to perpetrate a massacre — I turned my mind to what would happen when he realised that he wasn't going to be able to kill me there and then. If he was any sort of a tactician he would maintain his respectable front, purchase a book or two, then withdraw to plot anew. That was exactly the time that I needed to pounce — and I would track him to his lair.

But of course I wouldn't be able to achieve that by myself. I have already described my reluctance to drive in the dark, and the chances of me getting to the No Alibis van and completing my safety checks before he disappeared were quite small, even if he was an ancient crumbly. Besides, at certain times of the month I have an aversion to turning left, and this happened to be one of them, so there was a fifty-fifty chance that I would lose him if it was left up to me. One alternative was to call on my database of customers. They are not 'friends', as such, but they are loyal and supportive, and have certainly been an aid to me in previous investigations. However, if I issued an appeal to them, I knew I would necessarily have to be vague, so that although they would be keen to help, they would also want, *demand* to know why they hadn't been invited to the sale as 'favoured clients' and I'd end up having to sell off half my collection to them, and at a greater discount. I suppose I could have cherry-picked one or two of them — but word would inevitably spread; I believe they gossip about me behind my back, and quite possibly have an internet forum dedicated to it.

At that precise moment I happened to glance out of the window and across the road to Alison's jewellery store.

She has one of those old-fashioned display windows, which instead of going straight down to the pavement, is about three-quarter length, with brickwork below and a windowsill sticking out in front. Inevitably people sit on this, and she spends half her life shooing tramps, drunks, kids and old people off it. A gang of steeks had proved particularly obstinate, and despite having been moved on by the police several times, had taken to sitting there at every opportunity. Alison was convinced that they were planning to smash the glass and steal the jewellery, but I doubted they would be so obvious — more likely they were there for one of two reasons. The first was because it was directly opposite the Wine Mark off-licence they were barred from, so it was a good vantage point from which to observe muggable customers. The second was because they wanted to look at Alison, because she was so pretty.

In escorting Alison back to her shop I had had to walk their gauntlet of fear several times. They had said nothing to *us,* but as soon as I left her inside it was a different matter. Several times I was subjected to severe verbal abuse while I waited to cross back to No Alibis. They called me knob head, and prick face, and Pinocchio, peg leg, gimp, dummy, retard, spaz, queer, faggot, dyke, carpet-muncher, fudge-packer, smack head, crack head, meth head, slut, slag, scrubber, bitch, schizo and Catholic. But it was water off a duck's back. I heard worse at home.

On this occasion, however, I thought that their very *steekness,* their street nous, might allow them to blend in and follow my nemesis without arousing suspicion, either on foot or in one of the cars they routinely stole for joy-riding escapades.

Today there was just the two of them, so the prospect of putting my proposition to them wasn't quite as daunting as it would have been with the whole gang present. Anyone else attempting this might have opened with a 'Wassup, bro?', but that is not only demeaning but quite ridiculous to someone of my background and education.

Instead I ushered them into the shop, took up position behind the counter, one hand on my cleaver, and asked them if they had ever heard of the Baker Street Irregulars.

'What the fuck are you talking about?' was their considered response.

I explained that Sherlock Holmes employed a group of street urchins to help him out from time to time.

'What the fuck are you talking about?' was their considered response.

'You calling us fucking urchins, Holmes?' one asked.

I explained that I was willing to pay them money if they would do something for me.

'Fuck off, you fucking pedo,' was their considered response.

It was a game, a verbal jousting, we were establishing boundaries. It was like a mating ritual, without the mating, or cats pissing out their territory. As part of this one of them lifted *The Criminal* by Jim Thompson and licked it. It was necessarily a slow process, but gradually they came to understand what I wanted of them, if not why, and lacking money for drink or drugs, they became quite amenable to the idea. There was some good-natured joshing over their fee — my first suggestion that payment be made in book tokens redeemable only in these premises was greeted with much humour — but eventually we settled on straight cash, half now, half later. They were to hang about in their usual spot outside Alison's, and as my nemesis was leaving I would give them a thumbs-up through the window and they would follow him to the Eagle's Nest.

Everything was falling into place nicely.

29

The clock was ticking, and all but one of the players were in place. I was behind the counter, one hand on the cleaver. DI Robinson was towards the rear of the shop, looking through three shelves of signed first editions, Jeff was kneeling on the floor beside a box of books, giving the impression of recording newly arrived stock, and Alison was in the kitchen, with the door open, washing dishes, but with one submerged hand gripping a steak knife. Across the road my Botanic Avenue Irregulars loitered outside the jewellery store, apparently sniffing glue.

Seven o'clock came, seven o'clock went. By 7.15 p.m. DI Robinson had two books in his hands and looked about ready to approach the counter. I made eyes at Jeff and he confounded the critics by understanding: he quickly produced a dozen more signed first editions for DI Robinson to peruse; he knew they were valuable because I kept them in transparent plastic envelopes so tight that they discouraged examination; I knew they weren't because they were signed by Jehovah's Vengeance Grisham.

Across the road one of my trackers suddenly lay down

on the footpath.

Alison appeared in the doorway and said, 'Why don't I make us all a cup of—'

Buzzzzzzzzzzzzzzzzzzzzzzzz.

She stopped. DI Robinson glanced up. Jeff *stared.* I took several moments to examine my computer screen, to at least make it appear like I was fairly nonchalant, then looked to the door.

There he was.

An old man in a good suit. Silver hair cut close.

The Valium was useless.

Buzzzzzzzzzzzzzzzzzzzzz . . .

I pressed the door release. As he entered I said, 'Sorry, I was miles away there.'

'No matter.' He waved the apology away, as if he was swatting a fly. He stepped towards the counter with his hand extended. I was unprepared for this sudden familiarity and had to quietly let go of the meat cleaver in order to offer my own hand. I managed to set it down, but my nerves were such that in reaching across the counter my knuckles caught the top of a stapler and knocked it over the edge. My nemesis quickly diverted his hand and caught it before it had travelled more than a few inches.

He might have been an old man, but he had the reflexes of a juggler.

He set it on the counter, smiled and then offered his hand again.

We shook. His grip was strong, his skin cold.

'Thank you so much for seeing me,' he said.

'My pleasure,' I replied.

Neither of us volunteered our names. That itself was no indication of anything: bookselling could be a secretive business.

He looked around the store. 'This is a nice shop,' he said, his accent thick. 'I thought we would be alone.'

'Stock-taking,' I said, 'unavoidable, I'm afraid.' His eye lingered on DI Robinson. 'Another collector. Once he heard I was opening late, there was no stopping him. You guys are very persuasive.'

He nodded. I became aware for the first time that there was a bulge in his jacket, his left inside pocket. My immediate conviction was that it was not a wallet. Knowing what I thought I knew about him, I thought I knew what it was.

'No matter,' he said.

If he made even the slightest move for his gun I would have the cleaver out and plunged into his chest. Attack is the best form of defence. If it turned out to be a wallet I wouldn't get many marks for customer service, but at least I would be alive.

I had dismissed the possibility of him carrying out a massacre — but I suddenly thought . . . *why*? Three people were dead already. Another four wouldn't make much difference. You may as well be shot for a whole flock of sheep as a lamb.

'I wanted to show you something,' he said.

He began to reach inside his jacket.

Everything went into slow motion.

My hand was back on the cleaver, but I just couldn't move it. Instead I heard myself saying: 'Is there anything else I can help *you* with, *Detective Inspector?*'

There was no reaction from the old man at all other than to delve deeper into his jacket pocket, all the time his eyes boring into me.

'No, fine here thanks,' said DI Robinson.

The old man *didn't care* who he killed.

I had to do it. I had to do it *now*.

Now!

Stab, stab, stab, stab, stab, stab, stab . . .!

But I still could not move. Alison, Jeff, DI Robinson, none of them were any use, none of them realised what was happening, none of them were close enough to stop this old man producing his weapon.

His . . . small, crumpled, leatherbound book.

'Oh my,' I said, 'oh my oh my.'

He nodded. He thought it was an expression of appreciation instead of one of utter relief.

Unless he was going to poke me in the eye with it, I was safe.

I quietly set down the cleaver.

'I was wondering if there might be any value to this?'

I took the volume from him and gingerly opened it. It was a Bible. In German. But written inside the cover, in pencil, was:

Auschwitz 1944

Christ! He was playing with me. There was a cold sweat on my back, but not as cold as this guy: a Nazi, profiteering sixty-plus years down the line, the Bible's true owner mangled in a mass grave. I had both hands on the book, a thousand miles from my cleaver.

'Very nice,' I managed to whisper. 'How did you come by it?'

He gave a little shrug. 'I do not like to talk about it.'

There was complete and utter silence in No Alibis. Even the clock on the wall above Columbo seemed to have stopped.

From his position on the floor, bending over a box of books, Jeff said quietly, 'We have ways of making you talk.'

The Nazi turned. He put a hand to his ear. 'I am sorry . . . my hearing is not so good . . . what did you say . . . ?'

I did not wish Jeff to be shot through the head merely for being an idiot. I stepped in, the distraction somehow enabling my voice to recover. 'He said, we sometimes need to talk about a rare book, how you came by it, establish its provenance — it helps with the valuation. This obviously has some historical significance . . .'

'Ja, ja,' he said. 'I do not wish to sell. For insurance purposes, no?'

I nodded. I turned the book over in my hand. Despite

being small, it was surprisingly weighty. The edges of the pages were flecked with gold. All I knew about gold in the camps was that fillings had been ripped from the mouths of both the living and the dead.

'Well,' I said, 'we specialise in mystery fiction, our rare editions are really all in that genre, but if you give me a few minutes I could check its value on the web.'

He studied me. 'That would be very helpful, thank you. The web, I do not understand!'

He smiled. False teeth. False *smile*.

I indicated the shelves behind him and said, 'Perhaps you might find something that appeals, while I do this . . . ?'

The Nazi surveyed me for a long moment before nodding and turning to study my books. I glanced at Alison, now standing in the kitchen doorway. She raised her eyebrows. I gave her a helpless gesture. Jeff was also looking at me. He showed me his fist and gave a slight nod. *Do you want me to give him a dig?*

What to do?

What did his giving me the Auschwitz Bible mean? Was it a warning? A precursor to extreme violence, or was he saying, I know who you are and what you've been doing; if you continue you will end up just like the others? Why give a warning at all? Was it because we weren't alone? No — he had brought the Bible with him, so perhaps the warning was preplanned. Or was it his cover story, to get into the shop, to buy him time to work out how he was going to kill me and make his escape undetected?

As all this pinballed through my brain he reached up to a high shelf to lift down a book. In stretching, his bare arm emerged from both his jacket sleeve and shirt cuff and for the briefest moment I saw, tattooed on the inside of his forearm, a series of half-faded numbers.

My mouth dropped open.

Oh . . . my . . . God . . .

'Excuse me,' I said. The man turned. His face was grey and his eyes baggy. 'Were . . . were you actually *in* Auschwitz? I, uh, couldn't help notice your

I tapped my own arm. He looked puzzled for just a moment, and then laughed suddenly. 'Ah!' he said, coming back to the counter. 'My true identity is exposed!'

It didn't mean that he *wasn't* the killer, but suddenly everything seemed different, lighter. I relaxed the grip I had renewed on the meat cleaver.

He stood before me and pulled his sleeve up again, studied the number briefly, before allowing it to fall back into place. 'It was a long time ago. In that place, we were not allowed books. We were not allowed *anything*. But somehow, there *were* books. They were our escape. Ever since I have loved books. This Bible, I brought out with me. To remind me.' He nodded at me for several moments. I didn't know what to say. Alison crossed to the counter and stood beside me. 'This is your wife, no?' he asked.

'No,' I agreed.

'Not yet,' said Alison. She put her hand out. 'I'm Alison.'

As they shook, his eyes moved to me. 'I am sorry, I should have introduced myself properly, earlier. But I wanted to see what type of a man you were, this bookseller who would do my wife such a kindness.'

'Your . . .'

'My wife is Anne Smith. Anne *Mayerova*. I understand you may have saved her life.'

30

As soon as Mark Smith — Mark *Mayerova* — left No Alibis, I stood in the front window and waved frantically across the road, trying to catch the attention of the steeks in order to stop them following the old man. They were both clearly the worse for wear. Each had a plastic bag clamped to his face. They moved round in hazy circles, giggling. One of them spotted Mr Mayerova, and prodded the other, who prodded back. One of them looked towards the shop and saw me, and I made a cutting motion across my throat and immediately regretted it as he began to check his pockets for his favourite knife. I moved to the door and looked along the footpath to my left, just in time to see Mr Mayerova climb into the back seat of a Jaguar about twenty yards away. As it began to pull out it braked suddenly as the two steeks threw themselves across its bonnet.

Then they rolled off the other side and lay on the ground laughing.

The Jaguar blasted its horn once, then slid smoothly away.

My Botanic Avenue Irregulars were completely useless. In the morning they would remember nothing about the incident, apart from having a vague recollection that I owed them money.

I withdrew to the relative safety of the shop. DI Robinson was now at the counter with his selections. He had chosen W.R. Burnett's *The Asphalt Jungle* from 1950 and Jim Thompson's *The Grifters* from 1963. They were good picks, but it would be hard not to in my shop. I gave him a decent price and we played the old receipt game again.

He said, 'I couldn't help overhearing some of that. Must make you feel good when someone comes in and thanks you. My game, you only ever hear complaints.'

My exchanges with Mark Mayerova had been quite vague, and he had spoken relatively quietly. The two had combined to give the detective only a rough idea of what we'd been talking about, and no indication at all that the case had anything to do with the murder of Malcolm Carlyle.

So DI Robinson went on his way asking to be kept up to date about any future sales, and pretty soon after that I let Jeff go as well. He was looking thoughtful. He had listened mesmerised to the old man as he talked about life inside the camp, about being separated from his wife, and the joy of their reunion back in Czechoslovakia after the war. Each had been told that the other was dead. With all the chaos at the end of the war, getting back to Prague had been something of a nightmare — yet they both managed to arrive at their old apartment within hours of each other.

That left just me and Alison.

I said, 'You had tears in your eyes.'

'I love a good love story.'

'Usually someone dies in a love story.'

'You're a real the-glass-is-half-empty kind of a guy, aren't you?'

'I'm a realist.'

'Do you think you could have survived a death camp for me?'

'No.'

'Well that's about right. You wouldn't have survived five minutes. You would have freaked when you discovered they didn't serve frappuccino.'

'I wouldn't have *been* in a death camp. I would have been in the resistance.'

She laughed. 'Yes, you would. Conan the Librarian.'

I raised an eyebrow. She raised one back. It was like high-stakes poker, with eyebrows.

'What are you going to do now?'

'Think,' I said.

'About?'

'The Case of the Dancing Jews.'

'You mean it's back on?'

'It was never really off.'

'Well I'd love to join you,' she said, 'but I've work to do.'

'At this hour? I thought we might discuss

She shook her head. She wanted to get drawing. Mayerova's story had inspired her and she wanted to get something down on paper while it was still fresh. I was mildly disappointed but also pragmatic. It wasn't as if she was swanning off with someone else. Yes, I did want to think about the case. But I also wanted Alison to myself. I wanted to pull the shutters down and talk about concentration camps and murder and the who, what, where, when and how of it all with her. But it wasn't to be. Instead, before she left, she kissed me *deeply*.

That means, with tongues.

I was in shock.

I sat behind the counter, shutters down, light on. My mind kept flitting back to Mark Mayerova, and his wife, and how romantic it all was and how right Alison was: I *was* a glass-half-empty kind of a guy, and maybe I should take a leaf out of her book and try to look on the bright side. But then the more I thought about it the more I thought, maybe not. Mark Mayerova and his wife had survived the war, they had moved to Northern Ireland, and then after forty years of marriage and two grown-up children they had split up. He hadn't gone into why, and he clearly retained a lot of feelings for her, but it was another practical example of why I was perfectly right to gravitate towards misery. Things always fell apart. It was the nature of life. And death.

I took out a notebook. Beside the serial number that had been tattooed on Anne Mayerova's arm, I wrote her husband's serial number. I had only seen it for a few moments, and the ink was badly faded, but I have become an expert at memorising such sequences. So I now had two concentration camp numbers: it hardly constituted a collection, but at least there was a finite number of them. How much more interesting to find a pattern in those numbers than in the ever-expanding universe of car registrations.

I also wrote down the licence plate number of his Jaguar.

It was MM3.

Personalised.

In a way he had an excuse for it, unlike all those other posers. In the camps almost every facet of life had been designed to remove individuality and personality, to impose anonymity; they had reduced everyone to a number. His personalised number plate was just one way of telling the world that even when a government imposed a number on him, he was determined to stand out.

He was a good talker — spare with his words, but the ones he chose had been evocative. He was obviously grateful for what I'd done on behalf of his wife and didn't seem to think that we were wrong to be concerned for her safety. The Odessa, he said, was a very real organisation, and even though he had not heard of it being active in recent years, it might very well still be. But he certainly couldn't throw any light on what his ex-wife's big secret might be.

'And perhaps now we never will know,' he had said, with a sad shake of his head. 'She really is not well. The periods when she is lucid, they grow shorter and shorter.'

'We were lucky then,' I said. 'Hearing her story first-hand.'

He looked at me for a while. 'Sometimes,' he said, 'I think it should all be forgotten. We saw too many things.'

I asked him if he thought she would be able to attend the launch of her book, and he seemed surprised that it was happening at all. 'I had thought they had decided not to publish.'

'No, no — the publisher has bounced back. He sees it as a bit of a tribute to his dead . . . his *missing* wife. But it should be a good night. If Anne can't make it, you should absolutely come in her place, perhaps say a few words?'

Mr Mayerova nodded slowly. 'Perhaps, perhaps. Though what I know about dance - very little!'

He chuckled.

It was only after he'd gone that I realised he'd left his Auschwitz Bible behind. I had a phone number for him: he said he could never remember his home number, but if I looked up Smith Garages in the Yellow Pages one of his sons would pass on any updates I had on the launch of *I Came to Dance*.

'I came here in 1946,' he said proudly, 'and with what little money I had I bought a car. Sold it the same day and made a nice profit. Been doing it ever since. But I only work one day a week now - the boys think I. . . how do you say it . . . *cramp their style!*'

So I could have phoned him. But did not. The Bible was probably worth a few thousand pounds, but twice that wouldn't make up for even half of the stress I'd experienced because of *The Case of the Dancing Jews*.

I would deny all knowledge.

We book-collectors have an expression: *finders keepers, losers weepers.*

Not long after ten o'clock I switched off the computer and the lights in the front of the shop, and took my empty Diet Pepsi can and Twix wrappers into the kitchen. If I'm working late, and particularly in the summer months when it's still bright, I slip out the back way and down the alley to the No Alibis van. I had a box of books under one arm and a bag of rubbish for the bins in the other. I'd just dumped the rubbish and was turning into the alley proper when a voice to my left said, 'Hey.'

I turned into a blur of movement and a sudden impact on my left cheek. I flew backwards, books in the air, and landed hard on the glass-strewn lane. Knees thumped into my back, pinning me to the ground, and a hand pushed my face roughly into the gravel.

'Got you now,' the same voice hissed.

I was so *stupid.* I'd protected myself against a perceived threat just a few hours before, only to discover it was a harmless old man. And now I was alone, and walking dangerous back alleys without a care in the world, and suddenly the real killer had me. He had just bided his time until he could get me alone to finish me off.

But it is never too late to beg.

'I'm sorry, I'm sorry, I'm sorry, I'm sorry . . . please don't . . . please don't hurt me . . . please don't . . . I'm sorry . . .'

'You will be, you fucking

The load lightened, for just a moment, and then I was flipped over on to my back. He sat on me again. A rough-looking character, younger than me, his eyes fired up, his face thunderous, his breathing adrenaline-fuelled. No obvious German accent, but that meant nothing. Probably he was a master of accents and disguise and surprise and *death.* His fist closed again, but as he aimed another punch at me I cried out: 'Please don't! Not my face! I'm a haemophiliac! If you break my nose they won't be able to stop the blood!'

He hesitated for just a moment, which I took to be a good sign, before redirecting the punch to my arm. But before he could land it I cried, 'Please don't! I have brittle bones! They'll never be able to repair it . . .'

Again he delayed. 'Shut your fucking mouth!'

'I can't,' I cried, 'I have verbal diarrhoea

It was a whine too far. He punched me in the chest. He slapped me in the face, my head moving left, right, left again as the slapping continued. Tears in a grown man are not particularly cool, but I had no option. I was not in a position of strength.

'Please, I'm *really* sorry

He pulled me up by my shirt collar. 'What're you sorry for?' he demanded.

'Everything!' And I meant it. It was about survival. *Everything* covered everything. 'I don't care what you did or what your secret is, I don't care about the war or the camp or what happened . . . just don't kill me. I just sell books, I can keep my mouth shut, I—'

'SHUT UP!'

He shook me, hard. 'I ought to smash your fucking face in. It took a lot of organising to get those fucking trousers, you hear me?'

I nodded, but my mind was racing.

Trousers?

'And now she's dumped me as well, and the boss has sacked me, and it's your fucking fault for sticking your fucking nose in. Where the fuck are they anyway?'

He gave me another shake. 'Where are *what?*' I cried.

'The leather *fucking* trousers!'

I stared at him. It wasn't the assassin! It was the *boyfriend. The Case of Mrs Geary's Leather Trousers* back to haunt me. I couldn't help myself. I laughed right in his face.

'Nobody wanted them! I threw them out! They cut the

hole off me!'

He slapped me again, but it didn't matter! He wasn't going to kill me over a pair of bloody trousers. I was alive! I had a future!

'You fucking little shit! Where's your wallet?' He pulled open my jacket and reached inside. He pulled out my leather wallet and opened it. 'Is that *it?*' he growled.

'I live frugally,' I said.

'Into the fucking shop, open the fucking till or I swear to—'

'There's nothing there! I went to the night drop at the bank hours ago!'

'You're a fucking liar!'

'I'm not, I'm not, you can check if you want!'

He let out an anguished yell. 'I've lost my girl, I've lost my job, and now you've no fucking money?' He grabbed suddenly at my other pockets. 'Tell you what I'm going to do,' he spat, pulling out my van keys. 'I'm going to take your fucking wheels, man. Now they're my wheels. And if you go near the cops with this, if you squeal to anyone, I'm going to come back and I'm going to burn your fucking shop out with you fucking in it, do you hear me?'

'Yes! Take it!'

He pushed himself up and off me. I turned to one side, coughing. He could *have* the wheels. I was alive. The No Alibis van was three years past its MOT date and its tyres were threadbare. It was a death trap.

He jabbed a farewell finger at me. 'I'm fucking warning you!'

I just smiled stupidly at him. As he disappeared round the corner I lay back on the gravel and glass, breathing hard, and laughed and laughed.

31

I like the night, always have. I've never been scared of the dark, and quite often prefer it. I particularly like the streets at night. I like the idea of being able to walk and not be seen, or if seen, not in detail. People examine people too much. My creative writing guru Brendan Coyle thought he'd come up with something unique in describing *the writer's muscle*, but he was just putting into words what everybody does every second of every minute of every day anyway: they look at other people and they judge. The sexy girl, the old man, the fat thighs, the dodgy hairstyle. I don't like people looking at me and thinking *anything*. The night suits me: hood up; nail out; I walk for miles.

I stand behind trees.

Just stand.

This city has changed so much. It used to be divided, now it's divided into quarters. War zone to gentrification. T.B. Sheets to continental quilts.

In the night I have watched badgers snuffle and foxes quest. Sleeked cats. I have listened to lovers' tiffs and secret singers. I have haunted deserted mansions and paced wet-plastered new builds. I have written *Please Clean Me* in the grime of white vans and put nuts on neglected bird tables. I have imitated Spitfires on manicured lawns and pruned roses while gardeners slept. I have felt the dew settle.

Never once arrested for loitering with intent, for Peeping Tomness, never once threatened with an exclusion order, or probation, or made the subject of a curfew or community service.

Lately I have stood in the shadows close to Alison's house and watched her move from room to room. I have seen the effort she puts into her art. I have watched her lose herself in thought while cooking and then listened to her tantrum at her burned dinner. I have watched for her lovers and found none, and I have pondered for hours why she chose me.

That night, after the attack, I could easily have knocked on her door. I bruise up easily and well. And I had my story prepared. As soon as Alison finished peppering my poor face with kisses I could give a blow-by-blow account of my battle to hold on to the No Alibis van. *I look bad, but you should see the other guy. I would have made a citizen's arrest but the sneaky bastard blindsided me; before I could recover he had the keys and was away.*

But I didn't. I watched. I made mental notes of the cars parked around. I didn't locate any personalised number plates.

I am not odd. I am protecting her. Who else is going to do it? I could have been in there with her, but you cannot look from light into dark, you cannot see the devil coming. If you dwell in the darkness, you can see in the dark, and look into the light. But in choosing the darkness, you know you are destined to walk alone.

I walked home. It was a little after three a.m. on a summer's morning and a hint of the approaching dawn was already in the night sky. In the old days there would have been milk floats.

I was tired. If I was lucky, once I'd jotted down the number plates stored in my head, there would be a couple of hours' sleep.

Tired and *stupid.*

My earlier fight in the alley should have taught me to be alert at all times, but particularly when approaching places where I was *expected* to be. When I got to my corner, I should have held back and checked the plates, and the doorways, or gone in the back way, but I just walked straight up, yawning, and failed to spot that there was someone in the car parked directly outside my front door.

I was just reaching for my key when a voice said, 'You're out late.'

It *shook* me. I turned slowly, fearing the worst.

DI Robinson was just climbing out of the car.

Christ.

'Out for a walk,' I said.

He nodded towards the house. 'I tried the bell, but nobody answered.'

'She'll be asleep.'

'That's . . . Alison?'

'My mother.'

'I rang for a long time.'

'She won't answer the door after dark. What are you doing here?'

'Wanted a chat.'

'It's very late.'

'You're the one out walking. We should go inside.'

I looked up at my home. I was trying to remember the state of it and if there was anything lying around that might disturb him. But no, I'm pretty careful. I nodded, and he followed me up the steps. I opened the door and led him down the hall and into the kitchen. I indicated for him to sit at the table. I filled the kettle and stood facing away from him while I waited for it to boil.

'You have books everywhere,' he observed. 'You can't

have read them all.'

'Most,' I said.

'I'd never get any work done,' he said.

'It *is* my work. You would expect a surgeon to keep up to date with the latest developments. And a stockbroker to keep an eye on the markets.'

When I turned with two coffees, he got his first proper look at me in the light.

'Been in a fight?' he asked.

'Yes,' I said, 'with a door. A bit clumsy'

'Look like you've been in a fight.'

'You should see the door.'

'I enjoyed looking at your limited editions earlier. I like the shop. Did anything unusual happen after I left?'

'Like what?'

'You tell me.'

I sat at the table and stirred my coffee. He knew something. He knew that I knew he knew something. But I had started with a lie and was prepared to see it through.

He studied me. Maybe he had overheard more than I thought last night and it had just taken a while to distil itself into a theory. Perhaps he'd found the missing file on Rosemary and realised there was a connection.

'Where's your van?' DI Robinson asked suddenly.

'Gone,' I said quickly. 'For scrap.'

'Scrap? Why would you do that?'

'Because it was old and decrepit and useless. It kept breaking down. And I haven't the sense to fix it myself. It was costing me a fortune.'

'It was there last night.'

'Yeah, he only collected it later on.'

'Who he?'

'No idea. Someone who heard on the grapevine I was looking to get rid of it.'

'How much did he pay you for it?'

'He didn't. I gave it to him. It would have cost me more than it was worth to have it towed away, so he came and took it off my hands.'

'It didn't look that bad.'

'The paint job was holding it together. Riddled with rust. Why are you so interested in my van at three in the morning?'

'A couple of hours ago I got called out to a park in West Belfast. There was a van on fire. Real inferno. Your number plates.'

'So he got rid of it. I would have thought you were a bit above attending burning vehicles.'

'Thing is, there was someone in the front seat.'

'Someone in the front seat? You mean . . . ?'

'Dead in the front seat. Burned to a crisp.'

He didn't say anything for really quite a long, long time. It might only have been seconds, but when there's a feeling of dread growing on you it can feel like an eternity. He kept looking at me. I kept my gaze steady in return, although hopefully not mad steady. I think I'm quite difficult to read. Inside everything was racing. *Dead? Burned to a crisp?* How was that possible? Only a couple of hours ago he . . .

I knew how it was possible. I absolutely knew.

'Some of my colleagues checked the plates, made the connection, called me in. I took a look at the guy and guessed it wasn't you, wrong body shape.'

'Was he murdered?'

'Why do you ask?'

'It seems like a natural thing to ask. Was it an accident?'

'Too early to say. An accident. Suicide. Murder. It just seems to me like death is following you around.'

I took a sip of my coffee. 'I don't know about that.'

'Malcolm Carlyle. This guy. Is there anything you want to tell me, because it might save a lot of time and effort and do you some good in the end.'

It would have been easy to tell him about the guy who had stolen Mrs Geary's leather trousers, about the real reason I'd invited him, a cop, to the book sale, about Mark

Mayerova, and Anne Mayerova, and the concentration camp, and the disappearance of Rosemary Trevor, and the death of Manfredd, and my discovery of Malcolm Carlyle. But I couldn't tell him. Because he was right. Death was following me around, and if he knew the full extent of the violence, sitting where he was sitting, I was the obvious, easy connection. He proved as much with his next question.

'So where were you tonight, one a.m.?'

'Alison's.'

'Your girlfriend?'

'I just looked in on her.'

'She'll corroborate.'

'If she knows what's good for her.'

'You think this is funny?'

'No. Sorry. I'm just . . . *shocked.* I was only talking to the guy a couple of hours ago. Presuming it's him. And he's dead? Jesus.'

'I'll be talking to the pathologist in the morning. I'll be wanting a statement from you anyway about how he came by the van. But I'd think about things if I were you. There's something going on that doesn't feel right. I know you get off on your little cases, but sometimes when you throw a stone in a pond there are ripples, and when it sinks to the floor it kicks up a lot of dirt. Do you know what I mean?'

I nodded.

He got up. 'Thanks for the coffee. And apologise to your mother for the disturbance.'

Apologising to Mother. That would be a first.

I sat in the darkness of the front room for a long time and watched the street outside. Leather Trouser guy had been angry, he'd lost his girl and his job and was short of money. But he had not seemed suicidal. Unless the dire state of the van had been enough to finally tip him over the edge. No — he had been murdered. The killer had presumed it was me in the van, had followed it and torched it but made the basic error of not actually checking for sure that it really was me. I had a period of grace, when he would think that he had done his job. At least until the police released the identity of the victim. Then it would start all over again. There was no longer any doubt.

I had known this as soon as DI Robinson told me. So why hadn't I confessed all? Weren't my fears of being framed for murder based on *nothing much*? Why, when I was allergic to stress, was I making a point of encouraging it? How many warnings did I need?

There were no answers. There was just something dragging me along. Something unknown. The victim inside me.

I phoned Alison. She answered groggily. 'Brian?'

After a moment I said, 'Who's Brian?'

'What? Hold on, who . . . oh. I'm sorry. Asleep. Dreaming. What time is it? What's wrong?'

'I need a favour.'

'At . . . six fifteen?'

'If anyone asks, I was with you tonight.'

'Anyone?' She sounded more together. 'Who's going to ask, the postman?'

'No . . . you know. Something's happened.'

'What?' Not only *together*, but *alert*. '*What's* happened?'

Concern. I liked it. I told her about leaving the shop, and getting jumped, and fighting to save my van, but losing, and being upset about it, and going for a walk and losing track of time, and coming home to the news that my assailant had been burned to death and DI Robinson suspected me of murder and I had no alibi. 'But you know I wouldn't hurt a fly,' I said.

'I know you wouldn't. Of course you can say you were here. If he asks I'll tell him we made love for hours on end.'

'Who's Brian?' I asked.

'My husband,' she said.

32

'When I was twelve I was bitten by an earwig. I hoped it might have been radioactive. I spent several months thinking that I might turn into Earwigman.'

'What special powers would Earwigman have?'

'Big pincers. Flight. And I could crawl into the ears of my enemies and lay eggs.'

'If you're trying to inspire me to a new comic creation, I'm afraid you're well wide of the mark. I'm into gritty reality.'

Well, she *had* it.

In spades.

And talking of spades, that's exactly what we could have used, if we'd been so inclined, to dig a big hole and bury ourselves, or had we done that already? We were on the beach. Fourteen miles from Belfast, her little car sitting on the sand. No Alibis was shuttered, and my only feeble excuse was that there was a killer on the loose with my name in his little black book. It was the first time the shop hadn't opened on time since I'd gone into business by myself. Mother was always angry that her prediction that

I'd be out of business in six months hadn't come to pass. I was *so* determined to prove her wrong. I thought that if I once weakened, and began to close up at every sign of illness or on every Blue Monday, a creeping lethargy would irrevocably lead to the fulfilment of her prophecy. Yet here we were, thoughts of bookselling a million miles away, crowded out by paranoia, confusion and jealousy.

I hate beaches. I hate sand in things. Alison wanted to get out and walk, but I insisted on staying. I wasn't just thinking of the sand. I was thinking about telescopic sights and the end of *Get Carter*. I also hated the fact that she was married to someone called Brian, and had previously had sex with him, and perhaps recently as well.

She said, 'How do you think someone as pretty as I am could get to my age without being married?

I shrugged.

'Wait'll you meet the kids,' she said.

She was funny, but I'd a face like the Tomb of Ligeia. I hated Brian, but I wasn't scared of him. I *was* scared of someone trying to kill me. I could not reopen the shop unless I had some kind of security. I could not walk home. I could barely risk crossing from the shop to a waiting taxi for fear of someone *taking me out* before I got inside. And what if the taxi driver turned out to be the killer? That was how the Shankill Butchers had done it. Or what if the taxi itself was an evil Transformer? Alison, on the other hand, could probably fend for herself. She had hands and feet that could kill. My hands were brittle, and unless my Nazi assassin was allergic to verrucas then my feet were useless as well. I was utterly defenceless.

'In America,' I said, 'people don't have verrucas.'

She looked at me, eyes scrunched up. 'What?'

'They call them plantar warts. Same thing, but confusing.'

'Alison calling Planet Earth, are you receiving me? We're here, lovely beach, sunny morning, we should walk and talk this through.'

'Which through?'

'Whatever you want. Me and Brian. You and your ability to attract mayhem and death. Depends which you think is the most relevant.'

'When I was younger I had this recurring nightmare where I was forced to count the grains of sand on a beach. I've been wary of them ever since.'

The real problem was that ever since, whenever I see a beach, I get tempted to attempt it. But I would have needed someone to stop the tide, because it could really bugger things up.

'Do you know something? I think you've been saying *no* to things for too long. It's just a walk on the beach, you know? Have you ever skied?'

'What? No, of course not.'

'Climbed a mountain?'

'No.'

'Run naked through a field of corn?'

'*No.*'

'Hurled eggs at an Ulsterbus?'

'No. Of course not.'

'Man, dear, you only live once. Do you know what I think? I think you're like a bottle of Coke someone shakes once in a while. There's turmoil in there . . .' and she poked me gently in the chest, 'and I bet you would just explode into life if someone came along and took your top off.'

There were dog-walkers carrying bags of crap dotted about the sand. A teenager in a rubber suit was carrying a surfboard and sail towards the waves. Elderly couples were taking their constitutionals on the promenade.

'Brian came along and took your top off.'

She sighed. '*Yes.* Amongst other things.' She shook her head. 'Look at you, you look *hurt* by that. Do you expect all of your women to be virgins or something?'

I liked the phrase *all of my women*. It was so ridiculous.

'No,' I said. 'That would be unrealistic.'

We stared ahead for a little while. Then she blew air out of her cheeks, opened her door and snapped, 'Well, *I'm* going for a walk. Are you coming?'

I was halfway through saying, 'But what about snipers?' when she slammed the door shut and started walking.

I folded my arms and waited. She would be back.

But then I got to thinking that when she did return she would find the passenger window frosted and me with a neatly drilled hole in my forehead, because it might be just the opportunity the assassin was waiting for. The Russian sniper Vasily Zaytsev had shown infinite patience in the maelstrom of Stalingrad; how much easier must it be for my nemesis, nestled into the wild grass on a pleasant summer's morning on the County Down coast? He probably had a flask and sandwiches. It might only be slightly safer, walking along the beach, but at least I would be a moving target, and if I kept on the seaward side of Alison and close to her, there was a fair chance he would hit her by mistake, which would at least give me the opportunity to make a run for it. The sea would be my best chance of escape. I would probably drown, or suffer a stroke because of my morbid fear of jellyfish and riptides and sharks and seaweed, but *probably* was better than *definitely*, which would be the outcome of his second shot ramming into my brain if I stayed on the sand mourning for a lost love, or vainly trying to take shelter behind her lifeless body.

So I *ran* after her, my knees clicking and my calves straining. When I drew level she didn't acknowledge me, but there was definitely a little smile. I thrust my hands into my pockets and said, 'I really don't mind about Brian. Where does he live?'

'Why?'

'Just interested.'

'It doesn't matter. He's history.'

'So why did you say Brian when you answered the

phone?'

'I was half asleep.'

'But he must call you sometimes, for you to think it was him.'

'Yes, he does.'

'Did he beat you?'

'No! He's a perfectly normal human being, and I was in love with him when I married him, but it didn't work out, and we still talk from time to time. I don't hate him, there's no reason why he shouldn't phone me, and no reason why I shouldn't think it was him when I answer the phone in the middle of the night, okay?'

I nodded.

'Is he an alcoholic?'

'No!'

We walked on. I kept my eyes on the promenade, about fifty metres away from us. There were dog-walkers there as well, and several of those little electric golf carts that disabled people con out of the government.

She said, 'What are we going to do about *The Case of the Dancing Jews?*'

'I don't know.'

'We're not really any the wiser, are we? We don't know that the burning man in your van is the same man who stole it, and we don't know if he committed suicide or was murdered, or if he was murdered, if he was murdered by the same guy who killed Rosemary and Manfredd and Malcolm Carlyle, or indeed, if they were murdered at all. As I see it, the problem is that each individual death — and we don't even know that Rosemary is dead, really — has a perfectly plausible explanation. Even this guy in your van. Let's face it, they found him in West Belfast, they'd set you on fire there for looking at them the wrong way. There's never a bullet, there's never a witness, it's only when you put them all together that you see a pattern, but maybe there isn't really one.'

'There is. There definitely is.'

There are always patterns. They just aren't always obvious.

'But maybe it's like people's names,' Alison continued. 'You know — there are millions of Smiths, and you could argue that they are all connected, but they're not. They just have a common name. And what do you call that game they play, the Kevin Bacon one?'

'Six degrees of Kevin Bacon. Any actor in Hollywood can be connected to Kevin Bacon because of the number of films he's made and the actors he's worked with, usually in six moves.'

'That's a pattern, but it doesn't mean that Kevin Bacon is responsible for every Hollywood movie. What if *our* Kevin Bacon is just that, someone you can connect to the deaths, but he's not responsible for them?'

'Okay,' I said. I actually quite liked that. But for the fact that we weren't dealing with Hollywood movies. We were dealing with real live dead people. The stakes were infinitely higher. Or lower, depending on what value you put on life or movies. 'What do you suggest? Ignoring the threat? Just go to work as normal, and then if someone comes through the door and blows my head off, at least you'll be able to acknowledge the fact that you were wrong and the pattern was the pattern was the pattern.'

'Well, what do you want to do? Hide in a deep hole until he dies of old age?'

'See, even you're saying there is a he.'

'Just for talk's sake. I don't know if there's a he. It might be a she. It could be *me*.' She raised an eyebrow. 'Or it could be a whole team of them. Or it could be no one, that we're just seeing Kevin Bacons.'

We walked on some more. I wasn't familiar with this or any beach, so it was worth keeping an eye on the incoming tide in case we were cut off and drowned like Chinese cockle-pickers, or stung to death by Portuguese man-o'-war jellyfish.

'Okay,' Alison said, *'if* there's a he — and let's call him .

. .'

'Fritz,' I said.

'. . . Fritz, for now, let's think about what he might do next. If he's got some kind of hit list, if he's intent on wiping out whoever might know Anne Mayerova's secret, even if they're not aware of it, who's actually left? You — but at the moment he thinks you're dead. Me? Well I'm about twenty-eight degrees of Kevin Bacon, an afterthought at best. So we don't really need to be so jumpy, at least for a little while. Then there's Anne Mayerova herself. But not only is she reasonably secure in a mental hospital, she's also fifty per cent do-lally and getting worse every day. She's no real threat. What about her ex-husband?'

I thought about that for a moment before shaking my head. 'He's been with her all these years and hasn't spilled the beans.'

'Okay, so it's whoever Fritz believes knows the contents of the book that's in the real danger right now . . .'

'A book that will never be written.'

'. . . and that can only mean

'Daniel Trevor.'

'Exactly.' She stopped. She gave me a *look*.

'Why are you giving me a *look?*'

'Isn't it obvious? If Fritz is ticking boxes, and the only one left to be ticked is Daniel Trevor's, then if we want to identify Fritz, if we want to stop him, if we want to prove one way or another whether he exists or not, and we don't want to call in the police because we'll look like idiots and might yet be arrested for hanging pine trees on Malcolm Carlyle, then we have to go down to his stupid bloody artists' retreat ourselves. We have to confront Fritz. We have to unmask him. The only way we're going to solve *The Case of the Dancing Jews* is by going down there and setting a trap for him.'

'Fuck *off*,' I said.

33

I didn't like the way she was *moving in*. Mother had warned me about women who used their siren lure to get their way, to steal your wallet, your heart, your soul, who parlayed hormones into lifelong commitment, and I think she was speaking from the perspective of having done it herself. Father had nothing much to offer beyond straight laces and a Lambeg drum, but she devoured him nevertheless, and afterwards he was never the same, he was harder, colder, and I think some small part of her regretted it. Alison was a nodding acquaintance who had propelled herself into position as my sidekick, but she was like a one-legged black lesbian greasing her way up the promotional ladder not because of her talents, but because she ticked all the right boxes and there was nobody with the gumption to stand up and pull the ladder from under her, causing her to fall and break her neck or at least cause the kind of spinal injury that would require a body cast. She had been my sidekick for barely a week, yet instead of being content to nod mindlessly along, looking to me for direction and instruction, she now thought she could decide how cases would be dealt with, where we would go, who we would talk to; she thought she had the experience, the insight and the courage to deal with the criminal masterminds when it was me who had the knowledge, who had read all the books. She sold bangles.

She had needlessly complicated my life, and all because I had taken pity on her being excluded from a creative writing course. Everything that had followed had followed because of her. I was all for dumping *The Case of the Dancing Jews* at its very earliest stages, while she was the one who'd led us deeper and deeper into the mire. She had forced me to go to Purdysburn to interview Anne Mayerova, to break into Malcolm Carlyle's next door, and now she had kidnapped me and was driving me to the Beale Feirste Books retreat in the wilderness of County Down knowing *full well* I was incapable of using public transport to return to No Alibis. At least there I would know my surroundings. I knew the escape routes. There were always civilians passing by or occasionally actually in the shop to deter assassins. I could call on the protection of my Botanic Avenue Irregulars, or my friend DI Robinson, or the Traders Association, or I could harness the power of the internet to track down and expose the killer. There was no risk of being attacked by a cow *there*. Or a goat. Or a pig. Or a donkey. Or a bee. On Botanic Avenue I could not suffer a catastrophic wheat allergy or lose my arms to a combine harvester.

She had turned my head. How had I solved my previous cases? By a cool appraisal of the facts, by using my customers as my eyes and ears, by the application of logic. Had I ever previously thrust myself into danger? Once or twice, perhaps, but only by accident. I hadn't *hurled* myself towards it, the way I was now, travelling at speeds in excess of thirty miles an hour on twisting roads around the corners of which we might at any moment plough into tractors driving two abreast, or sheep.

She was talking about setting a trap for Fritz. I couldn't

set a trap for a *mouse*. Did she think we were going to camp out there until he just showed up? I had a shop to run. A mother to support. How could we ever trap an *assassin*, unless we challenged him to some kind of trivia quiz? She had *no idea*. The only trap she'd ever set was the one that ensnared me.

She said, 'Why are you holding on to the door handle?'

I let go of it. 'I'm not,' I said.

'Do you know the address of this place?' I shook my head. 'We can ask.'

'We're bound to come across it.'

'We'll stop and ask someone. It'll save time.'

'There'll be signs.'

'Okay,' she said, '*I'll* stop and ask.'

When we came to the outskirts of Banbridge, Alison pulled into a Shell garage. While she was in the Mace shop asking directions, I realised that she'd left the keys in the ignition. I could just drive off. I would be saving my own skin. Self-preservation is man's primal instinct, although it seems rare in women. So as not to totally rule out the possibility of having some kind of sexual relationship with her at a later date, I could claim it was an emergency, that Mother had fallen and was lying bleeding and needed my help. Or that I had a migraine. That *voices* had told me to drive off. But as I computed these possibilities she bounced back into the car and said, 'It's not far.'

We drove on. I sneezed.

'You okay?' she asked.

'Hay fever,' I said.

I had been expecting some kind of garage-based business with a ramshackle B&B attached, but the Beale Feirste Books office and retreat was entirely different — a huge mansion with a dangerous-looking lake out front.

'Golly,' Alison said, 'I *know* this place.' I was still getting over her saying *golly* when she added: 'I came here when I was a girl. It was open to the public. Whatchamacallhim used to live here, you know, the actor . . . ? *Irish* actor.'

'Give me a clue,' I said.

'Sir Terence something . . . way back in the fifties . . . I think he left it to the National Trust or something . . .'

'So Daniel Trevor doesn't own it?'

'Maybe he's like the custodian. Or he could have bought it, maybe it wasn't paying its way. I mean we can't remember the actor's name, so maybe nobody else can either. Does it make any difference?'

I shrugged. Probably not.

We parked facing the house, and were just discussing what we were going to say to Daniel when he flew out of the front door and across the gravelled courtyard towards us, waving excitedly.

'Well, someone's pleased to see us,' said Alison, rolling down her window.

But when the publisher bent down to us, he didn't look happy at all. 'You can't park here!' he cried, his face engorged. 'The poets have to be able to see the lake! Take it round the back!'

He turned on his heel and stamped back towards the house.

Alison turned to me and performed the universal sign for wanking.

By the time we eventually made it inside, having parked in a bog of a field, and tramped mud through an open-plan olde worlde kitchen heavy with beams and dominated by a cream Aga, Daniel had calmed down a bit. 'Sorry about all that,' he said, vigorously pumping my hand, 'but the poets . . . any distraction and there's hell to pay. Come in, come in, welcome to Beale Feirste Books. To what do I owe the privilege? Have there been any developments? You will stay for dinner? We always have great *craic.*'

If there's anything that can freeze my blood, it's the notion of great *craic.* I *abhor* the word. It conjures Tourist Board images of beefy men in white Aran sweaters downing pints of Guinness and roaring on dense rugby players and some soup-voiced harlot inviting you to come to Ireland to enjoy a bit of it. *Craic* was disparate strangers being forced together for no good reason and being pressurised into having a good time.

'Sounds like a plan,' said Alison.

'Love to,' I added, 'but we have to get going.'

'What? You've only just . . .'

Alison laughed. 'He's only winding you up.'

I looked at her. I was *not*. No Alibis had been shut all day. I had none of my medication with me because I had not expected to go on a safari into the wilderness. And what if Mother even now was lying on the kitchen floor, her head split open and the grey matter spilled across the linoleum? What was Alison *thinking* of? She wanted to warn Daniel about Fritz? Fair enough. She wanted to check out the house, survey the surrounding land for camouflaged enemies? *Okay.* But in the name of God get me home before nightfall. I could not cope with widespread dark. I could not handle forced bonhomie or watching strangers eat food at close quarters. If she wanted to save Daniel Trevor she could do it by herself, on her own time. Good Jesus Christ, it was an old enough house to have *bats*. They had *radar*, they could find you in the fucking dark.

Daniel clapped his hands together. 'Excellent! You settle yourselves in there, get yourselves a wee drinkypoo, I've some paperwork to finish off, and then once the poets knock off around six, we can have a chat, then after that maybe we'll get this party started!' He smiled enthusiastically and punched me lightly on the arm, caring not one iota that I was a borderline haemophiliac and could easily have bled to death right there on that spot. 'Be good for you to get a little culture in your life, eh?'

He sauntered off out of the kitchen. I stared after him, seething.

Then from behind, a different voice said: 'Every time I

hear the word culture, I reach for my revolver.'

We turned. Brendan Coyle, writer, teacher, was framed in the back door. Cocksure. Or just cock.

'Mr Goebbels, I believe,' I said.

'Actually,' Brendan responded, coming fully into the kitchen, 'that's a bit of a misconception. He said it, but he was misquoting the Nazi poet laureate Hanns Johst. What *he* actually wrote was, *Whenever I hear of culture, I release the safety catch of my Browning.* Although on the whole, I prefer the Goebbels version.'

He smiled pleasantly and came towards us with his hand outstretched. I glanced at Alison. I could tell exactly what she was thinking. How come an Irish writer like Brendan Coyle knows so much about Nazi poets?

I reluctantly shook Brendan's hand; it was fleeting. He took much longer to welcome Alison. He took her hand between two of his.

'How absolutely *lovely* to see you again,' he purred. 'Didn't we have a mighty *joust* last time?'

'Actually,' Alison purred back, 'it was a bit of a walkover.'

He looked pretend shocked and winked at me. 'Isn't she the feisty one?' He laughed uproariously, released her hand, and passed on through the kitchen.

I did not much like Brendan Coyle. Or Daniel Trevor. Or poets. Or old houses. Or the countryside. Or my sidekick. But it seemed that for the next few hours at least, I was stuck with them, come hell or high water. And with my luck, it would be both.

34

Even before I started taking my medicine, I never had any sort of capacity for or predilection for alcohol. I simply cannot handle it. People do not understand this. They will say, 'Go on, just have one. Let your hair down. Stop sitting in the corner like a sour-faced shit.' But I'm a stubborn soul and I would rather remain in the kitchen at parties, with the stacked plates and the dried-out chilli, than force myself to become *what I am not*. Besides that, with the regime of medication I'm on, even the merest sniff of alcohol can make me extremely ill. I had, for obvious reasons, like complete frickin' ignorance of what lay in store for me, neglected to bring my pills and potions and lotions and salts and suppositories and rubs and powders and sachets, although there was probably enough in my system to see me through to the autumn. But at least half of my medicines were liable to make me drowsy if I so much as sniffed alcohol. If there was a party starting and Fritz showed up halfway through it, and I had to make a break for it, the mere act of breathing in amongst drunks would rule me out of attempting to drive a getaway car or even a piece of heavy farm machinery.

The 'party' Daniel Trevor had predicted was in fact four poets, a sculptress, a screenwriter, a composer, a passing novelist in Brendan Coyle, a jewellery shop assistant/sidekick with ideas above her station, Daniel himself and me. There were many bottles of wine, candlelight and some kind of a casserole deposited in the middle of a long oak table by a cook called Emer, whom everyone referred to as Fanny, who quickly got off-side. Far from being the cultural oasis Daniel had predicted, the talk seemed to be mostly of football and tax evasion. Alison sat beside me, Brendan on her other side. She talked to him a lot. Although she barely spoke to me, once in a while she subtly elbowed me, to what end I wasn't quite sure. If she meant it to be somehow *inclusive,* she was failing miserably. Why not turn to *me* and talk? She could have probed *my* unknown depths instead of wallowing in the shallows of Brendan Coyle's suggestive banter. To distract myself, and at the insistence of the oversized sculptress, whom I was attempting to talk into making a life-size sculpture of Kojak for outside No Alibis, for free, obviously, I accepted a glass of wine. One of the poets suggested that he write a sonnet based on *The Murders in the Rue Morgue,* which I could have stitched by a stitcher and framed and hung in No Alibis, and I said no, I didn't think so. He poured me a second glass of wine, red this time, and asked if I didn't agree that poetry was proof that God existed, and I said no, that nettles probably were. The screenwriter asked what my favourite films were and I told him that this changed on a weekly basis, but that if he was interested I could show him the charts of my favourite films that I had maintained since 1978, and he seemed to think I was joking. The composer said she would put the Poe poem to music and then when it was hung in my shop I could play a tape of her composition at the same time and it would be very Zen. I wanted to head-butt her and say, 'Stitch that.' I drank some more wine and watched the back of Alison's head as she nodded and giggled. I hated Brendan Coyle. He was the type of man women said they hated, they absolutely hated, they absolutely and categorically hated, and then they went to bed with him. I was the type of man women said they hated, and then they went home. I could not for the life of me understand the difference between us, apart from his good looks and celebrity, although it was literary celebrity and therefore tiny. I was pretty sure if he was asked what his favourite film was in March 1983 he wouldn't have had a baldy notion.

It was dark and smoky in the room. There was a log fire burning. The conversation had become a hubbub. I love the word *hubbub*. Hubbub, hubbub, hubbub, hubbub, hubbub. Hubbub, hubbub, hubbub. Hubbub, hubbub. I was trying to catch what Alison and Brendan were talking about, but the hubbub wouldn't let me, that and the mild form of tinnitus I suffer from. The poet opposite me launched into a diatribe about *something,* but it just sounded like bollocks, bollocks, bollocks, break for sip of wine, bollocks, bollocks, bollocks. I nodded a lot and despite putting my hand over the rim of my glass another poet poured away. Alison laughed at a Brendan joke, but then gently placed a hand on my leg. What was she *doing?* It was like petting a golden retriever while having oral sex with someone. Except I wasn't a golden retriever, I was a pound puppy, crossbred, ears so long I tripped over them, temper so vile I was doomed to spend the . ..

The doorbell rang. The hubbub was so great I thought for a moment that I was the only one who heard it, but then I saw Daniel begin to rise from his seat.

'Don't answer it,' I said.

'Why on earth not?'

'Because,' I said, making *eyes.*

'Oh stuff and nonsense,' he replied. He pushed back, staggering slightly.

I curled one hand around my knife, the other around

my fork. In a tight corner I would also have found a way to wield the spoon. My eyes flitted to Alison. I was gratified to see that my former sidekick was now also fingering her butter knife, although she could easily have been doing that all along as a precaution against Brendan's advances. He hadn't made any yet, but like the Normandy landings, they were inevitable. She squeezed my leg again with her free hand; Brendan was still talking away, but she was watching the doorway. If Fritz came through, we would make a fight of it. Or she would distract him while I escaped and went for help. I checked my emergency exits: back door, stairs, window. But what if they were already covered? What if it wasn't just Fritz? Maybe there was a whole troop of them. *The Eagle Has Landed in Banbridge.* If the secret was big enough, what was to stop them killing *us all?*

Above the din, louder voices in the hall.

Then a burly figure filled the doorway, his hair long, his chest barrelled, a leather jacket unbuttoned. My heart *raced.* He had a bullfrog neck and big hands. He surveyed the table and shook his head. He reached inside his jacket.

'Ah, for fuck's sake,' he said, withdrawing a bottle of wine, 'youse might have waited. I'm fuckin' starving.'

He stepped into the kitchen, pulled an empty chair away from the wall and tucked himself in between two of the poets. I looked at Alison, and we both breathed a sigh of relief. Brendan, seeing that Alison was distracted, said, 'Hello, Kyle,' down the table and got a gruff nod in response.

'Let me guess,' I said, 'another poet.'

Brendan shook his head. 'Not a bit of it,' he said, lowering his voice. 'That's Daniel's son. Big strapping lad, isn't he? I expect . . .' And a second figure now appeared in the doorway, this time a woman, tall, with short dark hair and strikingly attractive. '. . . Michelle won't be far behind, and there she is. The daughter. Aren't they a fine-looking pair?'

This was confusing. 'I thought his children were like . . . toddlers.'

As I recalled, one of the reasons he hadn't gone with his wife to Frankfurt was to stay and look after the children.

As Michelle squeezed in another chair at her brother's side, Brendan leaned towards me. Alison leaned back. 'Not a bit of it. They started young. Both at Queen's now. But they *behave* like toddlers, I'll give you that. They have all the social attributes of poets, but unfortunately there's not a stanza in them. They are averse to verse. I think Daniel is very disappointed. He spends a lot of time bailing them out of trouble.'

Daniel's kids were now pouring wine into pint glasses. The hubbub increased; Kyle and Michelle were very much at home, and the focus of attention: the life and soul. Daniel sat at the head of the table, puffing on a cigar, nodding beatifically. He seemed remarkably content for a man who had so recently lost his wife. Perhaps it was the alcohol.

It was past eleven, and the bright summer evening had finally turned to night. The bats would be out. And the cows of darkness. I was well past medication time, but somehow it no longer seemed quite so important. Missing one set of pills, one application of lotions, would not make a great difference, not in the grand scheme of things. I was quite relaxed, actually, maybe even a tad woozy: if I did try to escape on a tractor later, I would be *very* careful. We had come to discuss Daniel's personal safety, and Alison had planned on setting a trap for Fritz; perhaps that was still her plan, but as far as I could see, which wasn't very far admittedly, what with the myopia and the candlelight and the wine, she was making a bit of a hash of it, unless she was planning some variation on the penis fly trap, and then it was probably going quite well, as long as the penis she intended to trap was Brendan Coyle. *She* was pouring *him* more wine; their two heads were very close together; any closer and she would have been whispering in his mouth; but I wasn't jealous. She was working; she wasn't seducing him, she was eliminating a Nazi apologist from her enquiries, she was extracting DNA from the source, not relying on some retarded snail trail.

I was distracted then by activity at the far end of the table. Kyle was on his feet and leaving the kitchen. He returned carrying a keyboard, which he proceeded to set on a stand and then plug in. The others began to move their chairs out from the table for a better view. Daniel clapped his hands together and cried, 'Right then, who's first!'

There is a particular type of dread that comes with the sudden realisation that one is expected to perform in public. I detest show-offs. I despise dinner parties not only because they require human interaction but because they can also occasionally descend into the kind of farce I was now about to witness. Untalented dreck, convinced by alcohol and inflated egos that they can entertain, get geed along by other drunks just waiting for their own opportunity. It is always pathetic and always embarrassing and I knew that given the choice, taking part myself or having Fritz come through the door, blasting away with a machine gun, I would choose to welcome him with open, albeit bleeding, arms.

I drained my glass and poured another. As I set the bottle down Alison grabbed my hand.

'What're you going to do?' she asked eagerly.

'Get my coat. We should be hitting the road.'

'I mean *do*. Sing. Can you sing, handsome man?'

I swallowed. 'We have to talk to Daniel, that's why we came. What if Fritz is out there?'

Her eyes were blurry. Or mine. 'He'll have to wait his turn like everyone else.'

Brendan Coyle's chair scraped back on the stone floor and he strode to the front. The other guests applauded. My heart sank. I *knew* his voice would not be a quivery falsetto or a ghastly rasp; it would be deep and proud and manly. Women loved him, men admired him. He had had Alison's attention all night, *knowing* this was coming; it would be the final nail in my coffin. He would have her up the stairs in no time, bent over a chair, taking her roughly from behind while looking at his own reflection in the dresser mirror. I watched in confounded awe as Brendan crouched beside Kyle, now sitting behind the keyboard, and whispered something in his ear. Kyle began to play. A hush fell. Brendan put his hand to his chest.

Oh, Mary, this London's a wonderful sight
With people here workin' by day and by night
They don't sow potatoes, nor barley, nor wheat
But there's gangs of them diggin' for gold in the street.

His voice was smooth, and beautiful, and haunting. The bastard.

At least when I asked them that's what I was told
So I just took a hand at this diggin' for gold
But for all that I found there I might as well be
Where the Mountains of Mourne sweep down to the sea.

His voice was full of *toil*, and *tears*, and *despair*. Even I was misting up.

There was an awed hush around the table.

As he took a deep breath, preparing to launch into the second verse, Brendan nodded gravely around his audience. His delivery had been so intense and profound that his listeners would surely die of grief before he got much further. But just as he opened his mouth to assault our senses anew, Alison cupped her hands together and shouted through them: 'Wanker!'

There was a moment of shocked silence, and then an explosion of drunken giggling. Brendan, flummoxed, didn't know whether to laugh or cry. In a desperate attempt to retrieve the situation he nodded quickly to Kyle, who had stopped playing. Kyle counted him in again, but as Brendan began to sing, one of the poets shouted, 'Big wanker!' and this time *everyone* laughed.

A third poet, one I'd not previously spoken to, barged forward, spilled half his drink over the keyboard and then announced in an American accent, 'It's a fuckin' party, man, let's party! Beach Boys!'

Kyle looked lost for a moment. He looked to his father, who raised his fist, hesitated, then, like Nero, raised his thumb skyward. Kyle began to play 'California Girls'. Once it got going, almost everyone began to sing along. There were two exceptions: Brendan, glaring along the table at Alison, who smiled triumphantly and nestled back into my arms.

And me, obviously.

Alison held my head up over the rim of the toilet. She was saying, 'Who shook you up and then took your top off? Bloody hell, I didn't know you really could sing.'

'Uggggggggggggghhhhhhhhhh . . . ?'

There had been more wine. A lot of it. It had interacted with some of the strongest medicines available on prescription, and many herbal remedies that were not. Sometimes when you say herbal remedies people think it's just code for dope, but I don't take dope. When I say herbal remedies I mean remedies made from Mother Nature. I take extract of artichoke to reduce cholesterol, cranberry for urinary tract infections, echinacea extracts for colds, elderberry for avian influenza, feverfew for migraine, black cumin to fight off cancers, pawpaw for worms, pokeweed for acne, peppermint oil for irritable bowel, *Rauvolfia serpentina* for sleeplessness and anxiety and high blood pressure and St John's wort for depression. There are others I couldn't think of right there and then, a deficiency I'm now trying to cure by taking *Salvia lavandulaefolia.*

But *singing?* That wasn't me. That definitely wasn't me. She was drunk and confused. A lot of people had sung, I remembered that much, but I hadn't sung. I couldn't have sung. I only know the lyrics to one song, and only those because my father played it repeatedly, and I mean *repeatedly,* when I was a teenager. I think it was his attempt to exorcise the devil in my soul, or to at least force me to move out.

'I've heard of songs being reinterpreted,' Alison said, patting what was left of my dank hair, 'but that was incredible. I came all out in goose bumps.' I threw up again. 'That's it,' she said, 'get it all up.'

She thought I was drunk. She had no idea. I was suffering an extreme reaction to my medication. I could quite easily have died at that moment, or descended into an irreversible coma. I needed an ambulance and a drip and a stomach pump. But then, through the confusion and dizziness and nausea, I also had to consider the fact that I was lying in her lap, just the two of us, and it was quite comforting, and if I was going to die, then this was the way to go, resting on the svelte thighs of someone I loved and not in some barely sterile hospital bed or on my face in the mud at the hands of Fritz and his paratroops.

'I love you,' I said. 'I really, really, really, really, really love you.'

She smiled down at me.

'And you're my best friend. And you're the best private eye in the business. We'll show them, we'll fuckin' show them.'

Alison mopped my brow with toilet roll. She said, 'You sang it for them. Now sing it for me.'

'What about Fritz?'

'Screw Fritz. Sing it again, Sherlock, sing "Lady in Red".'

I looked up into her red eyes and dark fillings. It was just the two of us, lost in music, on a bathroom floor, in

Banbridge. My voice was a dying rasp, but it didn't matter
— I knew that I would never be happier.

'*Lady in bed* . . .'

35

One should not take the loss of one's virginity lightly, but one should also acknowledge that no matter how meticulously one plans for it, those plans can be overtaken by circumstance, from fire, flood or hurricane to the shifting of tectonic plates or the application of large amounts of alcohol. One should not expect that the loss of one's virginity should necessarily follow in the wake of a white wedding, but may pre-empt it or precede it, or both. One's virginity is as priceless as a rare first edition of Poe's *Fall of the House of Usher,* but unlike the Poe, it can never be replaced. Also, unless you have the reading speed of Charlie in *Flowers for Algernon,* you cannot read a Poe in one and a half minutes, but you can lose your virginity in that time, from first fumble to sincere apology.

In case there is any confusion here, I am not talking about Alison's virginity.

Having herself been married, and being, and continuing to be, attractive, I had absolutely no doubt that she had divested herself of her virginity at some earlier point; I did not directly address the subject, nor indirectly; I took it as a given.

On the subject of my own virginity, rest assured, this is not *that* type of book. I simply believe there is no place for that kind of detail between hard or soft covers. It is an odd world indeed where one does not so much as blink as the serial killer carefully removes the skin from his victim in order to make a fashionable suit, but one can still blush to the core when anything goes on in that geographical area one might refer to as *south of the border*. Suffice to say that I did not expect fireworks to go off, but as I lay back, my head throbbing and my stomach still tumbling from the wine, I was a little surprised to discover that the price I was paying for the gift Alison had bestowed upon me was a mild form of tinnitus in my right ear, a perfect match for the constant *drrrrriiiiiing* I experience in my left. It was as though she had upgraded me from broken mono to broken stereo. It was only when this ringing in my right ear stopped abruptly thirty seconds later that I realised that what I was hearing was a phone ringing in the room next door, and my only thought then was that if I could hear the phone ringing so clearly, then what had whoever was in that room heard of our sex making?

We lay back on the bed, perspiring. The room was apparently on the top floor of the Beale Feirste Books retreat, although I'd no memory of getting there. I think Alison may have carried me. I could not remember removing my clothes. I think Alison might have completed that task as well. We lay in the semi-darkness, for it was very late, or very early, and the blinds were open, and the dawn was creeping towards us. I wanted to bundle her up and squash her down and carry her around with me in a pendant around my neck. That way I could take her out whenever I met an acquaintance or a stranger and say, 'This is my girlfriend, we've made love and all,' and they would pump my hand and say, 'Well done, old man, splendid performance,' and I would glow.

'Tell me about your mother,' said Alison, stroking my

arm.

'No.'

She gave me a little pinch. 'Go *on*. Tell me about your mum.'

'There's nothing to tell.'

'When you had your orgasm, you shouted out, *Thank you, Mother.*'

'I did *not*. What did you shout out when you had yours?'

She was silent on this point. I couldn't be entirely sure that she had shouted anything, because of the tinnitus. After a little while she said, 'You know, whenever I call your house, she never answers the phone.'

'She has an aversion.'

'The couple of times I've been to your house, she's never there.'

'She is, she stays out of the way.'

'Do you know something, I like you for exactly who you are. I wouldn't want to change you. I've had normal before.'

I pondered this for a little bit.

She said, 'If there's anything you want to tell me about your mother, then tell me.'

'There's nothing I want to tell you about my mother,' I said.

'Okay.' She kissed me on the forehead, and continued to stroke my arm. In a while I drifted off to sleep. For once I had a happy dream, about getting married. It would be just the two of us, in a register office. Obviously, what with the travel, there would be no need for a honeymoon. We could trawl Belfast's less smelly second-hand bookshops for rare first editions and order comics for Alison on-line. In fact, there mightn't be time for any of that: she was probably pregnant already. We had not used any form of protection. I am allergic to rubber. I presumed Alison was not, as they say, *on the pill*. That would have suggested an amazing amount of foresight, or lax morals.

Although, now that I thought about it, it was quite possible that her luring me to Banbridge had been part of a plan, that all along her interest had not been in trapping Fritz but ensnaring me. She had not warned Daniel of the renewed danger he was in, nor taken any measures to safeguard him. That was twice she had failed to take responsibility for protection.

I dozed a little before waking to the question of her really being pregnant, and whether that would then give our unborn child rights over No Alibis? What if those ninety seconds of debatable fun resulted in me losing control of my pride and joy? What if the two of them worked in tandem to asset-strip me at their earliest opportunity?

I had not shouted my mother's name out during sex. That was part of the plot to unsettle me. To make me doubt myself. I had to be on my guard *at all times*. There *are* conspiracies out there, the skill is recognising the real ones from the paranoid ones. Some of them are so glaringly obvious. One glance at Gregory Peck with his dyed black hair and overgrown Hitler moustache in *The Boys from Brazil* was enough to tip *everyone* off to the fact that he was a bad guy. But the secret of a good mystery is that while you suspect all along that it might be the *best friend,* you don't really know until the final chapter.

I woke up in full daylight and with another erection.

I could see how they could become habit-forming, but I willed it away. I have perfected this technique. My father taught it me. I no longer need the bucket of cold water or his strap.

Now the erection was gone.

But so was Alison.

A quieter version of the hubbub was back, this time gently vibrating through the house while the artists ate breakfast. I would probably never eat again. I rolled out of bed and held my head in my hands. I *needed* my medication.

You can miss those babies out once, but any longer and it really messes with you. I get the shakes. And I sweat. And my spatial awareness is not good. My palpitations run wild. My teeth ache. My sinuses tug at my brain strings. I needed Alison to run me home. We would have to rush through our Daniel debriefing, or return later, but I had to *go*. I was suffering withdrawal. I could become catatonic, or just as easily manic, or the one followed by the other, or in either order. I would also be car sick. I was not in a good place. The fact that I had lost my virginity was slim compensation, because I could not remember any of it, so in a sense I really had *lost* it, or it had been stolen, pickpocketed by an expert who even now was downstairs stuffing her face, and she would have no sense of shame at all. Perhaps the laughter drifting up the stairs was at my expense. Perhaps when I showed my face they would burst into sarcastic applause. The poets would compose an ode to my lost virtue, and the sculptress would fashion an erection in sarcastic tribute to me from Quaker oats and burned toast.

I struggled down the stairs, but in catching my breath on the first-floor landing I was more than relieved to spot Alison outside, walking by the lake. Though it was a bright summer morning she had her hands thrust deep into the pockets of her zipped-up jacket, and her head was bowed in thought. I had a sudden paralysing notion that her experience in bed with me had been so harrowing that she was walking the lake trying to compose a form of words that would not only let me down gently but also rid her of me for good. But she wasn't a master of words. She could much more easily have drawn me a picture, and how cruel would that be? I would throw it down in tears, and she would reclaim it and display it in a gallery. I would become the poster boy for bad sex. If it were me, I would just get in the car and drive off. But she was classier than that. She would even give me a lift home. She would say, 'We can still be friends,' when she knew it was a lie. She probably knew that I would make a doll of her and stick pins in its eyes and pass disparaging remarks about the provenance of her jewellery and arrange for someone who didn't suffer from vertigo to daub offensive graffiti about her on flyovers. And she didn't care, because she knew she could do better than me. Better than a one-third share in an independent bookshop. She had bigger ambitions. Like Borders.

I slipped out of the front door so as to avoid the catcalls of the kitchen. I hurried, as far as my hardening arteries would allow, after the object of my occasional affections and probable mother of my child. When I caught up with her, on the far side of the lake, she did not look up. I fell into step beside her.

'Morning,' I said.

'Morning,' she said.

'Did you have breakfast?'

'Yes. Scrambled eggs. They're in the bushes about a hundred yards back.'

'Morning sickness,' I said.

'I wish,' she said.

Further on, I said, 'If you want to get it over with, you should say it now. I understand. I'm used to it. Or, when I say I'm used to it, I'm not used to it, because I'm rarely in this position. In fact, when I say rarely, I mean never. I'm never in this position. But you should, nevertheless, get on with it. I have to get home. I have to get my medication. Say it now.'

'Say *what* now?'

'What you have to say.'

She stopped. She looked at me. 'How do you *know?*'

'I just know.'

'Okay then. You asked for it.' She took a deep breath.

Before she spoke, I cut in with: 'I wanted to thank you for last night, and apologise. I want you to know that no matter what happens I appreciate it and I'm prepared to give you any number of book tokens if you don't take the shop away from me and give me some sort of access to the child.'

She shook her head. 'You are *extraordinary.*'

'Sorry.'

'I think it's why I love you.'

I nodded. 'But . . .'

She screwed her face up. *'But . . . ?'*

'But . . .'

'Is that what you normally say when a girl tells you she loves you?'

I studied her. If you don't know people the way I know people, you might have taken her at face value. But I am wise enough to know that all protestations of love are merely in furtherance of a plot to achieve goals and rewards: you build them up and you knock them down; you encourage the mouse in with cheese, and then you decapitate it. She would not find me that easy to play. I knew every plot in every book. I could bluff with the best of them.

She said, 'Are you not going to say anything?'

'I love you too,' I said.

She smiled widely. 'Then give a girl a kiss.'

So I did.

Then after a bit she said, 'Sorry about the taste of boke.'

By our second lap of the lake, hand in hand, I was itching to go. *Literally* itching to go. I was going cold turkey, with side orders of fleas and shingles. Alison did not seem to understand. She seemed happy just to be alone with me in such congenial surroundings, which they *were not.* There were flies and bugs and stagnant water, which, with the onset of global warming, could at any moment give itself up to some new and untreatably malign form of malaria. There were trees swaying in the breeze that could snap on our heads and somewhere in the far distance the buzz of a chainsaw and *who knew* how many he had killed already? By this stage we were no longer alone. One of the poets had appeared almost opposite to us. The path around the circumference of the lake was not tremendously wide, but this poet, the American, had veered off it and was now crouched perilously close to the edge of the water — it was not deep, but it was murky, and there were fish, and he could easily have toppled forward and knocked himself out on a rock and drowned or been eaten, but nevertheless he reached out, meticulously chose several pebbles, then straightened and began to skim them across the water towards us with what I could only take to be some sort of baseball expertise and a blatant disregard for the obvious safety issues. He waved at us once, and I glared back. If one of his boulders jumped up and out of the water it could quite easily have caused a serious head trauma, leading to paralysis and a slow wasting away. It was needless gung-ho-ery, and it was a blessed relief when we finally moved out of range.

Alison squeezed my hand and kissed my cheek as we walked on, but before we'd gone very far the American disturbed us again by shouting from across the lake. I thought for a moment that the stupid fool had actually fallen in, for we could see that he was now up to his knees in the water. He was gesticulating wildly at us; as he did so he did actually lose his footing and went down on his arse; but almost as soon as he did he scrambled madly backwards until he was right back up on the path again, but he was still pointing and shouting rather incoherently. He was certainly upset enough for Alison to hurry along the path towards him - while still keeping a tight grip of my hand - and the closer we got the more we realised that far from causing a big fuss over nothing, as Americans will, there was actually something very badly wrong. It therefore seemed ridiculous to me that we were actually going *towards* him, when that something could very easily turn out to be upsetting or contagious or dangerous. We should immediately have gone in the *opposite* direction, to seek proper help, or at least sought safety in the branches of a tree. But no, Alison drew me relentlessly forward. The American poet, normally so eloquent, was now only managing to point and splutter. Despite having the kind of wide mouth and Mormon teeth that were perfectly suited to insincere smiling, he was grim faced and harrowed.

Alison let go of my hand. I stayed where I was, while she ventured forward to the side of the lake. Almost immediately she let out a small cry. But it didn't stop her. She stepped into the water, and waded out several feet. I could see now what she could see. There was something large and dark floating just below the surface. Alison glanced back at me. 'It's Daniel Trevor,' she said in a brittle voice. 'It's bloody Daniel Trevor.'

36

I did that rare thing, I listened. Poets, cops, kids, undertakers. I heard them all compare notes. Daniel Trevor had drowned. He had stumbled into the lake while drunk. Or he had thrown himself in while in a blue funk over his wife's disappearance. There were no obvious signs of a struggle, no suggestion yet of a suspicious death. There was a pointless ambulance, there was a reporter from the local paper, but it was cut and dried. Cut and *wet*. But it stank. Stank as much as Daniel did as he was dragged from the goddamn stagnant lake, already bloated, his dressing gown saturated, pondweed straggling from him, his hair dank, the poets supporting his body, shoulder high, as if carrying a mighty hero from the field of battle, his daughter on her knees in hysterics, his son standing stunned.

He'd been pissed. He'd been the paternal life and soul of the party. He'd *chosen* to go out this way remembered well, in the company of the artists and poets he loved, his children singing and dancing.

Brendan Coyle was supposedly the last man to see him

alive. He was still drinking at three a.m. when he saw Daniel pass by the kitchen door. He spoke to him, but the publisher didn't reply. The time struck a chord. Daniel's room was next door to ours. My phantom tinnitus was a phone call. I had checked the digital clock by our bed.

A call to lure him outside?

How difficult was it to drown a drunk and not leave a mark?

Not hard, I was sure.

Especially not hard if you were practised at it.

I knew this much about serial killers. That once they had the taste for it, they were insatiable. That where there might once have been months between killings, this soon reduced to weeks, and days. It was called *escalation*. Fritz had killed Rosemary some nine months previously, then there was a long gap before he started picking up speed. Now he was stacking them up on a daily basis. Rosemary, Manfredd, Malcolm Carlyle, Leather Trouser Man, and now Daniel Trevor.

Alison was really shaken.

I was *literally* shaking. It was mostly the medication. But also it was the jitters brought on by further proof, as if we needed it, that we were in terrible danger.

I said to her, 'We have to get out of here.'

'Why?'

'Because one of *them* might be the killer.'

'He drowned. They said he drowned. Which one?'

'I have no idea. Brendan Coyle.'

'You think?'

'I don't know. *Yes.*'

'You're sure?'

'No. But we have to get out of here.'

I was doing the math. A terrible expression, but appropriate. While we had made love, Daniel Trevor was being murdered. We should have been alert to the danger. I *knew* sex and death and evil were on a par. It had been drilled into me since I was a toddler by my father. You could trace it all back to Eve. My father despised his own weakness in being seduced by my mother. I think they only had sex once. I was the product. That's how it happens. Now I was about to produce an heir conceived in the shadow of murder. The math could, quite easily, in a pessimist, add up to 666.

Doors slammed, engines started. The poets and the sculptress and the screenwriter were all leaving. From the window of our room the lake looked placid. Water was the great life-giver, but it also took it away with surprising ease, leaving behind no trace.

No chalk outline on a lake.

No scene-of-crime tape.

Nor, so far, any DI Robinson nosing around. It was probably a different police division, but I was pretty sure that word would soon filter back to him wherever he was and it would become his business. We needed to slip away *now*.

'Alison, *please.*'

'I can't believe he's dead.' She was lying on our bed, where we had created Damien. 'Before I met you, I'd never seen a dead body. Now I've seen two. You sure know how to show a girl a good time.'

'I'm sorry.'

She shook her head. 'You look so sad. It's not your fault. Come and lie beside me.'

'We need to go.'

'Just for a minute. I need a hug.'

I lay on the bed beside her. She put her arms around me. She started to kiss me.

People deal with death in odd ways.

I got a crick in my neck turning to watch the road behind us as we drove home.

Home.

Where the heart is.

No Alibis.

'Don't you have to check on your mother?' Alison asked.

'She is self-sufficient.'

'Do you want my mobile to call her?'

'She wouldn't answer if she didn't recognise the number.'

Alison nodded. 'I wish I didn't have to go back to work, but I have to or I'll be fired.'

'It's okay,' I said. 'I'll be fine.'

She said the jewellery store was fitted out like Fort Knox. Maybe it was. But it was nothing compared to No Alibis. When I lock down, it's like *Panic Room*. I knew I would be safe inside, as long as I kept my defences in place. That meant not opening for the public. Profits would take a hit, but I was prepared to make the sacrifice. I needed my medication, doubles and triples of which I kept in the shop, and located at emergency depots around the city, and I needed time for it to work.

But mostly, I needed time to think.

I took my pills. I applied my lotions. I drank coffee. I sat at the till, lights off, the only glow from my computer. It was time to sort this case out. A cool appraisal of the facts. But every time I tried to address them, to assimilate, to establish patterns, my mind wandered.

All I knew about Fritz was that he was out there.

Time dragged. From time to time someone battered on the shutters outside. I had CCTV coverage. He or she *looked* like a customer, but how did I know? The whole world was threatening to turn Fritz on me. If I shouted, 'Closed for stock-taking,' someone would know I was in there. Even when Jeff turned up for his shift, I played dumb. If he was stupid enough to be in Amnesty International, then he was stupid enough to give me away to Fritz. Alison phoned half a dozen times. She was equally jumpy. Every time a potential client came into her shop she found a spurious reason to retreat to the storeroom at the back.

In the middle of the afternoon, DI Robinson banged on the No Alibis shutters. When he couldn't gain access, my phone rang. I let it, and he left a message. Give him a call. My e-mail went crazy. Customers demanded to know if I was shutting down for good and if there was going to be a proper sale. I did not respond.

Instead, I reapplied myself to the facts.

I went over everything I knew about the murders.

I examined my lists of car licence plates.

I became an expert on modern dance.

I knew everything there was to know about Auschwitz. I worked through the night and on into the next day.

If not for my brittle bones and poor circulation I could probably have gained a place at Anne Mayerova's former dance school based on my extensive research alone. Or I could have made a documentary for the Shoah Foundation.

But I was no closer to identifying Fritz.

I have often seen in movies journalists and writers falling asleep at their typewriters, and have always thought, how ridiculous, it's practically impossible, but that's *exactly* what I did. If someone had made a tracing of my forehead in the immediate aftermath they would have found the faint impression of a reversed *qwerty* appearing on their paper. It was partly the effort of my investigation, partly the lingering hangover. But mostly it was to do with the double dose of medication I'd taken to catch up.

When I woke nine hours later I could barely move my neck. I'd knocked the remnants of the Starbucks coffee across the counter and drooled extensively. There was a fresh flurry of angry e-mails waiting for me, including one from the late Daniel Trevor.

I stared at it for a long time without opening it. It had arrived during the night, but that didn't necessarily tell the full story Sometimes e-mail is instantaneous, occasionally it meanders around for days. He might have sent it to me last week, or on the day of his death, or he might have decided to send me some vital information seconds before his date with destiny. Perhaps he had identified the killer. He might even have sent it from beyond the grave. AOL's tentacles reach everywhere. I phoned Alison for advice. She was just getting up for work. She said, 'Ugghhh . . . Brian?'

I put the phone down.

She phoned me back. 'Sorry,' she said. 'What's up?'

I would have huffed for longer, but I was too worried about the e-mail. I quickly explained.

'Well open it!' she exploded.

'But he's *dead:*

'Yes he is, so open it.'

'But what if . . . ?'

'What if what?'

'What if it's actually from Fritz? What if I open it and there's some kind of automatic response which alerts him to the fact that I'm in here answering my e-mails and he firebombs . . . or what if there's some kind of virus that melts my computer, or melts *me?* Did you ever read Stephen King's *Cell?* If he can have mobile phones that cause their owners to murder—'

'Will you just open the fucking e-mail?'

I took a deep breath.

I double-clicked.

'Well?'

'It's from his son, Kyle.'

'Oh. Anticlimax.'

'He says the funeral's today and he hopes I can attend, and he's discussed it with his sister, and he intends to continue the publishing business and wants to go ahead with the launch of the dancing book. What do you think?'

'Fine, but for the funeral being today. Isn't that indecently quick?'

'I don't think so. Hindus do it as soon as they possibly can.'

'Was he a Hindu?'

'No, but if he was a Catholic, they do pretty much the same.'

'Hindus do it because they're generally in a hot climate, to stop the body going off. Why do Catholics do it so fast?'

'Gets them to the drink quicker, I suppose. Does it matter? It's today. You have to come.'

'I've had too much time off as it is.'

'I can't go alone.'

'Why not?'

What could I say? I have a morbid fear of graveyards, and funeral parlours, and the smell of formaldehyde, and shaking hands, and wreaths, and ministers, and pews, and coffins, and hearses, and undertakers, and people who show too much emotion, and people who don't show enough, and corteges, and walking behind a coffin, and being asked to lift a coffin, and wood, and dead bodies, and death, and soil, and inscriptions, and worms.

'I would appreciate the company,' I said.

37

Johnny Carson used to say that the annual Oscar show was two incredible hours wrapped up in a four-hour package. Much the same could be said of Daniel Trevor's funeral, except there were no trophies given out, unless you counted the urn after the cremation. It went on, and it went on, and it went on, with tedious musical interludes.

The Church of the Holy Redeemer off the Antrim Road was filled to overflowing. Because of Alison's insistence that she could only get off work at lunchtime, we were late arriving and forced to listen to most of it over loudspeakers outside. Another late arrival, but a little ahead of us in the crowd, with his back to us, was DI Robinson. There was a breeze, but it wasn't cold; there were clouds, but they weren't grey. The business of Belfast went on undisturbed while Daniel Trevor, after a career of publishing between hard covers, was dispatched between them himself.

They sang, Tell Me the Old, Old Story'.

Many references were made to the untimely nature of Daniel's demise, but there was no suggestion of suicide or murder. It was a tragic accident. He was described as devoted to his wife, but otherwise she was hardly mentioned. Occasionally there were heartfelt little gems amongst the eulogies, but it was mostly the poets who dominated and exploited the proceedings. Half a dozen felt sufficiently moved by the occasion to pen and perform pale knock-offs of W. H. Auden's 'Funeral Blues' and all that palaver about stopping the clocks, which did, almost, they were so insipid. While I knew that Daniel was a leading mover in the Northern Irish arts world, and a respected publisher, it seemed to me that most of those present were treating it as an opportunity to network. I would not have been surprised if deals were signed.

When the service came to its finale, the removal of the coffin for the drive to the crematorium at Roselawn, we watched with heads only slightly bowed. Kyle was amongst the pallbearers. So was Brendan Coyle. I was not intending to join the other men in walking for a short distance behind the coffin, but Alison pushed me forward. I moved uncomfortably amongst the black suits. There was a smell that fell halfway between cologne and embalming fluid. I wondered if one of the mourners crowding in around me was his killer. I wondered if he was behind me, beside me, ahead of me, if he was aware of me, if he was shocked or startled by my presence, or if he knew all along and was just waiting his opportunity to strike me dead.

As the mourners began to disperse, some to return to work, others to follow for a second short service at the crematorium, Alison slipped her hand into mine and said, 'That was sad.'

'Pointless,' I said.

'We were paying our respects.'

'We were exposing ourselves. It isn't safe, we should be more . . .'

And as if in answer to my fears a car pulled to a stop

beside us, just a little bit along from the church gates. It was a blue Jaguar with blacked-out glass. A rear window peeled down. Alison had already taken a fearful step closer to me, and I had taken one back and across so that I was behind her. At least if there was a gunshot I would be shielded from the full force of it.

'Mr Mayerova,' said Alison. 'Wasn't sure who it was, blacked out windows 'n'all.'

I moved to her side, flushed with relief.

'Dreadful business,' he said, 'young man like that.'

'Mr Mayerova,' I said. 'I didn't realise you were at the service.'

He gave a short smile. His front teeth were capped, but his gums had receded off them, revealing the yellowed roots of the originals. 'Old age and creeping infirmity have their advantages, I got led to the front. Nearer thy God to thee, *ja?*'

I nodded. He nodded. The Jaguar revved suddenly. I glanced at the driver: short back and sides, and one side of an angular profile.

'Patience, Karl, patience,' said Mr Mayerova, reaching forward to gently pat the man's shoulder. Karl did not look round, or react. 'I am sorry. My son is always in a hurry. Even at a funeral.'

Karl's eyes flitted towards me in the mirror.

And my blood froze.

'I called at your No Alibis yesterday,' said the old man, 'but it was closed.'

'Yes,' I said, my voice suddenly a dry croak, 'family illness.'

Alison's hand found mine again. She squeezed and it was as if we had formed a circuit of tension, flowing from me to her and back.

'I am sorry to hear that. Well, no matter, it was unimportant. I understand that the launch of my wife's book is to go ahead at your premises?'

I nodded.

'I was not sure of the . . . *appropriateness*? My wife is unwell, and with the passing of Daniel Trevor . . .' He waved a hand. 'Well, no matter. We shall be there.' He nodded at me, he nodded at Alison, then he reached forward to tap his son on the shoulder again. The window zipped up, the car revved once more, then smoothly turned back out into the traffic.

I stood looking at the personalised number plate.

Alison pulled at my hand. 'Did you see . . .?' she asked.

I nodded.

'It's too much of a coincidence,' she said.

I nodded again.

'He looks more like the mother than the father.'

I half turned to her. 'I'm sorry, what?'

'What did he call him, *Karl*? He's the dead spit of his mother, I should have recognised him."

My brow furrowed. 'What are you talking about?'

'What are *you* talking about? It's *Karl*. You notice he wouldn't turn towards me at all? But I recognised him straight off, very distinctive. Karl is the fella I told you about. The lovely and handsome customer who asked me out. He came into the store and invited me to dinner.' Her eyes were full and wide and still focused on the Jaguar, which was already just a distant speck. Her cheeks had coloured. 'Of all the jeweller's in the city, Mark Mayerova's son walks into mine, charms the pants off me and asks me out. What are the chances of that? Is that not odd? Is that not creepy? And not long after I turn him down, your van goes up in smoke with you inside it, for all he knows. Does that not turn your blood a little cold?'

'It does.' It had. 'But that's not what I was talking about. Did you not see the mirror, the rear-view mirror?'

'*What?*'

'Hanging from it, a Pine Fresh tree. Same make, same size, same colour as the ones on Malcolm Carlyle. And the Mayerova's family business is car dealing, no doubt with access to vast forests of Pine Fresh trees.'

We looked at each other.
'Fuck,' she said.
'Fuck,' I seconded.

38

In the trade, it's what we call a breakthrough. The private eye trade, that is. In the book trade, customers who don't whine about the weather would be considered a breakthrough. Needless to say, even though our new chief suspects had already disappeared from sight, we quickly made ourselves scarce. I was for returning to the panic room and not emerging until the next millennium; but Alison drove us to the NCP car park on Great Victoria Street and from there we walked to a Holiday Inn Express. I sort of hoped we might get a room, but instead she steered me into the lounge area to the left of reception and ordered coffee and sandwiches from a Pole.

While we sat and waited for lunch to arrive we said, 'Fucking hell,' quite a lot.

When the sandwiches were consumed, and my coffee ignored — it *certainly wasn't Starbucks* — we finally addressed the herd of elephants in the room.

'Mark Mayerova,' I said.

'And his son Karl.'

'The Pine Fresh tree.'

'If I'd gone out on that date, I may not have returned.'

'If you'd gone out on that date, we wouldn't be sitting here.'

'He would have murdered me.'

'*I* would have murdered you.'

'That's sweet. But I'm not sure you're capable of it.'

'You wouldn't like me when I'm angry.'

'I'm not sure I even like you when you're placid.'

'You love me.'

'Love is a funny business. He seems like such a pleasant old man.'

'A pleasant old man with a German accent, it's a bad combination.'

'There's nothing to say he's involved. It could just be the son.'

'You think about it, whoever is doing the killing has shown tenacity, and cunning, and ruthlessness. If Fritz wanted to protect the secret, he should have gone to the source first. Anne Mayerova. Security at Purdysburn isn't much more than some fat ex-lollipop men, he could have been in and out no problem. But not if it's his wife . . .'

'Or his mother.'

'Or them working in tandem.'

'I thought Karl was warm and charismatic, but did you see how cold he was in the car? He didn't even *look.* And me so pretty.'

'And his dad is so confident we haven't a clue what he's up to that he thinks nothing of cruising up to us for idle chit-chat, and all the time he has us marked for death.'

'He doesn't know who he's dealing with.'

'Neither do we. But we will.'

'You're sure about that?'

I nodded. I was sure. I could do facts. I could do internet. I could call on my database of loyal customers. Even, if all else failed, the Botanic Avenue Irregulars. The fear and alarm I'd felt on seeing the Pine Fresh tree hanging from the rear-view mirror had slowly evaporated and was now being replaced by a growing thirst for knowledge and a confident awareness that for the first time there was a realistic prospect of *The Case of the Dancing Jews* actually being solved, and on *my* terms.

'But now,' Alison said, 'I have to get back to work.'

'You can't. Not now.'

'I can. Right now.'

'But what if . . .'

'He won't. *They* won't. Not so soon after the funeral. We have a period of grace.'

Perhaps I had not explained *escalation* properly to her. But then I remembered that Fritz had so far attempted nothing in broad daylight. If he now chose to alter his modus operandi he would more likely come for Alison before me — she had recognised Karl, and he was quite probably aware of it.

'Okay,' I said, 'go back to work. But be careful.'

'And what about you, are you going to open the shop?'

I looked at her for a long time before nodding. It was hiding in plain sight. And I would also be able to keep an eye on her across the road. If they came to kill my Alison, it would at least give me time to make a run for it before they decided to cross the road for me too.

Jeff rode shotgun. Or rather, he idled on a chair by the door. He knew exactly who he was watching out for, because I'd given him printouts from the net. A few clicks had led me to Smith Motors, one of the largest car showrooms in the North, and they had several pages devoted to *meeting the staff*. There was a fairly recent photo of their retired founder, Mark Mayerova, one of a grinning managing director, Karl Mayerova, and one of his brother Max, chief sales executive.

I called Alison, and watched her come to the phone. 'I don't think it was Karl who asked you out,' I said. 'I think it was his brother. They're not twins, but they're virtually identical. That's why he didn't seem to recognise you.'

'Are you sure?'

'No, but it's a distinct possibility. And listen to this: *Every year Max travels to all of the great motor shows so that you don't have to, including London, Paris and Frankfurt, ensuring that you are the first to know about the latest innovations in the world of . . .* Did you get that?'

'Frankfurt. Do the dates match?'

'No. Not really. Frankfurt Motor Show is the biggest in the world, it runs until the end of September; the book fair starts two weeks later. But it establishes a familiarity with the area. If he was wanting to get rid of Rosemary, and he heard through his mother that she was going to Frankfurt, then what a perfect opportunity. Follow her there, get her alone, knock her off, slip out of the country.'

'Oh God,' said Alison, 'I'm all out in goose bumps.'

'Goose bumps is a misnomer. They only occur in mammals,' I said, 'so geese can't get them.'

'Shut up,' said Alison, 'and call me back when you find out more.'

She hung up. I could see that a customer had entered her shop, and at the same time Alison was disappearing into the strong room at the back, leaving another member of staff to deal with him. A few moments later I saw her peeking out before emerging back into the body of the shop. Despite her supposed period of grace, she was as nervous as I was.

Max Mayerova was the killer, then. Possibly in tandem with Karl. And perhaps under the command of their father Mark. Or individually, or any combination of the above. It still remained circumstantial, and coincidental, but many patriots have been put away for less.

The temptation once again was to call DI Robinson, but what if that only got me into even deeper trouble? I had no evidence. And I hadn't completely ruled out the possibility that he himself might be in with them. All you ever heard from detectives were complaints about the mountains of paperwork they had to do, yet DI Robinson apparently had the freedom to saunter around pretending to be a book–collector and having cosy chats with me in the middle of the night when all he really had to do was haul me down to the station for a grilling. He didn't seem particularly stupid, but with Malcolm Carlyle dead, the body in the No Alibis van and me sporting all sorts of bruises and lacking an adequate alibi, he still hadn't given me the third degree. What if the real reason he hadn't taken me in was that he was working for any combination of the Mayerovas and he didn't want there to be a record of the police investigating me? Who was liable to know more about killing people, a cop hardened on the streets of once troubled Belfast, or the owners of a car showroom?

So I wouldn't be handing *The Case of the Dancing Jews* over to the police any time soon. If DI Robinson was dirty, then I was certain that I would disappear for ever as soon as he got a whiff of my intentions. If he was dirty, perhaps he was laying off me for a reason. Maybe once he was in the employ of the Mayerovas, or any combination of them, he suddenly became interested in their big secret and thought he could squeeze it out of *me* in order to blackmail *them*. I can stand anything but pain, so I would give it up willingly at the first whisper of a Chinese burn, even though I still didn't know exactly what it was. However, since I had now identified the Mayerovas as certainly the source of the murders, I was convinced that their secret would soon follow.

I called Alison. I told her my suspicions about DI Robinson.

'You're barking,' she said. 'Phone me back *when you find something out.*'

She was right.

I had to focus.

Jeff, overhearing, said: 'All cops are dirty,' before adding: 'Are you going to marry her? If she talks to you like that now, in the first flush of romance, think how she's going to treat you once you're hitched.'

I thought about that for a moment. I had no better example than my own parents' troubled marriage. Father was trapped into wedlock and terrorised for forty years. He took his anger out on me, with a strap, and a stick, and a boot, and a large orange Space Hopper. But then again — Alison was nothing like my mother. Her barbs were playful, her putdowns came with a knowing smile, and I never had sex with my mother. Besides, Jeff was jealous of my success with women.

'Mind your own business, Jeff, and keep your eyes peeled for Nazis.'

For protection he had a hurly stick, which he wasn't sure how to hold, and my meat cleaver. He tutted, and muttered, '*Nazis.*'

I was convinced that the secret at the heart of *The Case of the Dancing Jews* had to be buried amongst the deportations, the death camps or the chaotic aftermath. It was about Anne Mayerova, her memory, her unwritten experience and the fear of what would happen if it ever was written down. Was it something she had witnessed, something terrifying she had experienced directly, someone she'd recognised? The events I had to investigate were more than half a century old, with most of the Holocaust survivors either dead or doting, and all I had to go on were two names and two numbers tattooed into their forearms. But it was a start. And this approach suited me better. I did not have to deal with living people, I did not have to interact, I did not have to travel, there was no requirement to charm or schmooze, I did not have to expose myself to their germs, their emotions, their black memories.

Just me.

My internet.

My determination.

I unpeeled a Twix.

I snapped a can of Diet Coke.

I sat down at my PC, determined not to shift until I had solved *The Case of the Dancing Jews.*

39

I have always known that if you stare at numbers or letters or a combination of them for long enough a pattern will emerge. In this case, *The Case of the Dancing Jews*, it took five days and nights. A tsunami might have drowned the rest of the British Isles, a bubonic plague might have destroyed civilisation, but neither would have moved me from my position. My panic room is watertight, and I have been inoculated against everything, including inoculations.

Jeff *shone*. Instead of his occasional shifts, he worked from nine in the morning until six at night *every* day with no prospect at all of additional wages. Even when one of his fellow travellers in Amnesty International beseeched him to attend a particularly emotive protest (I believe some Kenyan was being forcefully repatriated despite the fact he was good at basketball) he stuck to his lack-of-guns, insisting that my investigation, my plight, my stand against the forces of evil was much more vital. I salute him. He deflected customer enquiries, answered the phone, and all the time kept the meat cleaver and hurly stick close by. Before he left at night he repaired to Starbucks and purchased coffees in the *right order* and secured sandwiches from Subway before locking me in. When he came in the morning he insisted on leading me into the back yard for some fresh air. It would have been like giving a prisoner in solitary some much-needed exercise, except this prisoner had to be coaxed out and once there was immediately desperate to return to his cell. I knew the solving of *The Case of the Dancing Jews* was within my grasp.

Alison, being a femme fatale, did try to lure me away on several occasions, but I remained sure and steadfast. She pecked my cheek and sent erotic e-mails, at first, but in the last couple of days merely stood in the shop during her lunch break and watched me. I caught her conferring with Jeff several times. I knew they were worried about the intensity of my investigation, that such concentration could not be healthy, but I also knew it was the only way to do it. I think, perhaps, that she also felt a little bit left out. I did not share what I was or was not learning, I did not divide the research or assign her a task. I couldn't. It was all going on in my head. *My* head. That's where the circuits were.

On the third day, Alison said, 'Should I call on your mum?'

'No, she's fine.'

My eyes did not leave the screen. I was scruffy and stubbly and smelly and sweaty. The bags under my eyes were the size of used teabags. And I knew more about Auschwitz than any sane man should.

'I don't mind. She might appreciate the—'

'Leave her be.'

'I'm only trying to—'

'Please . . .'

When I happened to glance up twenty minutes later she was gone.

Jeff, looking sullen, said, 'She's pissed off with you. You keep treating her like that, she'll walk for good. You should send her some flowers.'

I returned my attention to the screen. Alison would walk anyway. It was inevitable. I did not subscribe to the *treat 'em mean, keep 'em keen* school of romance because I did not subscribe to *romance*, full stop. I found flowers depressing and I was allergic to most of them.

'Do you want me to send . . .?'

'No. Leave it.'

He left it. I worked on through the night. She did not come across at lunchtime. Jeff gave me a *told you so* look, but said nothing.

I focused to the exclusion of all else.

Apparently, later that day, my Botanic Avenue Irregulars came into the shop and demanded money. Jeff punched one and wrestled the other to the ground before throwing them both out and I *did not even notice*.

Five days, five nights.

And then, at about five o'clock on the morning of the sixth day, my Eureka moment.

Suddenly the pattern stood out like a 3D image on a 2D screen.

I punched the air and danced around and opened another Twix. I had a big wholesale box of them. It was the breakthrough I'd been searching for — perhaps not the final solution, but the beginning of the end. Now I could focus. The players were all still in the field, but there was a growing clarity. At that moment all I wanted to do was tell Alison, I wanted to see her little face lighting up when I showed her how I had worked it out, but it was still so early and I was dog tired. Jeff had made up a little cot for me in the kitchen, which I had barely used, but now I crawled into the sleeping bag and closed my eyes. I thought if I got a couple of hours' sleep, then when he arrived to open the shop I could pop home for a shower and a change of clothes. I could take Alison out for a special breakfast by way of apology for ignoring her and she would forgive me because she knew my work was important, and then when I told her how I had cracked the case she would collapse into the arms of the genius and kiss me passionately.

Except, of course, that when I finally opened my eyes and checked my watch, it was nearly closing time again. I stumbled into the shop, shouting at Jeff and scaring rare customers away.

'I thought it was better to let you sleep,' he said weakly.

He was a moron, but loyal.

'Has Ali . . .?'

He shook his head. Across the road the lights in the jeweller's winked off and a moment later Alison and her manager emerged, locking the doors behind them. The manager walked off; Alison lingered. She glanced once towards No Alibis, then quickly away.

She was hurting, and huffing.

But as soon as I told her, everything would change.

I yanked our door open and hurried across the footpath. I was crumpled and rancid, but it wouldn't matter. I waved, but she did not see. I called, but a rumbling Ulsterbus drowned it.

Then she moved to the side of the road, and I saw her smile, and knew everything was right again, but for all of a second, because the smile wasn't for me, it was for the man getting out of the red Ferrari with the personalised number plates.

It was for Max Mayerova.

I was staggered. *Stunned.* Frozen to the kerb. Alison. My Alison. With Max Mayerova. One of the killers. Or *the* killer. My immediate and inevitable thought was that somehow they were in league together, that it had all been a massive plot to get *me*. The Second World War, the Holocaust and the dancing Jews were all created in order to manoeuvre me into a position where I could one day be annihilated by the forces of evil. I was the custodian of some unknown universal code. Everything revolved around me. For countless generations my enemies had been spiralling closer and closer and I had been aware of it all along without ever quite being able to put my finger on it. By my investigating *The Case of the Dancing Jews,* my galactic enemies had realised that they were about to be unmasked and had decided to call all of their agents to a secret meeting, but in the midst of their panic they hadn't been careful enough and now I had spotted two of them, supposed enemies, slipping off to plot my downfall.

Then I thought, no, that's bollocks.

Alison wasn't *in league* with them. She was hurt by my rejection and being the wilful, wonderful, stubborn pixie that she was had decided to show me exactly what she was capable of. She was meeting Max Mayerova in order to trap him into revealing himself as the killer or part of a killing team. She had made repeated efforts to get through to me, but I was so caught up in my own investigation that I hadn't realised how desperate she was to help. She was putting herself in the line of fire for *me.*

I could not allow it.

I had a sudden, God-like revelation, there and then, on the kerb, Botanic Avenue, Belfast, 5.15 p.m. of a sunny Wednesday, that she was the one for me, that all the barriers I had sought to put up, all the doubts and dismissals, all the anger and jealousy and paranoia, all those years of hate, were suddenly behind me. She was mine. She loved me. She may or may not already have been the mother of my child; but if she wasn't now she would be, and soon. All I had to do was stop this naive, lovely fawn from being carried away to her doom by a murderer. His Ferrari was already nosing out into the traffic.

I did the only thing I could.

I ran after it.

Despite my knees and arteries and heart and blood and ulcers and tumours, I charged along the footpath, pushing home-bound workers to one side, dodging prams and shouting, 'Alison! Alison! Alison!'

But to no avail.

Max was too quick, and the traffic too light.

A taxi pulled in at the far end of Botanic Avenue; a man in a monkey suit got out. *Literally* a monkey suit. Any other time it would have freaked me out, with his fake monkey hair and fake monkey features but *human* eyes, but he meant nothing. I jumped into the back seat of the taxi and snapped, 'Follow that car!'

The driver, a rotund man in a frayed shirt, glanced laconically back. 'Sorry, mate, I'm booked.'

'No!' I exploded. 'You have to *follow that car!*'

He looked ahead. 'Which car?'

'The red one. The Ferrari. *Please.*'

'I really am boo—'

'I'll pay double. Triple. Whatever it takes.'

He raised an eyebrow, and smiled. He put the car into gear and pulled out. 'That's what I hate about taxi drivers,' he said, 'they're so fucking unreliable.'

Despite the fact that it was a Ferrari, Max Mayerova was still inhibited by rush-hour traffic from showing what his car could do. Or perhaps he had no need to. He wasn't aware that he was being followed, and he had Alison exactly where he wanted her. He thought she had no idea who he was. He thought she was tangled in his web. I knew Alison was smart, but I didn't know if she was as smart as Max. Bodies were piling up and there was nothing to connect him to any of them.

Or there hadn't been.

The taxi driver's eyes occasionally flitted to me in the mirror, but he said nothing. He could, if instructed, have drawn level with them; he could have honked his horn and I could have gesticulated at Alison to *get out of the bloody car.*

Max Mayerova intended to kill her. I knew that absolutely.

But I did not tell him to draw level.

I told him to pursue, but at a distance.

There was still that part of me that wanted to watch,

and see, the voyeur.

What was Alison planning? How would it pan out?

After about fifteen minutes, though it was just over a mile in the heavy traffic, the Ferrari pulled into a side street on the far side of the Victoria Centre, and from there made its way into the Cathedral Quarter. The city now has a lot of these quarters, certainly more than four. I hate planners who mess with numbers like this. How are you ever supposed to see patterns when they don't adhere to the basic laws of mathematics?

Get over yourself.

Focus.

Your loved one.

Up ahead.

In mortal danger.

The street was cobbled and bare of parked traffic, so we were immediately more obvious. But still, just a taxi, en route to somewhere. The Ferrari disappeared into an alley about two hundred yards along. We slowed as we passed. It was jutting out of a parking bay a little bit up, and Alison and Max were climbing out.

'Go on past, slow,' I said.

There was just enough time to see them move towards a doorway; it was the rear entrance to some kind of commercial premises.

We turned the corner and I counted along to where I supposed the front of the building was: a restaurant called Comanche. I instructed the taxi driver to pull up just a little short of it. I now had a perfect view of two tables sitting in the large bay window, to one of which Alison and Max Mayerova were being shown.

Menus were distributed.

Wine was ordered and delivered.

I could see Alison's face, but not Max's. She seemed to be smiling a lot.

The taxi driver said, 'Meter's running.'

'That's fine.'

Big glasses of wine. A toast.

The driver said, 'Do you want to tell me what this is about?'

'No,' I said.

'Only if you're some sort of nutter and you're intent on murder or you're stalking someone, it could rebound on me.'

'I'm not a nutter,' I said.

'And if you don't mind me saying, you look like you've been sleeping outdoors and you're a bit ripe and I wouldn't be surprised if you didn't have a penny to your name.'

'I have money,' I said.

He nodded. He rolled the window down. He lit a cigarette. 'So is it your wife and this slick wanker in a Ferrari?'

'Something like that,' I said.

'Happened to me, except it wasn't a Ferrari, it was a Volvo. She was easily impressed. You just going to watch, or are you going to go after him with a wheel brace?'

'It's more complicated than that.'

'Because I have a wheel brace.'

'No, it's fine, honestly.'

'One whack, he'd be down. But then you'd have to do her as well. Chuck it into the river, they'd never find it, it'd be their word against ours, and they'd be brain-damaged.'

'No, really.'

He looked at me in the mirror again. 'That's good. See, I used to be in law enforcement.' He took a draw of his cigarette. 'Well, to be absolutely accurate, it was just enforcement. Debts and kneecaps, back in the good old bad old days, you know what I mean? Back then the cops never caught anyone, but these days they'd be all over you like a rash. I don't need that. Meter's still running.'

'It's fine,' I said.

An hour passed. Food was served. More wine was drunk. One bottle. Two. My driver grew fidgety. He told me about the last wise guy who'd stiffed him on a fare, and how he wasn't out of hospital yet. In fact, in my rush to leave No Alibis I had neglected to lift my wallet, and my keys, and my mobile, or any form of identification. Growing up, I had been aware of the local tradition of *doing a runner,* but under these circumstances it would have been laughable. My charge up Botanic Avenue had been my equivalent of an Olympic marathon; even someone as round as my taxi driver would appear as nimble as a gazelle up against me. He would squash me like a bug.

'Well, would you fucking look at that?' he snapped suddenly.

'What?' I leaned forward. Worries about my long-term health had shifted my focus away from the restaurant window. I could see Max sipping his wine; but the seat opposite him was empty. *'What . . . ?* Where'd she . . .?'

'Did you not see it? She got up, probably away to the ladies'. Soon as she was gone, he picked up her glass, turned to the window so the other diners couldn't see, put something in her bloody drink.'

'Seriously?'

'Swear to God. Like a powder. Swished it around. The fucking scumbag.'

I nodded enthusiastically. 'The fucking scumbag.'

'What do you want to do? You want me to call the peelers?'

I shook my head.

'You fucking wise?'

'We have to see what happens.'

I was being inclusive. He seemed to thrive on it.

'The fucking, fucking scumbag.' I could see the pulse beating rapidly on the side of his head. He looked back at me. 'I know what you're thinking, she's made her bed, now she can lie in it.'

Alison returned, all smiles. She drank. Dessert was served. She drank some more.

She was giggling an awful lot. Then she was resting her

head in her hands, still nodding at him across the table, but definitely affected.

'She's certainly a looker,' the driver said. 'So was my wife. From a distance. Up close, not so hot. Up close, she looked like someone had punched her, though I never did. But fucking drugging someone, that takes the biscuit.'

Alison reached for her glass again, and knocked it over. She was all apologies. She was in tears. He reached across and held her hand.

I seethed.

Wheel brace, wheel brace, wheel brace, wheel brace . . .

'He's one fucking smooth cookie,' said my driver.

Max paid the bill. They got up. Max helped Alison on with her coat. She staggered. They disappeared from the window. My driver, without waiting to be told, reversed the car back to the alley entrance and turned in. He sped along past the parking bay where Max's Ferrari was still sitting, with a black Laguna now alongside. He pulled into an open and empty double garage, expertly turned the car and sped back down the alley, stopping just short of the bay, so that we were idling like any other taxi for hire by the time Max and Alison emerged from the rear exit.

Alison could hardly stand.

She clung on to Max. Then she threw up.

The taxi man looked back at me. 'What are you waiting for? You're not going to actually let him go through with it?'

I shook my head. My hand was on the door handle. I could be upon them in seconds. I loved her. I loved her deeply. But I still didn't quite move. What if Max had a gun? If he was exposed now, in the midst of carrying out his latest murder, and particularly by me, then surely he would take his opportunity to finish us both off? Was there any point in us both dying? I was *defenceless*.

The taxi man gave me an exasperated look. 'If you're not going to, I'll bloody—'

'Wait. Look.'

The driver's door of the black Laguna had opened, and a huge man in a too-tight leather jacket and black jeans emerged. I thought that maybe he wanted to help, and that it might be instructive to see how Max reacted to him. They exchanged words while Alison threw up again. But then the new guy suddenly took a firm grip of Alison's arm with one hand and opened the back door of his own car with the other. He quickly bundled her into the vehicle, slamming the door behind her, before nodding across at Max and jumping back into the driver's seat.

'What the fuck?' said my taxi driver.

'What the . . . ?' I said.

The Laguna reversed out of the bay and moved past us. As it did, I ducked down.

'That son of a bitch,' said my driver incredulously, 'that son of a bitch has drugged her and now he's fucking passing her on to someone else. That's fucking trafficking! Can you fucking believe that?'

Ordinarily, no.

In this case, absolutely.

40

I wasn't sure at what point Alison's captor realised he was being followed. Most likely, it was a gradual thing. It was a fine summer's evening but traffic was light, making it more difficult to keep ourselves hidden, particularly because the driver ahead of us did not seem to be absolutely clear of where he was going. He stopped several times, and appeared to be examining street names, and then particular houses. He would reverse, and peer out, and then circle. After a while, and perhaps noticing us mirroring his every move, he appeared to change his mind and began to drive out of the city.

Out on the open road, though, there was no hiding place for us. The car ahead began to increase in speed, and we kept pace. When we hit a stretch of dual carriageway, Alison's captor overtook quite recklessly. But there was also a curious politeness to it. He indicated when he moved into the fast lane, and then he signalled again to move back. My driver did the same.

We passed through East Belfast, through Sydenham, on to Holywood, then veered off the dual carriageway and up into the Craigantlet Hills. The road became narrow and twisting, ditches and hedges on one side, stone walls and sharp drops on the other. My heart is usually in my mouth whenever I go over speed bumps, and here we were literally taking flight on certain humps, yet I seemed immune.

My driver drove with his window down and his elbow resting half out. The fucking monster isn't even taking her home!' he raged. 'He's taking her out into the country, he's going to kill her, he's going to bloody kill her and dump the fucking body! Well we'll see about that, we'll see about that!'

We were going so fast that the wind was howling in, carrying with it pollen and germs and bees. Yet I did not sneeze once. Even a few days ago I would have been traumatised — a *speeding* car, bugs, open spaces, trees, cows, fleas, ploughs, wheat — but now none of these perils seemed to be impacting on me. Perhaps there was a long-overdue sea change going on in my physiology, a kind of post-pubescent puberty in which long-held intolerances were suddenly vanquished.

Or I was just quietly slipping into a coma and my senses were dulling.

Or adrenaline.

Or love.

I'd never had love. Maybe that was what it did for you. It turned you around and made you less frightened of wasps. Maybe Chris de Burgh had it. Maybe he had also been afeared of trees and bushes and wildebeest until he found love. Or maybe it wasn't the finding of love, but the fear of once having found it, it being taken away that changed you. Taken away, stolen away, *murdered*. The way my Alison was being taken by this monster. The Creature from the Black Laguna. She was lying sick in the back seat, unable to help herself. She had to rely on someone else to save her, her hero, her prince; a flawed prince who had to overcome previously insurmountable obstacles like pollen to rescue her. I had to step up and be counted.

Meanwhile, my driver *rocked.*

Now that the chase was acknowledged, now that it was *official,* he kept on her captor's arse. Bumper to bumper at *speed.* More than once we scraped along a dry-stone wall, several times we narrowly avoided death by coming blind over a rise and almost smacking into a slower-paced truck or tractor.

And then, when we came upon a long, straight, downward stretch, Taxi Driver upped the ante. Another two minutes and we would be off the hills and into built-up Dundonald where our chances of losing him in traffic would immediately multiply. I could see it. *He* summed it up more succinctly by crying, 'It's now or fucking never!'

He pressed the pedal to the metal.

He sped up beside the Laguna on the wrong side of the road.

For a hundred yards we raced side by side.

Then my driver suddenly threw his vehicle to one side, knocking into the Laguna on the front right–hand side with just enough force to push it off course and send it crashing through a farm gate and careering across a field of sprouting cauliflowers.

My driver screeched to a halt.

He reversed at speed.

He turned into the field and gunned the motor towards our enemy. Vegetarian shrapnel sprayed up all around us.

The Laguna had come to a halt about a hundred metres in, its front wheel buckled and useless.

'Now we fucking have you!' my driver shouted as we skidded to a stop parallel to the driver's door. He sprang out with surprising agility. 'You get *her,*' he snapped, 'leave him to fucking *me!*'

He hurried around to his boot and yanked it open. He removed the wheel brace. The Laguna's driver's door was just starting to open, but my driver struck first, smashing through the window and braining the creature at the same time.

'You fucking sick fucking fucker!' my driver yelled.

I walked across to the Laguna and pulled the back door open. Alison was lying face down on the seat; she had been sick everywhere. She groaned. I dragged her out and she flopped down into cauliflowers.

'Please . . .' she mumbled, 'just leave me . . . just let me lie . . .'

I pulled her and I prodded her until she managed to get to her knees. She threw up again. I got her under the arms and whispered encouragement in her ear and she told me to *fuck off and leave me alone,* which wasn't the reaction I wanted but was a good indication that she was still Alison, that I wasn't losing her. I grabbed her under the arms and dragged her back to the taxi. All the while I heard a kind of a slapping sound; it sounded like Sylvester Stallone beating a side of frozen beef in *Rocky.* The monster would not look very pretty by the time my driver was finished with him. He might not even be alive.

I preferred not to look.

I faint at the sight of blood.

One advantage of coming down off the Craigantlet Hills was that the Ulster Hospital was literally only a few hundred metres away. It meant we were there in seconds rather than minutes, especially with the way my man drove.

We pulled up in the emergency parking bay. My driver looked back at Alison, and then at me. His face was sprayed with blood. So was his shirt. And his hands. He looked like he'd had a bath in an abattoir. He was smiling. He was clearly insane. Yet he had saved my girl's life.

'That'll be sixty-seven pounds sixty,' he said.

I stared at him.

He stared back.

Alison groaned.

My driver winked. 'Only rakin',' he said. 'You couldn't

pay me for *that!* Like a walk down memory lane! Get her in
there, get her sorted.'

He put his hand out to me. It was thick with blood, and
mud, and cauliflower, and a tooth was sticking out of one
of his knuckles. I grasped it nevertheless, and we shook.

I never knew his name.

He never knew mine.

It was the world we moved in.

The taxi drove off. I settled Alison on the kerb because
she couldn't walk, and rushed in to the casualty
department and returned with a nurse and a wheelchair. I
told her that Alison was my girlfriend and that someone
had spiked her drink and she rolled her eyes.

'Are you sure?' she asked. 'Because ninety-nine per cent
of women who come through here saying their drinks have
been spiked are just pissed.'

'I'm *sure,'* I hissed.

I followed her through the swing doors. I tried to avoid
breathing. I did not wish to pick up bugs. Hospitals were
the home of MRSA and *C.difficile,* and those were just the
ones with bad press agents. There were thousands more
that would kill you as soon as look at you. Hospitals were
greenhouses for bugs, superbugs, and super-superbugs. My
huge intake of medication was no protection; all they did
was reduce the effectiveness of my immune system.
Walking into the Ulster Hospital behind Alison's
wheelchair was like signing my own death certificate.

Yet I did it.

She was helped on to a bed. I gave as many details to
the nurse as I could, and then the locum doctor tried to
ask her some questions. Her responses were largely
incoherent. She had hold of my hand and wouldn't let go.

Instead the locum asked me what had happened. I told
him her drink had been spiked.

'Are you sure?' he responded. 'Because ninety-nine per
cent of women who come through here saying their drinks

have been spiked are just very drunk.'

'*Yes,*' I said, 'I'm *sure.*'

'You do seem sure.' He nodded. 'Do you happen to know which one - GHB, ketamine, roofies?'

His clear implication was that if I knew for sure she'd been drugged, then I was responsible for it.

'No,' I said, 'I have no idea. Just . . . fix her.'

He raised an eyebrow. 'Well,' he said, 'there's a simple enough test.' He plucked one of her hairs. 'I'll send it for analysis; in the meantime let's see what we can do to make her more comfortable. If she has been . . . *spiked* . . . it could be eight . . . maybe twelve hours before she's on her feet again.'

'But she is . . . she is going to be all right, isn't she?'

The locum gave me a long look. 'That depends,' he said, 'on whether she's been spiked or not.'

I could have throttled him.

Or, more likely, not.

I just shook my head and looked back down at my love. She was already asleep. And yet her grip had not loosened one iota. If the superbugs showed similar determination, I really was screwed.

41

There were no beds to be had elsewhere in the hospital, not because they were overcrowded, a big fat nurse gleefully told me, but because half a dozen wards were closed due to a *C.difficile* outbreak. So Alison remained on a curtained-off bed in A & E while I moved between a red plastic seat by her bed and the waiting room. Several times I approached the Coke machine but backed away because the thought of all the sick fingers that had pressed its buttons made me feel ill. That and the air-conditioning and the smell of disinfectant, which, clearly, wasn't strong enough. The locum doctor I'd seen did not return to update me, and every time I re-entered Alison's cubicle nurses looked at me suspiciously, apart from the big fat one who seemed to think I was quite cute. She was probably out of her head on purloined drugs.

An elderly man in a dressing gown and slippers sat down beside me in the waiting room, despite there being other chairs. I immediately felt uneasy. What if he collapsed and I was forced to give him the kiss of life? No, in fact, nothing would force me to give him the kiss of life.

He could lie there until someone else noticed. I'd done all my saving for one day.

He said, 'Everything all right, son?'

'Yeah, fine.'

'You don't look fine. Waiting for someone?'

'Yeah.'

'I've a bed here in casualty because everywhere else is full, but there's no bloody TV. So I sit out here, annoying strangers.'

I nodded.

'Do you want a nut?' he asked. He offered me a plastic bag. 'My daughter brought them, but I don't like nuts.'

Ordinarily I would have told him to catch a grip, but I hadn't eaten since God knows when and I was starving. My mother used to say, 'You're not starving, people in Africa are starving. You're just hungry.' But no, I *was* starving. She knew nothing about Africa. I looked at the bag. I have been cursed with every allergy under the sun, except for a nut allergy. Ironic, you might say.

'What's wrong with you?' I asked.

'Slight stroke. Number five.'

Strokes, I thought, were not contagious. I took the bag. I opened it and put one of the nuts in my mouth. It tasted of nut, with something extra, quite sweet.

I was on my third when the paramedics came rushing in, pushing a trolley with the Creature from the Black Laguna on board. My locum came shooting out of another set of doors. He briefly examined the Creature's bloodied and bashed head and immediately instructed the paramedics to bypass A & E and to take him directly to theatre. The locum gave a slight shake of his head as the trolley zoomed away and in turning made eye contact with me. Briefly. He disappeared back through the doors.

The stroke victim said, '*He's* not long for this world.'

I nodded. And thought: good riddance.

I went to hand the bag of nuts back to the stroke victim, but he shook his head and told me to keep them.

When I stepped back into Alison's cubicle, the fat nurse was just finishing changing her drip. She smiled warmly on her way out. I sat down. I ate a nut. I closed my eyes. I wondered what the taxi driver would say to his wife when he walked through the door covered in blood. If he went directly to his next customer, the customer would climb in one side, and immediately climb out the other.

I drifted.

I was holding Alison's hand when she made a sudden lurch, which woke me. I glanced at my watch: three hours had passed. She blinked groggily, then looked around her, clearly disorientated. She focused on me, then away and back. 'Where . . . where am I?'

'It's okay. You're in hospital. You're safe.'

'Safe? Hospital? What's going on . . . where . . .?'

'You're all right. Max Mayerova slipped you a Mickey Finn.'

'Mickey . . . who?'

'He put something in your drink. GBH, Kitekat, roofties

'I don't under

'He spiked your wine, he took you outside, he handed you over to someone else, someone who was going to kill you. I followed, I got you back

She looked lost. 'Wine . . .? I remember, I remember . . . the restaurant

'I saved you.'

'No . . . no . . .'

'Yes, really

'No . . . you didn't . . . *no* . . .'

'He can't harm you now, sweetie, you're safe with me . . .'

'No . . .'

'You really are.'

'No . . . Brian, where's Brian?'

Oh *fantastic*. My moment of triumph and the bloody ex

266

is once again her first thought. I had given her everything, or some small part of everything, and she had slapped it right back in my face. Christ. She had absolutely no idea which side her bread was buttered.

NO.

Wait.

I should give her time, space. She'd just woken up, she was still drugged, she was rambling. About *him*. They must have spent a lot of time together. Having sex. It was ingrained. It was none of my business.

Alison squeezed my hand. 'Please, where is he?'

I grunted. I poured her a cup of water from a jug a nurse must have left while we were sleeping. Ice cubes plonked down into the plastic cup. I hoped the nurse had been wearing disposable gloves. Alison drank it down greedily. When she was finished she handed me the cup and pushed herself up into a sitting position.

'I feel strange,' she said.

'Of course you do.'

'But I've missed you.'

That was more like it. 'I've missed you too.'

'But you wouldn't talk to me. You wouldn't tell me what you were doing. That wasn't fair. That wasn't nice. I thought we were partners.'

Never partners, but it wasn't the time or place. I was constantly surprising myself - now I was self-censoring. I cupped my other hand around hers and patted it gently. I judged that she was now compos mentis enough to hear my news. My double whammy. Cracking the case *and* saving her life.

I was some pup.

'Alison

I paused for effect, but she leapt in.

'I didn't want to go behind your back,' she said, 'but you excluded me. I got angry. I wanted to show you what I was capable of by myself. That's why I arranged to meet Max Mayerova.'

'It was stupid and foolhardy,' I said, 'but also brave.'

'It was one of the most exciting things I've ever done.'

'If I hadn't been following you, you might be dead right now.'

She shook her head, and then looked woozy for several moments. She took a deep breath. *'No,'* she said softly, 'it wasn't like that . . . please believe me . . . I knew he was involved in the murders, do you think I was going to go out with him all alone and keep it a big secret? How professional would that be?'

Not very. *For a jeweller.*

'You mean you left a note or—'

'No! For goodness' sake! I was never in any danger.'

'He *drugged* you.'

'I half expected it.'

'But what if it had been poison and you'd *died?'*

'I knew he wouldn't do that, or I guessed, or I supposed. He couldn't have me dropping dead on the table, and anything that was slow release would mean a possibility of escape and being able to finger him before I died. No, I pretty much guessed he'd find something just strong enough to knock me off my feet.'

I stared at her. 'This isn't a game, Alison, he drugged you, he passed you along to his killer friend and—'

'No. It wouldn't have happened. Brian was there to protect me.'

'He . . . *what?'*

She smiled sympathetically. 'Oh look at you, such concern, you're so sweet, but really, I was perfectly safe.'

'Tell me that bit about Brian again.'

'He's just so dead on. Even though I can't live with him, he's always there for me. Look, I would have wanted you to be there with me, or watching over me, but you were incommunicado, so I arranged with Brian to follow Max's car, and then to phone me at a prearranged time. I used the excuse of a family emergency and Brian came by to pick me up. And good thing he did, because I could hardly stand.'

'It was very kind of him,' I said.

'Well if you were watching as well, then I was in several pairs of very safe hands. But you must have seen him. Black Laguna?' I kind of nodded and shrugged at the same time. Alison yawned extravagantly, and for several moments seemed to forget where she was in the story. 'Oh yes . . . he came and got me . . . put me in the back seat, but I was so out of it I couldn't tell him where I was living now . . . I was very groggy . . . he must have given up on me and decided to take me back to his place out in the sticks . . . and . . . and . . . that's where it gets a bit hazy. You said you saved me, but I was with Brian . . . did he bring me here? Or did you go to his house . . . did something happen there? I'm confused, I can't . . .'

'You need to rest,' I said. 'Plenty of time to explain in the morning.'

Alison nodded vaguely. She nestled back into the pillow. 'Rest . . . yes . . . but don't go away.'

'I'll be right here,' I said.

Here, or Bolivia.

42

I sat in the waiting room, nervously chewing my nuts. I was unsettled, I was anxious, but I wasn't to blame. Brian was in the operating theatre, for all I knew fighting for his life, simply because Alison had made the cardinal error of not letting anyone know that she had dragged him into *The Case of the Dancing Jews*. Absolutely *nothing to do with me*. He had been attacked by a taxi driver who had probably watched *Taxi Driver* too often. Brian was the unfortunate victim of friendly fire. Now that I thought about it, I was surprised by his size, and couldn't understand how, if she now had me as a lover, she could ever have been attracted to someone of his proportions. Maybe all women go through a phase of loving brawn over brain. In my few brief glimpses of him I had deduced that he didn't have the intelligence to tie his own shoelaces. The problem of course was that now he probably never would.

It was typical of life in general that at my very moment of triumph, when I should have been carried around shoulder high for cracking the case and overseeing the vanquishing of a villain, it had been snatched away from me. Instead of luxuriating in righteousness, in the victory of good over evil, I was sitting in a hospital waiting room chewing on an old man's nuts and worrying that my bloody handshake with the mental taxi driver meant that Brian's DNA had transferred to me and could thus tie me to what some cynical cop would doubtless consider to be attempted murder. Vigilantes have never gotten a good deal from the forces of law and order. They object to being shown how it should be done. I shook my head despondently. It was amazing how quickly things could change. One moment a nodding acquaintance of *I, The Jury*, the next it was *Me, The Scapegoat*.

The elderly stroke victim came back into the waiting room, spotted me, and despite my deliberately looking away when we made eye contact, shuffled across to sit beside me.

'Still here?' he asked.

'Yeah,' I said.

I sighed. I offered him his bag of nuts back.

He shook his head. 'Told you, don't like them. The chocolate was nice, though.'

'Sorry?'

'I sucked the chocolate off them and put them back in the bag. I hate to see anything go to waste.'

I nodded for several moments, then stood up wordlessly and hurried to the toilets, where I threw up.

I stayed in the cubicle for an hour. He might as well have injected me with his phlegm. For all I knew I had caught diabetes and emphysema and malaria and clots. The MRSA and *C.difficile* I'd already picked up were probably complaining about the overcrowding. I was dying. I was Frank Bigelow in *D.O.A.* I would walk into the cop shop and say, 'I want to report a murder.'

'Who was murdered?' they'd say.

'I was.'

Except I wasn't the victim of some criminal conspiracy.

I had been done down by old-man dribble.

Or had I? Maybe it was a conspiracy. What if he'd been sent in undercover to poison me? Why had he picked me out when there was any number of casualties he could have slipped his sucked nuts to? Max Mayerova had tracked me down to the hospital and come up with a devilishly fiendish method of killing me. Brian wasn't the assassin, it was an old man in a tartan dressing gown. He was Hyman Roth in *The Godfather: Part II,* on the surface a harmless old septuagenarian, in reality a ruthless Mafia boss.

I rested my head against the cubicle wall. I was sweating profusely. It was impossible to tell if it was just the aftermath of the throwing up or the poison at work. I might have twenty minutes left to me to pass on what I knew about the case, or the rest of my life.

What if, even as I sat there, Hyman was in Alison's cubicle, smothering her with a pillow?

I staggered out of the toilet and back out into the waiting room.

There was no sign of Hyman.

Panicked, I hurried back to Alison — and was relieved to find her sleeping peacefully. I collapsed back down into the chair by her bed. I studied her. She had rocked my world in a most unexpected manner. I thought about how things might have turned out if I hadn't had the support of my psycho taxi driver, if it really had been a killer instead of her ex-husband, if he had managed to lose me outside of No Alibis and her reckless attempt to prove her worth as a private detective had led her nowhere but a cold, hard mortuary slab.

There had been a lot of murders, but I had been quite detached from them. This attempt on Alison was different. This time it was personal. Just because she was still alive did not mean the end of it; there would be another attempt, and another, until everyone involved in *The Case of the Dancing Jews* was eliminated. If nothing was done, things would continue to *escalate*. I had already proved that the pen, the *keyboard* in fact, was mightier than the sword by cracking the case, but just because I knew, it didn't mean the guilty were going to throw up their hands in surrender; the information had to be passed on, and considered, and judged, and they had to be brought to justice. In the meantime, unless I came up with some means of transforming myself into a ninja in a few short hours, we were sitting ducks.

I needed help.

I needed to overcome a lifetime of mistrust and invest in someone with the power to make things happen.

I returned to the waiting room and crossed to the payphone. I punched in the numbers. I remember most numbers I have ever used. It was answered on the third ring.

I said, 'I'd like to speak to DI Robinson.'

'One moment, please.'

As I waited for much longer than *one moment* my eyes roved across the rows of chairs containing the fractured, the walking wounded, the dangerously drunk and the badly beaten survivors of a typical Belfast night, before coming to rest on a figure standing leaning against a pillar with his arms folded, watching me intently.

'DI Robinson,' I spluttered, 'how the bloody hell did you manage that?'

He said I was a stupid, stupid man and I had no idea what I was dealing with, and I countered that I wasn't a stupid, stupid man and I had a very good idea of what I was dealing with, I just wasn't equipped *to* deal with it and anyway there was a reasonable chance that he was up to his neck in it and his concern was a facade and a smokescreen and he'd actually been sent here by Max Mayerova or his dad or his brother to finish me off, and he said: 'What the fuck are you talking about?'

And I gave him a look that said, *You know.*

And he gave me a look that said, *What the fuck are you talking about?*

'I'm hauling your arse down to the station,' he growled.

'I'll never get there alive,' I said.

'What fucking planet are you on?' he asked.

'Similar planet to you,' I replied, 'but not as dirty.'

'Are you *on* something?'

I glared at him. Fact was I was *off* something. Everything. Once again I had missed my meds. I was sweating and itchy and the lights were too bright and I was being slowly poisoned by an old man's sucked nuts and might expire at any time and then Alison would be defenceless. I *had* to tell him, I *had* to trust him, there was nobody else to turn to. But I still . . . couldn't . . . quite.

'How did you even know I was here?'

'Because a doctor reported you for administering Rohypnol to a helpless young woman, enough to near as dammit kill her, and your name cross-referenced with my investigation and so I was called from my nice warm bed.'

'And here you are, all alone,' I sneered. 'How come you always travel in ones?'

'Cutbacks.'

I raised an eyebrow. He just kept looking at me. The stroke victim came wandering back in and sat in his usual chair. DI Robinson moved closer to me and lowered his voice. 'Because everyone else told me to let it go, there's no connection between any of these deaths, we have bigger fish to fry. But I know there is. So it's kind of my hobby.'

'Like collecting crime fiction.'

'So you sussed me out. *Whoopy-woo.*'

We glared. First ten seconds I can handle anyone, after that I'm like putty.

'I didn't murder anyone,' I said.

'Did I say you did?'

'You're implying.'

'Am I? *Did* you murder someone?'

'No.'

'Did you slip your girl roofies?'

'No, sir, I did not. But someone did.'

'And you know who it was?'

I nodded. 'Do you?'

'Would I be standing here if I did? Listen, beam back down to us, son, and we might be able to get this sorted out.'

It really was time to choose. It really was time to trust.

'Okay,' I said. 'But on my terms.'

He rolled his eyes. 'Why the hell should I care about your terms?'

I folded my arms and looked at him. After a while, and without further progress, I said, 'Okay. But do one thing for me. Then I'll tell you all about *The Case of the Dancing Jews.*'

'The . . .'

'Get some of your uniformed chums down here to stand guard over Alison.'

If I was about to take a long walk off a short pier I wanted there to be a record of it, some paper trail that said he was here and he was involved.

He thought about that for several moments before nodding. 'This,' he said, raising his mobile phone, 'had better be worth it.'

'It will,' I promised. I nodded towards the curtained-off cubicles. 'I'm going to say goodbye to her.'

DI Robinson sat down two empty chairs up from the stroke victim while he waited for a response on his phone. 'Don't be long,' he called after me.

'I won't.' I nodded back at his new neighbour. 'And watch out for the nuts.'

'I always do,' he replied.

43

I was once encouraged to attend a salsa class by Mother. She thought it would help me to experience social interaction with people who were not obsessed with 1940s pulp fiction or serial killers. But people who suffer from irritable bowel syndrome should not attend salsa classes.

When I come to power, all forms of dancing will be banned, especially salsa.

Naturally I shot down Alison's suggestion that we have some kind of dance performance at the launch of Anne Smith's *I Came to Dance* with the ruthless efficiency of a Jap on a whale cull. She argued that it would help to lull our targets into a false sense of security; I argued that much the same could be achieved by a few bottles of Concorde and a sausage roll. I won that particular argument because it was my shop and my rules. If any kind of inspirational performance was going to take place in No Alibis, then it was going to come from me. God knows I spent long enough setting it up, and learning my lines, and joining the dots, and rehearsing it all.

It was the day of reckoning.

Or, in fact, the evening of reckoning.

The evening of closure, and justice.

To get there, there was a bit of bargaining involved. When a squad of uniformed cops arrived at the Ulster Hospital to guard my loved one, when Brian came through surgery with flying colours, when I realised that for all his solo investigations DI Robinson knew virtually nothing, when I understood that he had never had the faintest notion of trying to frame me for any of the murders, I knew that the ball was very much in my court. I could have volunteered everything I had discovered during the course of *The Case of the Dancing Jews* at any point during the eight hours he kept me in a cold police cell without access to a lawyer or Twix, I could have given it to him all at once or drip-fed it one sentence at a time. But I held out. Of course it was vital that the bad guys be brought to justice, but it was also important that the glory wasn't stolen away from me. I wasn't in it for the glory, but if there was some glory to be distributed then I was bloody sure I was going to get the lion's share of it, having done the leg work, having suffered the outrageous slings and arrows of being pursued by Nazis, and having worked my fingers to the bone tracking down the truth over the information superhighway. DI Robinson had done nothing but look a bit furtive from time to time.

Also, I had a girl to impress.

DI Robinson got really quite angry at my decision to withhold my evidence until the night of the book launch. The longer I held on to it, the more difficult it would be to mount a successful prosecution, the more likely it was that DNA evidence relating to the murders would degrade, the more opportunity there was for those involved to flee the country or concoct an alibi. But I wasn't for shifting.

Agatha's many thousands of novels may be considered to be ridiculously old-fashioned, but the dame certainly knew how to wind up a plot. These days it's all SWAT teams and torture porn. Back then all she had to do was get all the protagonists into one room, present the facts, and then sit back and wait for the fallout. I saw no reason why, with proper undercover police protection, I should not reveal my findings in a similar fashion. Of course times have moved on, and too much talk can be confusing or put you to sleep, so I decided to present my revelations by way of a PowerPoint demonstration.

DI Robinson, my lovely Alison, and Jeff were 'in' on the fact that something was going to happen, but I was the only one who actually knew the details. Alison besieged me for information, but after the trauma of trying to tell her about my triumphs in the hospital I decided that once bitten, etc. and to keep it to myself until the big reveal. DI Robinson demanded it, but he was in no position to apply pressure. Jeff didn't seem to care one way or another. I loaded the images on to my laptop and rehearsed the presentation alone, projecting it after hours on to the bare back wall of No Alibis, with me safe in my panic room and also secure in the knowledge that there were uniformed cops on duty outside. I had twenty-four-hour protection. I was important. Alison also had protection, but not as much. DI Robinson even offered to extend it to my mother, because if the bad guys sensed that something was up, they might try to get to me through her. They might kidnap her and send her fingers through the post to me one at a time as a warning. I told DI Robinson not to bother investigating until they got as far as her thumbs. You need your thumbs. They are one reason cats can't make omelettes. Besides, Mother was well capable of looking after herself.

Thankfully Alison showed no ill effects from her experience with Max Mayerova. Incredibly, he sent her a bouquet of flowers and a note saying he hoped she'd recovered from her food poisoning, and he felt terrible about taking her to such a dreadful restaurant, and he hoped she would give him a second chance and soon. He had *no idea*. The fact that he sent them to the jewellery store, on the very day she finally returned to work, showed that he was still watching and waiting. It sent a little chill down both our spines. Alison brought the flowers across to show me and I immediately raged at her about the possibility of them being sprayed with deadly poison. She said, 'But Interflora delivered them,' and I said, *'Exactly.'*

I was still giving her something of a cold shoulder. I was absolutely and totally in love with her, but she had to *learn* that my emotions were not to be toyed with. She had betrayed me by going behind my back with Brian and Max, and it would take a lot of effort on her part to regain my trust. She certainly worked at it, mostly by throwing herself into the organisation of the launch party for *I Came to Dance*. I was glad of her help, for I have had very little experience of parties, having never had one as a child or been invited to more than a handful as an adult. My knowledge of choosing cakes, or chairs, or drinks, or canapés was negligible, and my knowledge of book launches even smaller. One of the many benefits of Northern Irish terrorism is that for more than thirty years there was an almost total lack of locally produced crime fiction. There was just too much distracting baggage to squeeze in. There was no such thing as an ordinary common or garden murder, it always had to do with this organisation or that, or one religion or another. There was never a simple *body in the library*, there were multiple body parts of multiple people blasted all over footpaths and the sides of buildings. There was just something about the sheer horror of it all that turned writers away from even attempting to chronicle it within the confines of the mystery fiction genre. There was also a very definite lack of interest from readers: if you walked out of your front door in the morning and there was a British soldier crouched with his rifle in your front garden, the last thing you wanted to do was read a crime novel in which a British soldier was crouched with his rifle in your hero's front garden. If people wanted to read crime fiction they generally wanted to escape to somewhere exotic, and that meant American authors, and when they found they had exhausted the so-called big names in the Main Street stores, they would go searching for alternative sources and eventually come across the nirvana of No Alibis. So the Troubles were actually great news for me, and I mourned their passing, because business was never as good again. However, this total lack of local authors meant that I was virtually never asked to host book launch parties, and thus I had to rely on Alison's greater experience to pull it all together while making sure to offer her only the occasional scrap of encouragement.

The first copies of *I Came to Dance* arrived on the morning of the party. I flicked through it rather disinterestedly — after all, that evening's event wasn't really about the book, it was about me, and what I had learned. All of the players had been invited and I was reasonably certain that they would attend. If any of them cried off, citing a migraine or a prior engagement, it would have deflated the whole carefully conceived and orchestrated denouement. Having to say 'so and so can't be with us tonight, but I would like to accept this murder charge on his behalf' would have been rather anticlimactic. The book itself was presentable enough, but I tried reading the first chapter and found it to be as dull as dishwater. Although prior to his unfortunate murder Daniel had provided me with a list of the leading lights of the dance community he wished to invite, and those invitations had in fact been sent out, in the few days immediately preceding the launch I had to go through the list again uninviting many of them. It is not a huge shop, and I had to make sure there was room for all those who were involved in *The Case of the Dancing Jews* and that they could be comfortably seated, not squished in with dozens of suck-cheeked former hoofers. There were some irate calls, but Jeff dealt with them, with only the very minimum of swearing.

Jeff and Alison were tasked with greeting the guests, while I prepared myself 'backstage' in the kitchen. They were as nervous as I was. I had to warn them several times about overindulging in the wine. I abstained completely. I didn't want it reacting with the antidepressants, or the antiepileptics, or the antipsychotics, or the antihistamines. I had several Starbucks lattes lined up, which I sipped one after the other. It was my way of chilling, like transcendental meditation, with added milk. As each guest arrived, Alison or Jeff made sure they received a glass of wine and were subjected to a high-pressure sales pitch. I had to shift books *before* I gave my little talk, because there was no knowing what sort of chaos it might descend into later. When one of our major players walked through the door, Alison popped her head into the kitchen to update me and I duly marked off his or her name on my mental list.

DI Robinson was one of the first there. He stood at the back watching everyone like a hawk. Every time I peeked out at him he was pushing himself up on to the balls of his feet, and then dropping down again, and then going up again, as if trying to fool anyone watching him into thinking that he was a former dancer recalling his glory days *en pointe*, whereas what he really looked like was an undercover cop with scratchy piles. Daniel Trevor's children, Kyle and Michelle, arrived, and apparently made noises about taking over the meeting and greeting, but were quickly distracted by the wine and thereafter busied themselves with making sure their father's final publication was properly displayed. Brendan Coyle arrived in a very smart and expensive-looking suit, and appeared disappointed to discover that the shop wasn't packed with nubile young dancers. The American poet who had discovered Daniel's body came in, already quite drunk. Brian, Alison's ex, came in on a pair of crutches, and with his head all swollen up. I had my reasons for inviting him, and was quite prepared to forget that he had had sex with my wife-to-be and that he had tried to implicate me in an attempted murder by hurling himself repeatedly at a wheel brace. Garth Corrigan, the banker for whom I'd solved *The Case of the Missing FA Cup*, arrived, all smiles, with his rediscovered love May holding his hand. Garth was one of half a dozen former clients whose services I'd called upon to help me solve the case. Another was Jimmy Martin, the graffiti-artist son of a dead graffiti artist, who came in rather sheepishly, not ever having been in a bookshop before; I'd traded his community service redecoration of my shop for something infinitely more useful.

As seven p.m. approached, Alison entered the kitchen, closed the door all but a fraction, and pressed her pale face to the tiny gap.

'What is it?' I asked.

'Max Mayerova. I saw him crossing the road. I couldn't just stand there and give him a glass of wine like nothing had happened. He tried to kill me.'

'You're safe with me,' I said.

She looked at me. 'I know that. Although you are a shit-magnet.'

'Thank you,' I said. I nodded at the door. 'He's not alone, is he?'

'No, the brothers are either side of the old man, helping him in.'

'Good. Excellent.'

She came across to me. She put her arms around my neck. 'I'm proud of you,' she said, and kissed me.

'Why? I haven't done anything yet.'

'But you will, and you'll do it well.'

'Do you think presenting my evidence in the form of a narrative poem is a good idea?'

'No,' she said.

There was no spotlight, no drum roll, not even a

microphone, just a low makeshift stage made out of the bases of two packing crates, a laptop, and a bare wall to act as a screen. As I emerged from the kitchen, the hubbub from almost fifty dancers, publishers, friends and murderers was considerable. They probably hadn't even noticed the soundtrack to the evening's proceedings, which was just high enough not to be subliminal: Talking Heads singing 'Psycho Killer', Elvis Costello's 'Watching the Detectives', Itzhak Perlman playing the theme from *Schindler's List,* plus Captain Sensible's version of 'Happy Talk', just to confuse anyone who was listening and looking for patterns.

I stood by the laptop and waited for silence to fall. And waited. I wasn't even *noticed* enough to be ignored. Eventually Jeff hammered a spoon against a wine bottle and shouted, 'Ladies and gentlemen, silence please, for a few words from our host, a man who needs no introduction.'

He left it at that, when an introduction was *precisely* what I needed. A build-up. Perhaps even a support act. There were no lights blinding me, but I blinked nevertheless. Sweat dribbled down my forehead. My pacemaker ratcheted and clanked. I have never been one for standing up in front of a crowd or even for myself. I was an internalist standing in the brogues of an externalist. I had my speech memorised, but forgotten. I had my pages before me nevertheless, but my eyesight was suddenly blurred. If I hadn't so recently met a stroke victim I would have thought I was having a stroke. My eyes settled on Mark Mayerova, sitting with the privilege of age in the front row. Max sat on his left, then there was an empty chair, and then there was Karl. With every other borrowed chair in the room taken, it seemed odd, until I suddenly realised that the empty chair was meant for the only major player who wasn't there, whom we had never expected to attend, Anne, Mark's ex-wife, the dancer and author herself. He had deliberately left it empty in tribute to her.

Touching, if I hadn't known what I knew, and had the knowledge of knowing what I knew; and knowing that he didn't know that I knew the knowledge that I knew gave me a renewed resolve to do *this*, to face my demons, and present my case.

That and seeing Alison smiling encouragement from the sidelines.

'Ladies and gentlemen,' I said, my voice now firm, and grave, my eyes focused, 'I want to welcome you to No Alibis and this reception to mark the launch of the first and probably last book by Anne Smith, the doyenne of modern dance in Northern Ireland.' There was an appreciative buzz amongst those in the audience who had a clue who she was. 'Hers is indeed a remarkable story.' I held up a copy of *I Came to Dance*. 'Unfortunately very little of it is contained within these covers.' The buzz grew deeper, and more urgent. 'Bear with me now, please, as I explain to you *The Case of the Dancing Jews.*'

44

'Bookselling is hard, ladies and gentlemen. It's relentless. The books just keep coming. Beans don't change, peas are peas are peas, but books are always evolving. There's bugger-all profit, the hours are extraordinary and the shoplifters are stupid, because you can just borrow the bloody things from the library. You can't borrow beans.'

I studied them. They studied me.

I nodded. 'No, sir,' I said, 'you can't borrow beans.'

Several guests, unfamiliar with my ways, glanced to the door, as if realising that they'd been hooked by a free sausage roll into attending a three-hour time-share sales pitch. Others, on more familiar territory, waited for me to get to the point. The Mayerovas never took their eyes off me.

'We do it because it's a labour of love,' I continued, 'we do it because we think it's important. And *here*, we do it because we like to champion the underdog, the bastard outcast of literature we like to call mystery fiction. I often say, give me a young man uncorrupted by the critics, and I will make him a crime aficionado for life.'

Alison cleared her throat. Feet shuffled. DI Robinson rose and fell.

I was not to be deterred. This was my time.

'I have made a lifelong study of crime fiction. I have read all of the great works, and most of the middling ones, and many of the minor ones, and a lot of trash besides. There is virtually nothing about the solving of fictional crimes that I do not know, and what are fictional crimes but factual crimes with hats on? It seemed only natural to me when, a few short months ago, I was asked to help solve a real-life mystery that I should combine what I have learned about crime as a reader, and human nature as a bookseller, in pursuit of a solution to a fiendishly difficult case. Since that first triumph I have investigated many mysteries that previously had confounded the forces of law and order, and there is not one that I have not solved. But my most testing case, my most harrowing, and without doubt my most dangerous, walked through these very doors just a matter of days ago and it concerned the man whom, together of course with our esteemed senile author, we have come here tonight to pay tribute to: Daniel Trevor.'

I pressed the miniature PowerPoint button in my hand, and a picture of Daniel Trevor appeared on the wall behind me. There were a few hushed *oooohs* from my captive audience. And they *were* captive. One of DI Robinson's undercover comrades had locked the front doors.

'Daniel Trevor . . . *murdered* last week.'

This got a bigger reaction. As did the next picture, which I immediately clicked up beside Daniel's.

'Manfredd Freetz of the Bockenheimer publishing company and a business colleague of Daniel Trevor's - *murdered* in Frankfurt.'

The hubbub increased. And again with the third photograph.

'Malcolm Carlyle, private eye, employed by Daniel and

murdered shortly thereafter, right next door.'

Although I did not look at them directly, it seemed to me that only the Mayerovas were failing to react to my revelations.

I clicked again. 'This is Terry McIvor — an innocent young car thief, hideously burned to death because he was mistaken for me.'

There were groans of horror, because the photo I put up *was* horrific. I had been unable to get a photo of Terry McIvor as he *was,* but some bright spark from his immediate neighbourhood had taken a photo of the burned corpse on his mobile and posted it on the internet even before poor Terry's family were informed of his death.

'Four murders, ladies and gentlemen, and that's without even mentioning the fate of *Rosemary* Trevor . . .' She appeared on screen, beautiful, right next to her husband. 'Daniel's wife, who remains missing presumed dead almost a year after she went to Germany on business connected to the *very book* we have come together to launch here this evening.' I looked up at the photographs for several long moments of silent contemplation before turning back to my audience. 'These deaths have all been made to look as if they might have been accidents or from natural causes or suicide. But none of them are; they are *murders,* murders carried out to protect a secret that has lain dormant for more than sixty years but which I can reveal here *tonight.'*

My audience gasped. I nodded around them, allowing my eyes to flit to Mark Mayerova for just long enough to establish that he was looking right back at me, and that he was neither shaken nor stirred, but cool, even relaxed, or at least he was striving to give that impression. His hand was clasped tight around his walking stick, the knuckles showing white.

'But I'm getting ahead of myself.' I clicked the PowerPoint button and a photograph of Anne Mayerova as a teenage dancer appeared on the wall just as the other murder victims disappeared. 'The author, one of the photographs from *I Came to Dance*. Shortly after this was taken she married Mark . . .' I nodded down at him. '. . . in Prague. Unfortunately no photographs of the big day have survived.' I clicked again. 'This is an artist's impression of how they must have looked . . . love's young dream. The drawing is by one of our finest young artists, who is here tonight . . . Alison, take a bow.' Alison smiled bashfully as most of the audience turned to look at her. 'Alison is also the author of a series of graphic novels and comics that are available here in the store.' I indicated the relevant area. It is always important to take advantage of such gatherings to try to shift stock. 'Back in Prague, meanwhile, conditions were deteriorating, with the Nazis in control and all Jews being forced to register for deportation. These two young lovers were about to be sent away, first to the ghetto at Terezin and from there, in the spring of 1944, to Auschwitz. Here they were eventually separated into the male and female camps. Anne herself was possessed of an incredible survival instinct and a spirit that would not be quashed. Even in the midst of the horror of that death camp, she found a way to dance.' I clicked on to the next picture. 'Yes, ladies and gentlemen, it is a little-known fact that even in Auschwitz . . . and in this artist's impression, again by our esteemed friend Alison, we can really appreciate how uplifting it must have been for those poor dying souls to see a truly great dancer perform.' I allowed them to think about that for a little bit before continuing. 'Remarkably, where millions died, both Anne and Mark survived the war and actually made it home to Prague under their own steam, arriving within hours of each other for a joyous reunion — which we see *here* . . . another masterful depiction by Alison.'

I beamed at her again, but she didn't seem quite so happy. She made an odd kind of face at me, jutting her head forward and screwing up her eyes, which I took to mean *get on with it*. But there would be no hurrying. It was important to explain the background.

'However, they found it difficult to settle in Prague, and with the Communists coming to power, they very quickly decided to move on. They had some obscure family connection here, so this is where they came, to our Belfast, which at the time must have seemed like a smart idea. They were determined to blend in and so changed their name to Smith. Mark set up the company we all know today, Smith Motors, while Anne turned to education, teaching dance both at a girls' secondary school and also in her spare time. Her success with this led to her forming her own dance school — and the rest, as they say, is history, all of it exhaustively chronicled in *I Came to Dance.*' The front cover appeared on the wall behind me, and was followed by a succession of photographs at regular intervals showing Anne with her students. These provided a changing background, calm and understated, while I delved further into dark matters. 'But you are no doubt wondering, how do we get from this lovely, copiously illustrated, value-for-money book to murder most foul? Well, ladies and gentlemen, it has all to do with Rosemary Trevor's accidental discovery that Anne had been in Auschwitz. Although it was not a secret, she had never publicised the fact, and in fact, somewhat bizarrely, made no reference to it at all in her memoir. Rosemary immediately realised that this was the *real* story, and attempted to get Anne to write it all down. From this moment on, her fate was sealed.' I nodded around the gathering. 'You see, certain persons knew that if Anne wrote in detail about what she knew, and particularly because her mental health was beginning to fail, she might forget herself and reveal the secret she had been keeping all of these years. What the killer or killers couldn't know was whether Anne had already revealed it, or exactly how much Rosemary knew. They decided that even if Rosemary or the people she spoke to didn't yet understand the significance of what they had heard, nevertheless they had to be eliminated. That's how important it was to them. At first this was just Rosemary herself, and then to play safe Manfredd as well — but once Daniel Trevor assigned a private investigator to the case, Malcolm Carlyle, and he began to uncover some of the background, he too became a target. After Malcolm was dealt with it all went quiet until Trevor, frustrated by lack of police progress, decided to employ, well, *me*. And that was really when things started to escalate.' I again nodded gravely. 'So what was this secret; what was so important sixty years after the fact, when most of those involved must surely already be dead, that so many murders had to be committed to keep it hidden?'

It was what we know in the trade as a rhetorical question. No hands were raised.

'Well,' I said, 'I visited Anne Mayerova and heard her story in her own words. I went over and over it in my head, but still couldn't decide what there was in it that was worth going on a killing spree for. And then one of our esteemed guests here tonight unwittingly gave me the clue that enabled me to solve *The Case of the Dancing Jews*. In fact, when he first walked into this store I thought he might actually be the killer — the clipped, efficient manner, the German accent — but then I relaxed totally when he reached up to lift a book down from one of my shelves and I saw the Auschwitz number tattooed right there on his arm.' I nodded down at Mark Mayerova. 'Perhaps you would care to . . . ?' I indicated my own arm. Mark Mayerova shook his head. 'Of course. This gentleman, in fact, introduced himself as Anne's husband Mark, and told me he'd come to thank me for taking the trouble to go and visit his wife in Purdysburn. It was only much later when I sat down to examine the facts of the case that the penny finally dropped. You see, I had jotted down the number tattooed on Anne's arm when I saw her, and I did the same for Mark. I'm like that with numbers. It's a little hobby of mine. I like looking for patterns. There are all kinds of patterns. You can find them anywhere. Not just numbers, but in tiles, and trees, and stars, and . . .'

My eyes fell on Jeff. He was shaking his head. I took a deep breath.

Concentrate.

'You see, as soon as I had those numbers, they just fascinated me, I had to know everything there was to know about them. I became obsessed by them. I learned that during the Holocaust, concentration camp prisoners received tattoos at only one location — Auschwitz. At first these were sewn into their prison uniforms, and then only for those who were selected for work details, not those going directly to the gas chambers. But so many were dying that there was no way of identifying the bodies after their clothing was removed, so the SS began to tattoo the bodies of registered prisoners in order to identify who had died. In the spring of 1943, the SS authorities throughout the entire Auschwitz complex adopted the practice of tattooing almost all previously registered and newly arrived prisoners, including female prisoners. In order to avoid the assignment of excessively high numbers, they introduced new sequences of numbers in mid-May 1944. This series, prefaced by the letter A, began with 1 and ended at 20,000. Once the number 20,000 was reached, a new series beginning with B was introduced. Some fifteen thousand men received B-series tattoos. Are you with me?'

Most of my guests had come to hear about Irish dance, and here they were stuck in the middle of the Holocaust. Some looked horrified, some looked blank; others were bored and playing with their mobile phones. But those directly involved were clearly fascinated.

'The point, my friends, is that when I saw Mark Mayerova's tattoo, and jotted the number down, I didn't give it a second thought. But as I looked into the history of Auschwitz, trying to define what the secret might be, it came to me that given the dates when Mark Mayerova was a prisoner there, his B-series tattoo could and should have been anything up to 15,000, so how was it that his number was actually B17007? The B numbers *didn't go that high*. Was it some kind of clerical error, perhaps?'

I looked down at Mark. No flicker of a reaction.

'Mmm,' I pondered. 'Germans, Nazis, not otherwise known for slipshod work. So, intrigued, I began to look a little more closely at Mark Mayerova, and of course that's not an easy thing to do, because the Nazis were aware as the war ended that they would be in deep, deep shit when it came out what they'd been up to in the camps. They did their level best to destroy whatever records they had. But some were ferreted away and over the years they've turned up here and there, and actually there's been a lot of competition between different organisations to get hold of them, organisations whose main purpose is to make sure that we never forget the Holocaust. It's kind of a friendly rivalry. I turned first to the International Tracing Service, which has managed to accumulate some fifty million pages of records. After that I consulted America's National Archives. Then on to several foundations in Israel. I had it confirmed, and reconfirmed, that a man answering to the name of Mark Mayerova died in Auschwitz in 1944. And there it is.' I clicked on the PowerPoint, where Mark Mayerova's name, and Czech origin, were very clearly listed on a photostat of a typewritten document. 'So how is it that Mark is still with us, here tonight? How did he miraculously escape? Have you anything to say, Mark?'

All eyes were upon him.

When he spoke, he was calm and collected. 'This is *preposterous.*'

His son Max suddenly jumped up and pointed an angry finger at me. 'Is this some kind of a joke? What the hell are you—'

'Just sit down.'

It was DI Robinson, up on the balls of his feet, speaking quietly but firmly. He moved a hand up to scratch his head, and in so doing, and quite deliberately, his coat fell open to reveal the holstered gun at his side.

'Let the man finish,' he said. 'You'll get your turn.'

Max glared at him. Karl leaned across and whispered something in his father's ear. The old man never took his eyes off me. Max reluctantly retook his seat.

I nodded at DI Robinson. 'So anyway,' I continued, 'I thought to myself, how could this be? *Another* clerical error? How bizarre. Naturally, I wanted to find out a little bit more. If Mark Mayerova was really dead, then who was this man who was claiming to be him, who was married to Anne Mayerova? And do you know something, for someone who established a garage here in the late 1940s, who has gone on to become one of our country's leading businessmen, he has been rather remarkably publicity-shy. There are many, *many* photographs of his wife in circulation, but virtually none of him at all. Of course we're all entitled to our privacy — but still. I thought it strange. So I went hunting. Or should I say, I engaged what I like to think of as my family of beloved customers to hunt on my behalf. You see, they come from all walks of life; they are butchers, bakers, candlestick-makers — well actually, mostly they are white-collar, but you get my drift. Amongst them is one particular little genius who works for the *Ulster Tatler,* a magazine that has been recording our social elite at play for decades. He was sufficiently interested in this case to take it upon himself to go through the huge mountains of back issues in search of Mark Mayerova. Nothing was filed, nothing digitised or on-line; he couldn't just type the name in, he had to go through every issue. The only guidance I was able to give him was the suggestion that the immediate post-war years might be his best bet, the years when this man who claimed to be Mark Mayerova was perhaps struggling to establish himself in business in our strange little country — he would have needed to make connections, to get his face known amongst our movers and shakers. Perhaps some society photographer managed to capture him unawares, or he was unable to back out of a hastily arranged group shot without it making him appear odd. And do you know something? My guy found it.' I clicked on the PowerPoint, and the front cover of the magazine appeared, with a photograph from inside it immediately beneath. *Ulster Tatler*, October 1950, Belfast Round Table Christmas Dinner, there he is, Mark Smith, as he became, second from the left, beside his rather beautiful wife Anne — if you don't mind me saying?'

I nodded down at the still remarkably impassive old man. He looked even thinner in the photograph than he was now. His shape was not helped by an ill-fitting suit.

'I was thus armed with a photograph of the man claiming to be Mark Mayerova, all thanks to my wonderful customer, who unfortunately can't be with us tonight, but rest assured, a book token has his name on it already. So what next, then? Well, perhaps you're ahead of me already, but I got to thinking: if he's not the real Mark Mayerova, who can he be? Another prisoner? Why would another prisoner need to adopt a false identity? Perhaps he had something to hide? What if he had been a kapo, a prisoner appointed by the SS to make sure their orders were carried out? Kapos had no choice but to obey such orders, or they themselves would have been killed . . . but some certainly went about their business with more enthusiasm than others. And come liberation they couldn't suddenly revert to being ordinary prisoners again, for those prisoners they had beaten and bullied would surely want revenge. So *there's* a reason to adopt a false identity. My next step was of course to establish whether the man impersonating Mark Mayerova really was one of these dreaded kapos and if whatever he had done perhaps even qualified him as some kind of *war criminal.* And the simplest and most straightforward way of finding this out was to send this photograph to some real *experts* in the field. I e-mailed it to the Simon Wiesenthal Centre in Los Angeles. Within two days, they responded.' I looked down at Mark Mayerova.

Icily calm. His sons were sweating, though, darting little looks around, particularly at DI Robinson. 'They had absolutely no idea who it was in the photograph.'

I kept him waiting.

'However, I don't give up easily. As I said, there's a lot of competition in the Holocaust business, so I sent the photo out to everyone I could find. And you know where it ended up? Almost full circle, back with the Wiesenthals. Only this time with his lesser-known brother, Erich, who ran his own centre out of Basle, Switzerland. He's dead now, but his sons continue to fight the good fight. Once they got a look at the photo, they said, we've been searching for this guy for sixty years. But no kapo he.'

You could hear a pin drop.

'Of course they weren't just going to name and shame him on the basis of a photograph. They said, we have his fingerprints on file from immediately after the war when he was briefly arrested.' I clocked the PowerPoint and a copy of the original arrest sheet, with photograph and fingerprints, appeared on the wall. 'If you think it's him, they said, if he's really still alive, we're going to have to get a new set to compare. As it happens, I said, I believe I have his fingerprints already.'

I clicked the PowerPoint, and the next image came up.

'This is the Auschwitz Bible Mark Mayerova himself handed to me in this very shop just a few days ago. The fingerprints were a perfect match.'

I clicked again.

This time the photo showed Mark Mayerova as he had looked during the war.

'Ladies and gentlemen, let me introduce to you SS Sergeant Major Wilhelm Koch. Otherwise known as the Mechanic of Auschwitz!'

45

So much happened in the next twenty seconds that it is much easier to list the events as bullet points. Which is quite fitting, really. In fact, it would be much easier to illustrate what happened by way of a graphic novel, because later Alison captured it perfectly, but there are copyright issues that prevent me reproducing her drawings here. Sufficient to say, it was chaotic for a while. These are *my* impressions of what happened:

- Karl Mayerova makes a run at me.
- DI Robinson takes him out with a rugby tackle.
- A lot of girlie-male dancers start screaming.
- Mark Mayerova aka the Mechanic of Auschwitz sits placidly throughout.
- Max Mayerova pulls a gun.
- He is wrestled to the ground by undercover cops, but not before:
- He fires one shot, which goes through the ceiling;
- Drilling a neat hole through a copy of *Weep for Me* by John D. MacDonald, though I won't discover this for six

months.

• The girlie-male dancers rush the door but are repelled by more undercover cops.

• My laptop is irretrievably damaged in the melee, forcing the abandonment of further revelations by PowerPoint demonstration.

• I suffer an asthma attack.

• The Mayerova brothers are handcuffed and held face down on the floor.

• The smoke alarm goes off, not because of the bullet, but because someone has taken advantage of the chaotic scenes to light up in the toilet.

• CCTV footage will reveal that the culprit is Brendan Coyle.

• Alison takes advantage of Max Mayerova being on the ground to kick him in the ribs.

Pandemonium is a word I like. I have a collection of words I like. Not many people know where it comes from. It is the name the poet John Milton gave to the capital of Hell in *Paradise Lost*. Pandemonium might be overstating things for what went on in No Alibis during those twenty seconds, but it certainly fits the source of all that trouble — what happened at Auschwitz, which *was* very much the capital of Hell. Like all cities, it needed someone to ensure that it ran smoothly. Much publicity has been given to the architects of the concentration camps and to the demon doctors who carried out experiments there, but very little to those who made sure the machinery kept working, who mended the fuses, who oiled the nuts and bolts, who ensured the gas pipes didn't rust. People like the Mechanic. A man who thought there was no contradiction between sharing his sandwich with a starving prisoner, and maintaining the ovens in which he or she would shortly perish. A man who could continue to sit impervious while everything erupted around him, a superior, supercilious and defiant smile on his white face.

When order was restored, one of DI Robinson's colleagues sought permission to lead all three Mayerovas away for questioning. The detective looked towards me, kneeling on the floor over my broken laptop. I looked back and shook my head.

'No,' he told his colleague, 'Mastermind has started, let's hear him finish.'

'But sir . . .'

The truth is that part of my agreement with DI Robinson was that I would be allowed to present my evidence in total before I handed it over to him. If he tried to stop me, I promised him that I would eat it. I was quite serious. Yes, I was keen to have the Mayerovas locked away, but I'd done all the donkey work and I was damned if anyone else was going to claim even a smidgen of the triumph. So, as people hesitantly retook their seats after what amounted to a short intermission, I stood before them again to continue my resolution of *The Case of the Dancing Jews*.

Of course I had not planned for that sudden explosion of violence, and there was a very real danger of the rest of the proceedings being anticlimactic; Agatha must have known, for there are few scrums in her books, at least before the ultimate denouement. If I wasn't to let it slip away from me I knew that I would have to deliver the rest of my evidence as quickly and economically as possible.

I raised my hands for quiet. I apologised for the disturbance. I told them that the Erich Wiesenthal Centre in Basle had vast quantities of damning testimony from prisoners at Auschwitz about the work SS Sergeant Major Wilhelm Koch had carried out at the camp. With parts in short supply and the number of murders being increased on an almost hourly basis as the war drew to a close, Koch had been instrumental in keeping the ovens and gas chambers functioning at a level of high efficiency. Several statements did refer to the preferential treatment he had given to a 'dancer' he took a shine to, and alluded to a sexual relationship. One claimed to have spotted him dressed in prison clothing immediately after the liberation. It seemed pretty clear to the people at the Erich Wiesenthal Centre that Koch had tattooed himself in a desperate measure to evade justice, and with the connivance of Anne Mayerova, who clearly owed her life to him, managed to escape the authorities. They made it as far as Prague, where he was quite probably recognised and they went on the run, eventually ending up in Belfast. Perhaps with the passing of the years Anne had found it increasingly hard to live with the fact of what her 'husband' had done during the war, and that led to their eventual separation. The fact that they had children, and the damage it would do to them if the secret came out, had undoubtedly led to her agreeing to keep it, and it was only with the onset of Alzheimer's that there was a real danger of it slipping out.

'Only Sergeant Major Koch or his sons can say how it developed after that - whether he told them his secret, or whether they discovered it through their mother — but what I do know is that they decided or agreed to protect their father — and through violent means. Perhaps it's in the genes. As for the evidence, that will lead to one or two or all of them being charged with murder — and that's forgetting for the moment the war crimes charges, although not *forgetting* them, obviously. It's not my job to prove any of this; I merely present what I have found and let others take it away and use it as they see fit. But I can give you some examples of the evidence I have found that at least suggests to me that the police will have little difficulty securing convictions. Like — Malcolm Carlyle's body was found hung with Pine Fresh trees to hide the smell. Each Pine Fresh tree happens to have its own serial number. Those on Mr Carlyle were from a batch sold to Smith Motors just over a year ago. Quite a coincidence, I'd say. One of my customers . . .' I nodded across at Garth

Corrigan, the FA Cup fan, who quickly sank down in his chair. '. . . is a banker who has gained access to the Smith-Mayerova bank accounts and can prove that Karl Mayerova flew to Frankfurt on the day of Manfredd's murder and returned the following day. That Max Mayerova purchased cigarettes using his cash card at a twenty-four-hour petrol station less than a mile from Daniel Trevor's house at four o'clock on the morning Daniel supposedly drowned. Another of my valued customers . . .' This time I nodded at Jimmy Martin, who smiled proudly. '. . . using his contacts in the painting and decorating industry was able to join a team working on a new showroom at Smith Motors, and gain access after hours to their computers. Now Jimmy won't mind me saying that he wouldn't know a hard drive from an orthopaedic shoe, but he was more than happy to smuggle out Karl and Max's computers overnight so that I could search them for incriminating evidence. And there was no lack of it. Boys, one should always remember that nothing ever truly disappears from a computer. If you know what you're doing, it's not hard to find. A few further tips for future reference - when planning a murder, do not use Google Earth to pinpoint the best access routes to your victim's house . . . that's Daniel I'm talking about . . . do not use e-mail to keep each other posted as to the movements of your intended victims . . . and most certainly do not describe my girlfriend, the girl I'm going to marry, as a sexy little thing you're going to have fun with before you plug her, because that only gets me angry, and you wouldn't like me when I'm angry.'

There was plenty of *stuff*, dozens of other e-mails, bank account details, receipts, invoices, a history of websites visited (including ones for the purchase of weapons), which together amounted, so far as I could see, to a mountain of incriminating evidence. There were also Brian's and Alison's statements about the attempted drugging, and lab reports of her hair sample showing

Rohypnol use. Now it was up to someone else to prove it in a court of law. That wasn't my job. There was no reason for me to hog the limelight any further. As far as I was concerned the bad guys were in handcuffs and they were going away for a very long time.

I was satisfied.

I was vindicated.

I was happy.

'Now,' I asked, 'are there any questions?'

I surveyed my frankly *stunned* audience. Towards the back, one young man tentatively raised his hand. I nodded for him to speak.

'Could you tell me how much the books are, and if it's possible to get one signed by the author?'

One must never overestimate the intelligence of one's customers; equally, business is business.

'Fourteen ninety-nine, and no.'

Another hand was raised.

'Are you serious about marrying your girlfriend?'

It was, in fact, my girlfriend.

I forced a smile. It was a rather poor attempt to shift the spotlight to her good self. 'It's not really the time or the place,' I said.

'But you brought it up.'

I shook my head dismissively. I turned to an impatient looking DI Robinson, then nodded down at the still-pinned-to-the-floor Mayerova brothers, and their impassive father.

'Book 'em, Robbo,' I said.

He did not look like he much appreciated it, or even understood.

46

As a lifelong studier of patterns, it is not difficult *at all* to establish the trends and fashions in mystery fiction. They tend to reflect society as a whole. The genre has become more violent, more pornographic, less literate, and there are a lot more serial killers around. One might debate whether mystery fiction influences society, or it is the other way around. Quite possibly there were always a lot of serial killers, they were just less well chronicled. However, one thing that does not change with crime or mystery fiction over the decades is that the public demands that in the next-to-final chapter the murder or crime be solved, leaving the final chapter to tie up the loose ends and to allow for some playful banter between the leading characters, who have probably fallen in love. These are the *conventions*. Occasionally there is a surprise ending, in which one or other of the characters the reader has grown to love turns out to be the killer after all, and has gotten away with murder, or reveals some unsuspected secret that leads one of the lovers to suspect that he or she is now in mortal danger. So it ends with an unresolved cliffhanger.

Generally I do not like such books and do not often recommend them to my customers. Life is too short to leave questions unanswered and it often makes me think that it is a case of the author simply not knowing how to finish his story rather than him being particularly clever. For example, Brendan Coyle.

At least here, in real life, there would be no unresolved endings. The SS Sergeant Major was arrested for being complicit in the murders involved in *The Case of the Dancing Jews.* DI Robinson turned up further e-mails showing that Smith/Mayerova/Koch had been the driving force behind the murders — while renewed forensic examination of the various murder scenes, now that he knew who he was trying to implicate, was yielding dividends that would mean he probably wouldn't have to rely in court on the evidence I had amassed through mostly unconventional methods. An extradition warrant had also been received for the former Mark Mayerova, naming him as a war criminal. Smith Motors remained open for a while, but the publicity surrounding the case meant a huge drop in custom. Some unknown (!) graffiti artist painting *These guys are fucking Nazis!* across their showroom windows didn't help business much either. As DI Robinson has hinted to me over a Starbucks coffee — I'm back to the top of the menu once again, and loving it — the Mayerova brothers aren't quite so menacing any more. They're blaming each other. It's all starting to come out, and he's quite hopeful that the location of Rosemary Trevor's body will soon be forthcoming.

As for me, I wasn't in it for the publicity, I was in it for the satisfaction of triumphing over evil and demonstrating that a life in crime fiction has its practical applications. Needless to say, members of the public with a mystery to solve have been making their way to my shop door in increasing numbers. As before, I do not accept all of these cases, preferring to cherry-pick those that are both the most challenging and the least dangerous. I do not intend ever to be involved in murder again, or with Nazis; there are plenty of missing trousers, dogs, lampshades and bicycles to keep a bookselling amateur detective busy for decades to come. As for Alison, after a period of sulking because I did not once refer to her in my performance — and it was a performance, every pause rehearsed, every pithy comment worked over — as my *partner* in crime-solving, or even as my *sidekick,* she has come around a bit. With my encouragement she has now gone part time in the jewellery store in order to devote much more time to her comic-book art. I have even helped her with a few scripts myself. She has not returned to Brendan Coyle's creative writing class, and is all the better for it.

I thought the business about me suggesting that I was going to marry her, which somehow crept out during my public resolution of *The Case of the Dancing Jews,* had slipped from her mind, but I should have known better. Though we resumed our courting and on occasion had the sex, she managed to keep the subject under her hat until some six weeks after the events surrounding the case. On an evening when she had said she wasn't coming out to play because she was working on a comic, she unexpectedly appeared at my front door, despite the fact that I have made it clear to her in the past that I do not welcome such surprises. I do not expect her to make an appointment, but some prior warning always allows me to get the house in order. In fact, the house is always in order, scrupulous order, but that is hardly the point.

Nevertheless, I welcomed her in, and I made her coffee, and I sat her down at the kitchen table.

'You look vexed,' I said.

'Are you ever going to marry me?' she asked.

I said, 'Whoa, hold your horses.'

I offered her a Jacob's Orange Club biscuit. She ignored it.

'Why would you say a thing like that in public and not mean it?'

'I was striving for effect.'

'Have you any idea how hurtful that is?' She shook her head. 'You don't, do you? You know what your problem is? You're an emotional cripple.'

'You shouldn't say *cripple*.' As an attempt at humour, it failed miserably. 'I am what I am,' I said.

'That night at the party in Daniel Trevor's house you were the life and soul, you were singing and laughing and joking and you got on with everyone. There was none of this *hate*.'

'I don't hate. I *suspect*. Maybe it's to do with what I do; when your life revolves around murder, fact and fiction, it's natural to—'

'It's got sod-all to do with what you do.'

'That wasn't me at the party. I was drunk. Do you want me to be drunk all the time?'

'It was a glimpse of who you can be, with the inhibitions down, with the paranoia in check, with your *suspicions* allayed. People aren't horrible, but you treat them like they are.'

That was, frankly, *ridiculous*. I give everyone a fair shake. The fact that they usually fail miserably is their problem, not mine.

'Well if I'm so dreadful, Alison, what are you doing here?'

She studied me. 'Because I see hope for you.'

'With you?'

'With me. Is that so strange? I think you're like a baby butterfly caught in a cocoon and you've never been able to break out.'

'*Chrysalis*,' I pointed out. 'The pupa stage of the butterfly is—'

'Shut *up*,' she said. 'I'm serious. You need to get away from here. It's . . . killing you. It's like a museum, or a mausoleum. You should . . . move in with me.'

She looked at the table. She picked up a Club. So that was what she was after. She was everything I had ever dreamed of, but still.

'I have responsibilities.'

'No you don't.'

'But M—'

'You don't have a mother.'

'Don't be ridiculous, everyone has a—'

'Stop it. Stop it now. Your mother is dead. She is your excuse for hiding from the real world. Do you think I don't know? How come she's never here? How come she never answers the phone? How come she depends on you for everything, and yet you spent days and nights in No Alibis without once going home to feed her?'

'Do you think I've *invented* my mother?'

'Yes, I do.'

'Do you not think she's upstairs now listening to every word?'

'Then ask her to come down.'

'She can't come down. She's infirm.'

'Then let me go up.'

'She doesn't like visitors.'

'Even the girl you're going to marry?'

'Especially the girl I'm going to marry.'

'She doesn't approve?'

'She doesn't approve of anyone.'

'Please,' said Alison, '*stop this* . . . I love you, and I know you love me. How often is that going to come along?'

'I *can't*,' I said.

She steamed. She blew air out of her cheeks. She pushed her coffee away. 'It's not exactly Starbucks,' she said.

'It's not even close.'

'You wouldn't have a Coke?'

'Diet?'

She nodded. I got up. I have forty-eight cans of Diet Coke in my fridge. In case there is a strike, or a plague.

When I turned with her can, Alison was no longer at the table.

'Alison?'

There had been no sound of the front door opening or closing. I hurried into the hall.

'Alison?'

I stopped at the bottom of the stairs.

Alison was already on the first-floor landing. She looked back at me. 'I'm going to have it out with her,' she said.

'You can't!'

'I have to!'

She hurried up the next set of stairs.

'No, Alison, *don't* . . .!'

I thundered up behind her.

'Come out, come out, wherever you are!' Alison cried, all the time rising higher, getting closer to Mother's room. She threw open every door that she passed. 'Are you in *here*? No! Are you in *here*?'

My legs are not good, and my breathing was laboured; she was young and lithe, and by the time she got to the top room, to Mother's room, she was still well ahead of me. She put her hand to the door. She hesitated. She looked back at me.

'No, Alison, *please don't* . . .'

But she was determined.

She threw the door open and strode in.

She was such a clever girl, but it was a tactical mistake.

You should never enter Mother's room alone.

22309005R00189

Made in the USA
Middletown, DE
26 July 2015